TOUCH OF DARKNESS

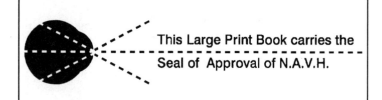

This Large Print Book carries the
Seal of Approval of N.A.V.H.

DARKNESS CHOSEN, BOOK 2

TOUCH OF DARKNESS

CHRISTINA DODD

THORNDIKE PRESS

An imprint of Thomson Gale, a part of The Thomson Corporation

THOMSON

™

GALE

Detroit • New York • San Francisco • New Haven, Conn. • Waterville, Maine • London

THOMSON

—————★————— ™

GALE

Thorndike Press® Large Print Core.

The text of this Large Print edition is unabridged.

Other aspects of the book may vary from the original edition.

Set in 16 pt. Plantin.

LIBRARY OF CONGRESS CATALOGING-IN-PUBLICATION DATA

Dodd, Christina.
  Touch of darkness : darkness chosen / by Christina Dodd.
    p. cm. — (Thorndike Press large print core)
  ISBN-13: 978-0-7862-9918-8 (alk. paper)
  ISBN-10: 0-7862-9918-5 (alk. paper)
    1. Archaeologists — Fiction. 2. Family secrets — Fiction. 3. Blessing and
  cursing — Fiction. 4. Large type books. I. Title.
  PS3554.O3175T68 2008
  813'.54—dc22   2007035076

Published in 2008 by arrangement with NAL Signet, a member of Penguin Group (USA) Inc.

Printed in the United States of America on permanent paper
10 9 8 7 6 5 4 3 2 1

This book is dedicated to Roger Bell,
retired Air Force pilot,
with thanks for his advice and critique,
and to his commanding officer,
Joyce Bell,
who always knows how to conjugate *lie*
and *lay,*
and who generously reads, compliments
and corrects.

ACKNOWLEDGMENTS

The Darkness Chosen project has been a joy from the start, and a lot of people deserve recognition for their deeds and misdeeds.

To tell you the truth, most of the misdeeds have been mine, so I'd like to express appreciation for my agent, Mel Berger, for his enthusiasm and support. Thank you to Bobbie Morganroth for a clean read; to Teresa Medeiros and Geralyn Dawson for their brilliance; and to the NAL production team, art department and editorial department for their inspired scheduling, design and innovation. And to all my friends who have listened to me endlessly enthuse about this project without yawning, gasping or giggling, thank you.

DARKNESS CHOSEN
FAMILY TREE

THE VARINSKIS

1000 AD—In the Ukraine
Konstantine Varinski
makes a deal with the devil.

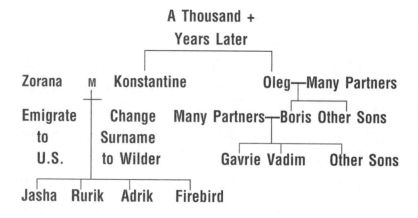

A Thousand +
Years Later

Zorana M Konstantine   Oleg—Many Partners

Emigrate   Change   Many Partners—Boris Other Sons
to   Surname
U.S.   to Wilder   Gavrie Vadim   Other Sons

Jasha Rurik Adrik Firebird

The Night That Started It All

"I want you to cover my back." Konstantine handed his brother the bottle and gestured down to the encampment in the valley below. "I'm going to take the Gypsy girl."

"We're not supposed to mess with the Gypsies." Oleg took a long pull of vodka. "Remember? It is written. Any woman is ours for the plucking, but not those *zalupa* Romanies."

Konstantine bared his sharp white teeth in what passed for a grin. "And I wonder why that is." The Varinski family had no rules. No rules at all. They could do what they wanted — rape, pillage, torture, murder — and no one could stop them.

But one ancient law existed.

They were not to take a Gypsy woman.

"Gypsies are filthy." Oleg spit in the direction of the camp, and the warm spittle steamed as it struck the frozen ground. This autumn was as cold as a witch's tit, with an early frost that had ruined the crops and put a hungry edge on everyone's temper. "You'll get a disease."

"What do I care about a disease? The only thing that can kill me, brother, is you."

"I wouldn't kill you," Oleg said hastily.

Oleg was the same age as Konstantine, and about the same size: six feet five, heavily muscled, with huge fists. Even better, Oleg was a great fighter. But he feared pain. When he had to fight, he would, but he didn't love it.

Konstantine *did* love it. He loved winning, of course, but more than that, he loved everything about a brawl. He loved strategizing while on his feet, figuring who was going to attack and how, calculating which of his enemies was easiest to crush and who required extra effort. Pain acted as a stimulant, and red was his favorite color.

Tonight Konstantine wanted more action. He judged there were probably forty people in the Gypsy camp: thirty men and women from ages fifteen to seventy, and ten children. "Have we not fought hard this night? Have we not washed our hands in the blood of our enemies?"

"They weren't our enemies." Oleg stared at the campfires below. "They were just another job."

"Whoever we have been hired to kill, they are our enemies." Konstantine took the bottle and drank until the vodka burned his gut, and handed it back. He didn't underestimate the Gypsies; they defended their own, they valued the girl, and most of all, they were dirty fighters. He appreciated that. He also figured with a little strategy, he could steal the girl from under their noses. "I am negotiating with a terrorist in Indonesia. Soon we'll go to war. Until then" — he started down the hill toward the encampment, the thrill of pursuit thrumming in his veins — "I will get me some Gypsy pussy."

Oleg smashed the bottle across his head.

Konstantine saw stars.

Tackling him behind the knees, Oleg brought him down, and wrapped a crooked elbow around his throat. "If you do this, you'll have to leave the clan."

"Who would have the guts to throw me out?" Konstantine looked into his brother's eyes in challenge. "Not you, Oleg."

"No. Not me. But maybe . . . maybe the Gypsy law came not from the first Konstantine . . . but from his maker."

"From his mama?" Konstantine's lip curled. "He killed his mama to seal the pact with her life's blood."

11

"No. From the devil." Oleg jerked on Konstantine's hair. "Did you never think of that? Did you never think the devil might have made that the condition of the pact?"

"Of course I did. Did you never wonder why? Why would the devil tell old Konstantine he couldn't have a Gypsy woman?"

"I . . . don't know."

Konstantine relaxed into his brother's arms. In a conversational tone, he said, "Did you see the Gypsy girl when she was in town?" He waited. "Well, did you?"

"Yes." Oleg was reluctant to feed Konstantine's obsession, but he understood it very well. "She's beautiful. But too small for you."

"High breasts, small waist, small hips, dark hair —"

"She'll grow a mustache soon."

"What do I care? I'm not going to keep her. But did you notice those deep, dark eyes that see everything? Do you know why her eyes are like that? Because she can see the future."

Oleg's guard slipped. "They're Gypsies. They lie so they can take the money from the gullible humans."

"No, I heard her people talking — they thought I was a dog. The girl doesn't tell fortunes. She has visions. I want her to bear

12

me a son."

"A son. You can't have a son with her. She's a Gypsy!"

Konstantine grabbed Oleg's wrist. "Think about it, Oleg. Open your tiny little mind. Imagine a son with my gifts and her visions combined. He would be powerful, so powerful the Evil One himself would fear him. That's why we're not to breed with the Gypsies. Because my child could take the devil's place as the leader of hell."

Oleg sat back, his expression appalled. "Sometimes, Konstantine, you're crazy."

And so swiftly Oleg never had a chance of holding him, Konstantine changed.

Where Konstantine had reclined on the brittle grass, a puddle of clothes remained, and over them stood a huge, muscled, brown wolf — a wolf who was Konstantine.

Oleg scrambled to regain his hold, but the wolf caught Oleg's hand in his teeth and bit down until the bones crunched.

"You filthy *govnosos!*" Oleg screamed.

Konstantine released. Sometimes Oleg had to be put in his place.

Loping down the hill, Konstantine entered the encampment. Almost at once, he caught the scent of the girl — a young body, fresh and clean. He gave the men a wide berth, wanting no trouble until he had his quarry in sight, and no one paid attention to him, for wolves traveled in packs, and lone dogs were nothing but a nuisance.

He followed his nose, and there she was, sitting with the other girls, listening and talking, laughing at the antics of another girl who modeled a fur hat, and all the while using a spindle to turn wool into thread.

He stood out of sight of her campfire, watching.

His intentions were cold and calculating, true; he wanted a son born from the psychic's loins. But the deed would be a pleasure, for the girl was very pretty.

Unexpectedly, cold crawled up his spine. *Danger.*

He glanced around. The men were drinking, and hadn't noticed him.

Oleg didn't dare interfere again; he was probably still nursing his hand and cursing.

So where was the threat?

There. On the far side of the fire. The old woman.

Blin! She was hideous, a hunched crone with eyebrows so dark and wildly curled he could see them from here. She had one of those soft, bulbous, old-lady noses that drooped over her wrinkled lips. Worst of all, beneath the wrinkles and the thinning hair, he saw the remnants of beauty. It was as if some evil spell had befallen her, and that spell was old age.

He was quite sure his brown coat and immobility hid him from human eyes, yet she looked right at him, her big, black-rimmed glasses magnifying her faded eyes. Slowly she lifted her hand and pointed her crooked finger at him.

A silence fell over the girls, and as one they turned to look.

"Varinski," she said, and the word was a curse.

"Don't be silly, old one. The Varinskis don't bother us."

"Varinski," the old woman said again.

How did she know? How did she recognize him?

Then the girl, the one with the visions, stood up, spindle in hand. "I'll go check, old one."

This was easier than he expected.

The girl started toward him.

He absorbed the wolf and once again became a man.

"No!" the old woman shouted with surprising power.

The girl turned and walked backward toward him. "It's all right. I've got to get more wool anyway."

As the old woman struggled to get to her

feet, the beautiful Gypsy walked right into Konstantine's arms.

She didn't scream; he didn't give her a chance. With one hand over her mouth, he wrapped his arm around her waist, lifted her, and walked toward the edge of the camp.

He was naked.

She wore a skirt.

This would be easy.

Then the bitch used her spindle to stab him in the side.

He dropped her and roared.

She screamed at the top of her lungs and scrambled to escape.

He caught a glimpse of the surprised men coming to life and charging toward him. Grabbing her arm, he spun her around toward him, and as she raised the spindle once more, he yanked it out of her hand and threw it at her rescuers.

"Poyesh' govna pechyonovo!" He laughed, took out the lead man, punching him into the middle of the charging mass of men. Tossing the tiny Gypsy girl over his shoulder, he ran into the darkness.

They couldn't catch him, those Romanies. They didn't have his stride, his lungs, or his instincts.

After a few attempts to knock him off-balance, the girl went still, but he didn't make the mistake of thinking she was resigned. She was simply waiting. Waiting until he stopped and she could fight him with all her breath and all her spirit. She made him want to laugh, this tiny thing who stabbed him with her woman contraption. She would be a pleasure to tame.

A half hour later, he stopped at a motel outside Poltava. He had an understanding with the innkeeper there — the innkeeper kept one cottage available for Konstantine, and Konstantine let the innkeeper live.

The girl was limp now, shivering with cold, and breathless from being knocked against Konstantine's shoulder. He shoved his way through the door and into the warmth of the room. He let her slide down his body and held her while she regained her balance, and waited while she examined him.

She didn't bother with the head-to-toe trick; she zeroed right in on his genitals and indifferently inspected them.

Most women either fainted or made cooing noises.

Then she scanned the rest of his body. Her gaze lingered on the bloody evidence of her spindle attack. She said, "So you can be hurt," and smiled.

She wasn't afraid. She was furious, and ready to attack. She was only five feet tall, containing eight feet's worth of defiance. She couldn't be slapped into submission; that would never work.

So he did something out of character.

He kissed her.

He didn't know why. He'd never kissed a woman before. Coitus didn't require that kind of intimacy. But something about this girl made him want to touch her lips with his, and he wasn't a man who deprived himself of his desires.

It was a lousy kiss.

He mashed his mouth on hers.

She puckered her lips tightly to repel him and, at the same time, pinched his arms with her fingers.

Yet . . . when her breath touched his face, sensation swept him. He didn't recognize it; it felt like a fire kindling in a stove that had never known flame. He slipped his arms around her back, seeking the source of the feeling.

She stopped pinching him and stood motionless. Then, oh God, then her lips softened and opened. She was like a ripe plum waiting for him to take a bite — which he did, the most gentle nip on her lush lower lip.

She jumped, and when he licked the place, she jumped again.

Her tongue touched his, and as swiftly as a forest fire, heat roared out of control. Their kiss became an exchange of tastes, touches, passions, souls. Their kiss consumed him, blinding him to danger and taking him to madness.

Never again would he take another woman. He wanted her, the Gypsy girl. No other woman would do.

When at last they pulled apart, breathless and amazed, he looked into her dark brown eyes, and he saw his destiny. That was why he had to have her.

That was why the devil had forbidden it.

When she spoke, her voice was husky and passion-filled. "My name is Zorana."

"Zorana," he repeated. He knew very well the magic held within a name, knew, too, that she had gifted him with a piece of her soul. He, like a wild beast giving its trust for the first time, answered, "My name is Konstantine."

"Konstantine." She nodded. Taking his hand, she led him toward the bed.

To him it seemed as if the universe had shifted, become a place where the old rules no longer applied and fresh bright hope, long snuffed, now sprang to life.

He was right.

But no mere man flouted the devil's authority without fearsome consequences. . . .

CHAPTER 1

"I've got the plane," Rurik shouted as he grabbed the controls.

A stark mountain face loomed before them.

The missile was almost on them.

He drove the plane up and to the side.

They weren't going to make it.

They weren't going to —

"Excuse me, sir, we'll be landing in a few minutes. You need to return your seat back to its full upright position."

Rurik Wilder jerked awake, heart racing, sweat sheening his body.

The stewardess stood in the aisle, giving him that phony half smile that said she didn't care whether she woke him up, that the seven-hour trip from Newark to Edinburgh had kept her on her feet the whole time, and had he even *heard* the kids rampaging up and down the aisle while their parents snoozed and everyone else complained?

He stared at her, bewildered, trying to orient himself.

"*Excuse* me, sir, we'll be landing in a few minutes. You need to —"

"Right!" He tried to look normal, grinned apologetically, and brought his seat back forward.

She walked off with that snap in her step that said she was not appeased.

The old woman on his left glared at him through eyes so dark brown they were almost black.

On his right, he felt someone's stare, and when he glanced over, the American girl averted her gaze.

Panic hit him, and he ran his hands over his face.

No, he might be a little wide-eyed, but his heartbeat was slowing and more important, his features were human.

He tried a smile. "Was I snoring?"

"You were sort of thrashing around. That must have been quite a nightmare." The girl was probably nineteen, with wide, soft brown eyes, a natural tan, and breasts that would win her fans around the world.

Too bad the only breasts that appealed to him were attached to a woman with big blue eyes, short, black, curly hair, a Nikon SLR digital camera always around her neck, and an ego-bruising way of disappearing when he least expected it.

Damn Tasya Hunnicutt. Damn the fascination she had exerted over him from the first moment they'd met. Damn her for being oblivious, and damn him for wanting her more, now that he'd had her, than he did before.

Tasya was his fate — and she didn't even know it.

"I always get that nightmare when I fly. Usually I won't sleep, but I left Seattle twenty-three hours ago and between layovers and a late plane going into Chicago . . ." He shrugged, playing it casual, pretending the dream was nothing but a nightmare concocted of jet lag and exhaustion.

The girl bought it, too, nodding sympathetically. "Is this your first trip to Scotland?"

He expertly interpreted every sound the jet engines made. "What? No. No, actually I've lived here for the past ten months."

At once she grew animated. "Cool! I've always wanted to live in a foreign country. I feel like it would broaden my horizons, you know?"

"Yeah, I've got very broad horizons." And a dead ass from sitting so long.

"What do you do there?"

"I run an archaeological dig in the Orkney Islands off northern Scotland."

The girl's eyes got huge and round. "Isn't that a coincidence? I've always wanted to be an archaeologist!"

You and everybody who ever read about the discovery of gold in King Tut's tomb. "That is a coincidence."

"What are you digging up?"

"Until we actually open it, we won't know for sure" — although he knew in his bones, and had always known — "but I believe it's the tomb of a Celtic warlord." He strained to hear the changes in the wing as they descended.

Man, he was pathetic. It had been five years since he'd sat in the pilot's seat, five years since he'd vowed never to fly again, and he still couldn't relax and trust the commercial pilots. If he could see out the window, he'd be better able to judge how the guy was doing, but Rurik was in the second seat in the middle section.

When he'd got the call from the dig, he'd grabbed the first flight out, and this was his punishment — a seat too narrow for his shoulders, knees up under his chin. But at least he was getting back in time to open the tomb.

"I know who you are!" The girl sat up straight, her eyes sparkling. "I saw you on CNN."

"Didn't everyone?" He'd seen the news coverage in the airport, too, and it had confirmed his worst fears.

"Mr. Hardwick was talking about you."

"Good old Hardwick." The foreman at the dig and, Rurik now realized, a grandstander with a thirst for publicity.

"You're the guy everyone thought was crazy who started digging around on the tiny little island and now they've found a huge stash of gold."

With the innate caution of an experienced archaeologist, he said, "Actually, I got funding from the National Antiquities Society, so I always had a team, and there's something that looks like gold, maybe, inside what looks like a tomb, maybe, but until I get there and we can finish opening it, we won't know what's really going on."

He needed to be there now, to see whether Hardwick had found the box Rurik had been searching for, the box containing a far greater treasure than gold.

"Wow. Just . . . wow." The girl's eyes were big and worshipful, and she offered her hand reverently. "I'm Sarah."

He shook it.

"Why do you have nightmares?" She smiled at him, and rubbed her fingertips over his white knuckles.

"Because I'm . . . afraid to fly?" Ridiculous, of course, but better than telling the truth.

"You poor thing." She smiled at him again.

It took that second smile before he realized — he had a nineteen-year-old making a pass at him. He jerked his hand out from under her touch. He glanced over to see if the dark-eyed grandmother had noticed.

Of course she had. She was glaring knives at him, her heavy black and gray eyebrows meeting over her narrow nose.

Sarah leaned toward him. "I could be a big help to you at your dig."

He averted his gaze, and mentally urged the pilot to put the damned plane on the ground. "I would love to have you, but we only hire experienced archaeologists. Besides, aren't you meeting someone?"

She shrugged. "Just my church group."

So she was nineteen, part of a church group, and trying to seduce him.

Great. Just great. He'd grown up knowing he was going to hell. He just hadn't realized the handcart would be doing 120 on the Road to Hell Autobahn.

"A church group is exciting."

"Exciting?" Her voice rose incredulously. "Have you ever *been* part of a church group?"

Why, no. No, he hadn't. Churches didn't exactly welcome a family like his.

The plane jolted as the wheels hit the runway — he was almost out of here. "Are you going to Paris? You'll love it. Grand cathedrals. Nice little churches."

Not that he'd ever been in any of them.

He got on his feet before the flight attendants opened the door. "Some great choirs. Don't forget to go to Rome. The Vatican's there!"

Another place he'd taken care to stay far away from.

While Sarah struggled to get her bag out of the overhead, he grabbed his carry-on and muscled his way past her.

His mother would have killed him for being such a jerk, and his brother would have died of laughter.

But my God. An underage kid making a pass at him — that officially made him a dirty old man at the ripe old age of thirty-three.

He hurried toward baggage claim.

A nineteen-year-old made a pass at him, and Tasya Hunnicutt couldn't get away from him fast enough. He'd gone home to his folks' place for the Fourth of July celebration that had started out great and ended in Swedish Hospital in Seattle, and at the same time, the tomb he'd been painstakingly excavating opened itself to reveal the glint of gold.

What a bitch of a month it had been.

Now it was going to take him a hard day of driving along increasingly narrow roads to get to the ferry at John O'Groat's and from there to the Outer Orkneys, and he'd be lucky if, when he made it, a gale hadn't kicked up, keeping the ferry in port.

Not that he hadn't been amazingly lucky since he started the dig. There'd been storms, of course — one didn't go through the winter in northern Scotland without some blistering cold winds and freezing-ass rain, but he'd had to knock off only a couple of days, and he would have had to stop work on Sundays, anyway. If he was a superstitious man, he would say that the dig served some higher purpose.

He hadn't *been* a superstitious man when he'd started working the site.

He was now.

Grabbing his bag off the carousel, he headed toward the car-rental counter, got the keys to a MINI Cooper, then stepped outside and put on his sunglasses.

"A beautiful day."

He turned to find the old woman from the plane standing beside him. She was short and stooped; the top of her head barely reached his shoulder. "Yes, it is." Which in Scotland even in midsummer was pretty amazing.

"But there's a change coming." Her voice was husky, heavily accented . . . and not Scottish. She sounded almost like his father — Russian or Ukrainian.

"Really?" He scanned the skies. "Are the forecasters predicting a storm? Well, it's not surprising, is it? After all, it is Scotland."

"A change in the earth."

"Huh?" He looked back at her.

"I can feel it in my bones." Her dark, dark eyes scrutinized him from head to toe; she saw beyond his clothes and skin, down to his bones, and she saw nothing that pleased her. "There's an upwelling from hell, and heaven's finger stretching down from the sky" — her voice dropped to a whisper — "and when the two collide, everything will be different."

"Sure." He edged sideways down the curb. "Well, I've got a long ways to go, so good-bye!"

"Godspeed," she answered.

Crazy old lady.

29

He squeezed himself into the driver's seat, and drove off.

How did he always attract the crazy ones?

But when he looked in the rearview mirror, she stood watching him. A ray of sunshine touched the silver in her dark hair. Irresistibly she reminded him of his mother, and the vision that had changed his life.

And a shudder crawled up his spine.

CHAPTER 2

Sunshine. Temps in the seventies. No wind. Not a hint of rain, and none in the forecast.

Rurik stood on the bow of the ferry — he was the lone passenger — and waited for his first sight of the Isle of Roi.

Yesterday, he had driven like a madman through the Scottish Lowlands, broad expanses of nothing, interrupted by golf courses, industrial towns, and whisky manufacturers. His own fatigue had forced him to stop in Inverness and crash in one of the bed-and-breakfasts, then rise early today to drive the Highlands, *Braveheart* country, crisscrossed by tiny one- and two-lane roads that twisted and turned, where his top speed was a crawl and he stopped for sheep crossings.

But even that delay had been minor. By afternoon, he'd made it to the northern coast of Scotland. It seemed as if the elements conspired to bring him to the dig as quickly as possible.

There's an upwelling from hell, and heaven's finger stretching down from the sky, and when the two collide, everything will be different.

His mother had said something like that, but unlike the weird old woman, Zorana was not weird or old or given to enigmatic statements, unless one considered *Load the dishwasher, you big lummox — I didn't give birth to you so I'd have another man to wait on* enigmatic.

From behind him, the ferry's first mate advised, "Ye'll na' get to the isle faster by pushing."

"Duncan. Hey, how are you?" Rurik grimaced as he shook hands with the weathered Scot. "I can't help pushing. I should have been there the whole time."

"Aye, ye stay here day and night and as soon as yer back is turned, yer team pulls the tablecloth out from under the china." Duncan joined him at the rail and stared at the choppy water. "Do ye know how many tourists we've transported in the last four days?"

"How many?"

"Enough to swamp the boat." Beneath his gray, trimmed beard, Duncan's lip curled in disdain.

"If the team had kept their mouths shut —"

"Ye canna' contain the rumor of gold, my friend. That's not changed in the last ten thousand years. Gold brings the greedy to gawk and covet."

"They didn't have to call a damned press conference." That was what stuck in Rurik's craw — seeing Kirk Hardwick on camera, expounding on the fabulous treasure of gold and knowledge.

"Hardwick does like his wee bit of attention and with ye gone, he's had it."

"I'll bet." The first hint of a shadow appeared on the horizon. The Isle of Roi.

"When I tell the American tourists the island is only seven miles across, and that there are no cars, they look as if my wit has escaped me." Duncan's shrewd eyes watched as the island took shape — flat on one end, rising slowly to a tall cliff on the other. "And the reporters! Squawking and laden down with cameras, each one trying to slip Freckle and Eddie a tip to carry their gear."

Rurik glanced back at the two crewmen. "Did they rake it in?"

"They liked the money. They didna' like being treated like the village idiots."

"How many reporters are there?"

"Four — two from Edinburgh, one from London, and a German from some international news service. Enough to write one decent story, ye'd think, but I've yet to see one." Duncan faced Rurik, leaned against the railing, and crossed his arms over his chest. "Now, when that sweet-faced dark-hair lass starts awritin', then we'll see something."

Rurik played dumb. "Who?"

Duncan wasn't buying it. "Ye know who."

"Tasya?"

"Nay, I dunna' know Tasya. I mean Hunni."

"Tasya . . . Hunnicutt." Everyone called her Hunni, and she responded easily to the endearment, smiling at everyone, charming men, women, and children alike.

Rurik couldn't bring himself to use her pet name so casually. It irritated him — she irritated him — like a grain of sand in a clam.

"Ah, is that her real name?" Duncan said. "I didna' know." The hell he didn't. He saw right through Rurik's pretended indifference.

"So she's here." Rurik would see her again, see her for the first time since he'd completed his carefully plotted seduction and they'd spent the night in Edinburgh together.

"Brought her across this morning. She said she would have been here sooner, but she was finishing the photos for her story in Egypt. She's a traveler, that one is."

That's for damn sure. A man would have to nail her feet to the floor to keep her in one place. "She hasn't been here long. Good."

"There's na' harm in the lass."

No harm? Rurik remembered all too clearly the harm she'd done him. The scent of her skin, the sound of her husky laughter, the sensation of her heated body against his, her taste . . . "She's too damned nosy for her own good."

"In a charming way — but then, I've got the hots for her." Duncan put his hand to his chest and sighed like a lovelorn lad.

Rurik clasped the rail as tightly as he could. He had to, or he would strangle Duncan.

Duncan rattled on. "There isna' a man on the island, barring that nancy-boy reporter from London, whose compass doesna' point north at the sight of her."

"She's got a bony face."

"She's got a face?"

Duncan's incredulity caught Rurik by surprise, and he laughed. Of course, Duncan was right. Why should any of the guys care what her face looked like?

Unfortunately for Rurik, he couldn't get Tasya's face out of his mind.

Her short hair was so black that in the right light, like in the pub after a hard day's work and a few hours' drinking, the highlights shone with all the colors and gloss of a raven's wing. Her cobalt eyes were surrounded by Snuffleupagus eyelashes, absurdly thick, sooty, and long. When she blinked, her lashes fanned the air, and when she looked at Rurik, her electric blue gaze sent a shock along his nerves.

And to be fair, her face wasn't really bony — sculpted would be a better word, with a broad chin that she used for emphasis — she lifted it when she was stubborn, turned it away when she had no intention of listening, pointed it at a guy when she wanted to make a statement.

When it came to her body . . . well, okay, Rurik understood why the guys made moaning noises about woodies and making a hole in one. She looked like a fifties film goddess, with generous breasts — Rurik gave her a C, and that wasn't a grade — a tiny waist, a glorious flare of hips, and great legs. Long, muscular, great, great, great legs. All of that was packed into about five feet five inches of dynamic action.

Cover all that with a nun's habit, leave nothing but her face peeking out, and no man would even notice her — except for him.

So, of course, Duncan promptly contradicted Rurik's wistful thinking with, " 'Tis her lips. . . . She makes a man think of sins performed sinfully, slowly, and often."

That perfectly described Tasya and her lips and the sex. . . . "She's a distraction."

"Aye, that she is," Duncan fervently agreed. "But she doesna' use her wiles for evil, Rurik. She'd na' do anything behind yer back."

Rurik had been unfair about her character. Probably. And for his own reasons. But when Tasya Hunnicutt observed the dig, it wasn't her passion for him that made her blue eyes grow gray and intense. He would swear she had more on her mind than making sure she got good photos and wrote the inside story. "She knows too much about the site."

"Ye mean, she knows as much as ye do," Duncan said shrewdly.

God forbid. Rurik stared at the oncoming island.

"She *is* a reporter, and her employer *does* fund the dig, so maybe it's her job to know too much." Duncan clapped his hand on

Rurik's shoulder. "If ye ask me, ye should just harpoon the Hunni and stop sulking."

Rurik whipped his head around and glared.

"It's not like the rest of us are getting any. Ye're the only one with any chance at all. Now, if ye'll excuse me, Cap'n MacLean'll be wanting my assistance bringing the ferry in." Duncan headed for the bridge, grinning.

Rurik faced the island, but he saw Tasya — and his destiny.

The Isle of Roi was shaped like a bony forearm, with the elbow end elevated out of the water. The tomb was on the high side, not far from the cliffs and a hundred-foot drop into the sea.

As the ferry closed on the island, he could see more detail — the blush of summer grass, the few trees, bent and blasted by wind, the white sand beaches beneath the cliffs. The place was a haven for seabirds; they wheeled through the air, crying of long migrations and short summers, and a single golden eagle flew high above them all, hunting . . . always hunting.

Rurik followed its arc, his soul desperate to take flight, to soar on an updraft until he reached the sun, then tuck his wings close to his body and plunge toward the ocean, the wind so strong it filled his lungs, the exhilaration sharp, keen, fresh.

With very little trouble, he could convince himself it was necessary. If he would just let himself, he could change his form, become a giant hunting bird. He had powers that no mere man should have, given to him by a pact made long ago between the first Konstantine and the devil.

Rurik's father said the change brought them closer to evil, but Rurik would use it for good.

That's what he'd told himself five years ago . . . and a good man had died.

No matter how much he longed for the joys of flight, since then Rurik had never turned.

Yet the power wasn't something he could lose. It was a hunger that grew every day, a craving in his gut he could barely curb — and that made it all the more dangerous.

Now, more than ever, his hawk vision seemed the best way to watch over his vital project, his long talons and swift dives combined with the element of surprise the likeliest defense.

Most important, he could tell himself the Varinskis had found him. . . . They had, after all, found Jasha, and it was only a matter of time before they tracked him down, too.

Tracking was what the Varinskis did best — or so his father said.

But it was what his mother had said that truly haunted him . . . he shuddered as he remembered.

He'd gone home to the Cascade Mountains in Washington for the annual Wilder family Fourth of July celebration, his first break since he'd begun work on the dig.

That night, after fireworks were over, the guests had departed, and the bonfire had burned low, this powerful vision had seized his mother.

And yeah, she was a Gypsy, and yeah, Rurik suspected she was a weather-worker. And yeah, their whole family was a little different from most American families — his parents had immigrated from the Ukraine and changed their name from Varinski to Wilder because the Varinskis were assassins and plenty pissed about his parents getting together, and his mother's Gypsy clan had been hot under the collar, too.

But except for the time when Rurik was eight and he'd shoplifted that Megatron Transformer from the Wal-Mart down in Marysville and his mother had made him turn out his pockets before he even left the store, he'd never witnessed any signs that

40

Zorana was psychic — until the night of the Fourth. Her slight body had exuded power, her usually feminine voice had grown deep and great. She'd looked at Rurik, and he would have sworn she could see the stains on his soul.

She had cursed the family with her prophecy. . . .

Each of my four sons must find one of the Varinski icons.

Only their loves can bring the holy pieces home.

A child will perform the impossible. And the beloved of the family will be broken by treachery . . . and leap into the fire.

The blind can see, and the sons of Oleg Varinski have found us. You can never be safe, for they will do anything to destroy you and keep the pact intact.

If the Wilders do not break the devil's pact before your death, you will go to hell and be forever separated from your beloved Zorana. . . .

And you, my love, you are not long for this earth. You are dying.

She'd been talking to Rurik's father, and as soon as she'd finished speaking, Konstantine had crashed to the ground, crushed in the grips of a rare disease that ate away at his heart.

Konstantine had always been one of the most hearty, commanding men Rurik had ever met. To see him stretched out on the gurney in Swedish Hospital in Seattle, IVs poked into his arms, a shunt in his chest, tubes running up his nose — in that moment, Rurik's understanding of the world had changed.

He had only a limited time to find the icon that would save his father's life and soul. If Rurik failed, destruction came to everything important to him. His family. His world.

Maybe the *whole* world.

The ferry took a sharp turn to the left, coming around the end of the island, and there it was, the village of Dunmarkie, nestled into the harbor and bragging of three dozen homes, a pub, and a market.

The streets were empty.

Rurik straightened.

As he'd done every day for the last twenty years, the captain efficiently brought the ferry into the dock. The crew hurried about, securing her moorings, setting the gangplank . . . and then they stood there, looking uneasily at the village.

"Where is everybody?" Duncan asked.

Rurik met Duncan's gaze. "Something's happened at the site."

42

■ ■ ■ ■

Rurik cleared the last rise, looked down, and swore.

His lonely, windswept archaeological site, with its gently mounded grave that was brushed alternately by the caress of the sea breeze and the roar of brutal storms off the North Sea, was inundated by people. Villagers, fishermen, photographers, and reporters — they were all there, tromping down the pale green grass and fragile flowers, overrunning his carefully marked sections, milling, talking, jostling for position.

Where were his workers? Who was in control?

Where was his superintendent? *Where was Hardwick?*

Grimly Rurik surged forward.

The crowd had already spotted him, and he heard his name repeated over and over again.

Ashley Sundean got to him first before he reached the edge of the crowd. She was an archaeology student from Virginia, here for the summer dig, a girl whose soft-spoken drawl hid a steel core and a hard head for drinking.

He stopped and faced her. "What is going

on here?"

"It's . . . it's so awful. . . ." She slumped before him.

"It sure as hell is." He saw the flash as camera lenses turned his way, and heard them start to click and whirl. "Start at the beginning. Tell me everything."

She responded to his command voice by straightening her shoulders and looking into his eyes. "About a week after you left, we were clearing debris in section F21 on the ramp."

He glanced down the hill toward the site. A year ago and twenty feet from the mound, they'd found a stone ramp sloping down toward the grave. Since then they'd focused their attention there, sifting through the dirt, working their way toward what Rurik believed was the entrance to the tomb. They'd followed the wide path of flat stones down into the cool, dark shadows of the earth. Twelve feet below ground level, the path ended at the corner formed by the two vertical walls that sealed the grave.

Ashley continued. "A storm came up. We set up a tarp, but the water kept dripping down our necks and the wind ripped off the corner of the tarp."

"So you quit work for the day."

"Yeah." She sniffed, dabbed her red nose

on her sleeve.

She'd been crying. Why had she been crying?

"It was a bitch of a night. Rain pouring down, and wind howling — the people in the pub said the banshees had been loosed and the world was coming to an end." She shivered as if the threat was real.

He felt no skepticism. How could he? Perhaps banshees were real — he was the last man who could discount the old legends.

"When we came back the next day, the sun was out. The light was bright and crisp. We could see for miles." She looked at the tomb as if she was remembering. "The tarp was gone. Some of the stones on the rock wall lay crumbled on the ground — and right as we walked up, the sun entered the tomb for the first time since the day it had been sealed — and the beams struck gold."

"So I heard. On every news channel in every airport."

Ashley rubbed a spot on her forehead. "I told him he should call you and then put the lid on it —"

"You told Hardwick?"

"Yes. And he didn't tell anyone, but the word got out with the villagers and from there, I swear, the rumor flew off the island without anyone saying a word." She scuffed her toe in the rough grass, holding back some . . . thing.

"But?"

"But once the reporters showed up, Hardwick couldn't take the pressure. He caved. He gave tours, he talked about the progress of the dig — he gave you all the credit. Really, he did." She touched Rurik's sleeve, so distressed he nodded acknowledgment. "He loved the limelight. We all did — it was cool to pull our heads out of the dirt and have reporters treat us like everything we said was important. But we didn't do anything wrong."

Rurik's gaze swept the crowd, noting the reporters now surging toward them. "Talking to the press may have been cool for you, but it didn't help the site." He started forward, ignoring the reporters, the tourists, the visitors who shouted his name.

Ashley hung on to his sleeve, letting him cleave a path through the crowd. "Hardwick said we didn't have a choice."

"Hardwick is an idiot."

Ashley's voice went up two octaves. "Don't say things like that about him!"

"He's supposed to be in control here. So why the hell not?" Rurik pushed through to the edge of the ramp. He took in the scene at the tomb wall — and knew the answer before Ashley answered.

One wall had been broken. The rock had crumbled on the ground. Inside, a window of gold beckoned . . . and the hilt of an ancient steel blade jutted from that window.

The point protruded from the back of Hardwick's skull.

And Tasya Hunnicutt, the woman whose careless courage filled him with fury and unease, struggled to lift the body free.

CHAPTER 3

Tasya Hunnicutt's eyes watered as she strained to lift Kirk Hardwick's limp body off the blade. She wasn't crying, exactly, but to arrive at the scene in time to see Hardwick reaching into the tomb to retrieve the first piece of gold, and trigger a thousand-year-old booby trap — that scene would play and replay in her nightmares. And in her line of work, she had viewed enough atrocities to people her nightmares; she hadn't expected one at an archaeological dig run by the cool, decisive Rurik Wilder.

But Rurik wasn't on location, and that accounted for the mistake that had cost Hardwick his life. Rurik wouldn't have allowed Hardwick to excavate the tomb while expounding for the cameras. The reporters would never have been able to bully Rurik into rushing the excavation.

She'd walked up, seen Hardwick kneeling

before the window that opened into the tomb, and heard him say, "Four to five thousand years ago, tomb mounds were constructed. Mr. Wilder's theory is that a thousand years ago, a medieval warlord called Clovus the Beheader took the structure and made it his own, stocking it with treasure in anticipation of his death."

Brandon Collins from the *London Globe* had shouted, "What led Mr. Wilder to that conclusion?"

"He did extensive research on Clovus and on the path of destruction he cut across modern-day France, England, and Scotland." Hardwick removed stones from the wall while Rurik's team of archaeologists stood back, frowning and watching intently, their arms crossed. "Mr. Wilder documented Clovus's slow disintegration from the most powerful and feared warlord of his time to a feeble man broken by illness, and he traced Clovus's retreat to this remote location —"

At that point, Tasya had leaped onto the stone path. She was the National Antiquities representative, the only one who had a chance of talking sense into Hardwick before he did harm to the site — and Rurik did harm to him.

That was why she saw the events so clearly: She'd been about ten feet away when

Hardwick interrupted himself and exclaimed with delight, "It's a treasure chest covered with gold!"

At that moment, an unseen wave of freezing rage from within the tomb engulfed her. She hadn't experienced such a shock of pure malice since the day the four-year-old she had been saw her world go up in flames. The cold took her breath away, blinded her, stopped her in her tracks.

By the time she could see and speak again, Hardwick had reached inside.

And the sword popped out of nowhere to pierce him right through the eye.

The dull glint of gold must have been the last thing he saw.

Hardwick died instantly, hung on the sword like some gruesome warning to all who dared assault the sanctity of Clovus's treasure.

The crowd gasped, murmured, shrieked . . . and shrank back from the edge of the walkway. Distantly Tasya heard the clicking and whirring of cameras and computers as the reporters and tourists fought to capture the scene and convey a story that in an instant had gone from fluff to spectacle.

No one came to her aid. They were afraid.

Tasya was afraid, too. To her, the open

grave exuded a palpable malice, as thick and green as poison. She breathed it in and urgently wanted it to clear, but the malevolence was old, potent, and endless.

Yet someone had to move Hardwick off the blade, place him on the ground, and give him the rest owed to the dead. Although she prided herself on her upper-body strength, Hardwick was both tall and pudgy, and every time she wiggled the body, the sound of the sword scraping flesh and bone made her want to throw up.

Then she heard it. The voice she'd last heard a month ago, calling her name in passion —

"Wait, Tasya, and I'll help you."

She glanced up. Saw Rurik striding down the ramp without a care for his own safety.

Two reactions hit her simultaneously.

My lover.

And . . .

The fool. The damned fool.

Releasing Hardwick, she launched herself at Rurik. She plowed her shoulder into his belly, sending him sprawling, and before he could catch his breath, she crawled on top of him and got in his face. "Have you no sense? There are more booby traps."

"Who's without sense, then?" His eyes, the color of raw brandy, blazed with irritation — at her.

If his behavior was anything to judge by, she had always irritated him. "I *am* being careful, not stomping on the path with my head held high, asking to get it chopped off."

"I've walked the path before."

"Yes, and when the first stone in that wall moved, everything in this grave went out of balance." She held Rurik's shirt in her fists and whispered softly, wanting none of the reporters to hear. "The old demon who's buried here is determined to make us pay dearly for the contents. Nothing's safe."

"Then what are *you* doing here?" His abdomen was solid. He was warm.

And she was cold and afraid. He felt like security to her.

That was wrong. So wrong. "What did you want me to do? Leave Hardwick to the carrion birds?"

He seemed to stop breathing, and his lids drooped, and his eyes grew . . . clouded, as if he fought to conceal some secret within him.

Hastily, she released his shirt.

No one knew better than she did that his straight, brown hair felt smooth when she tangled her fingers in it, that the taut body beneath his work clothes could transport a woman to ecstasy, that the tattoo that etched his chest, belly, and arm must have been a young man's foolishness, and that tracing it was a woman's. The memory of the pleasure they'd shared made her melt. The heat of possession, when he sought to brand her as his, had sent her running.

More than that — sometimes when she was close to him, she experienced the sting of something . . . frightening. Something that reminded her of that night of fire and destruction, fear, and unending darkness.

She eased herself off and away from him.

His eyes returned to normal, and they snapped with irritation. "Do you always have to be the one to fling yourself into danger? Can't you just once let someone else do the report on the massacre in Somalia or the plague in Indonesia?" He acted as if they'd had this fight a hundred times, when actually he'd never mentioned her work before.

They'd hardly talked before. Their mutual antipathy hadn't required words.

Neither had their mutual passion.

No. No memories. Not now!

She glanced up at the faces peering at them. The villagers were there. The reporters. The archaeological team. "This is no time for that conversation."

"When would you suggest we talk? After we've made love all night? No, wait. You don't stick around for a leisurely breakfast. You leave without saying good-bye." Rurik remained on the ground, mocking and, to all intents and purposes, relaxed.

He didn't fool her. Every muscle in his body was taut.

Because he wanted to grab her? To remind her that the last time she'd laid eyes on him, she'd been naked in his arms?

"Not now," she said between her teeth.

"Believe me, I realize that, or I'd be shining a light in your eyes while I interrogated you." Deliberately, he sat up, and rested his arms on his bent knees. "Tell me what happened here."

She was more than glad to change the subject. "Hardwick never saw it coming. He took one stone away and the blade popped out — it had been waiting for a thousand years for just that moment."

Rurik looked at Hardwick, and his face showed no sign of compassion. "The dumb son of a bitch."

"He didn't deserve to die for his stupidity. No one deserves that."

Rurik's gaze shifted to her. "No. No one deserves that. Unfortunately, it happens more than any of us like."

"Look, is every word you say going to be rife with significance?" She heard a murmur, glanced up at the lines of avidly staring faces, and realized her voice had risen.

"Shall we get him out of here?" Rurik asked.

He acted as if her unrestrained outburst had satisfied some perverse need in him, or proved something to him, and that made her madder. "Try not to get your head cut off. You might need it someday." She led the way back to Hardwick's body.

Rurik followed, keeping his profile low and his body tight, a man presenting a smaller target to his unseen — and long-dead — assailant. Grasping Hardwick under the arms, he lifted him easily, gently.

The tears prickled Tasya's eyes again and made her nose itch. It wasn't only sorrow and shock; seeing Rurik treat Hardwick as if he were a baby who needed his rest caused her a pang of tenderness alien to her nature.

Because how could a woman like her carry a suitcase full of tenderness on her travels? That way opened the door to heartache, and heartache interfered with work.

She wasn't a fool — she knew her work was important. Her photos shone an un-flinching light on war and poverty, and her stories chronicled injustice so unmistakably that she was persona non grata with some of the world's governments . . . and a heroine to others.

More important, when she succeeded in getting her book published with an accompanying blare of publicity, she would have improved the world, and gained the smallest, most juicy bit of personal revenge. All it took to place the book on the bestseller lists was the evidence that existed in this tomb.

She followed Rurik up the ramp, watching, listening, *feeling,* for more traps.

The crowd had fallen silent. Rurik placed the body on one of the carts the team used to cart debris away, and turned to the people who stood around.

Visibly, he gathered the reins in his hands. "Martha and Charlie, pick two of my crew to help you haul the body to the village and lay out Mr. Hardwick."

Martha was the owner of the pub/general store, about as in charge as anyone could be of Roi's two hundred fishermen, farmers, and elders. Charlie was the guy who dispensed religious advice, not a minister, but a learned man with a good head on his shoulders. They nodded, took Jessica Miller and Johnny Boden from his team, and headed for the village.

As soon as they topped the hill and disappeared from sight, the reporters started shouting questions.

He waved them to silence. "We want to offer Mr. Hardwick the proper respect, and at the same time save the site he worked so hard to excavate. Hardwick believed deeply in protecting our heritage and understanding the past, so I want everyone to stay back while I remove the treasure chest and any other valuables. Then we'll set a guard on them and the site."

Tasya watched as the reporters responded to his easy air of command, writing and recording every word he spoke.

From the first time she'd met him, she'd known he was a man born to authority. He led without ever looking back to see if anyone was following him — and they always were. His people worshipped him. She told herself it was because he'd been an Air Force pilot; she knew that because she hadn't been able to resist investigating his past. She resented that he could so effortlessly fascinate her while treating her like an insignificant pest, a squealer sent by the National Antiquities Society to police his efforts.

Then . . . they made love, and he proved

he'd been paying closer attention than she had imagined.

My God. When Rurik Wilder showed his interest in a woman, in *her,* she fell like a ton of bricks. When she discovered that all the businesslike indifference he had displayed was nothing but a facade he used to challenge her, to lure her into his arms . . . okay, she'd run. Run like a scared rabbit.

She still thought her flight had been the best, most intelligent decision she could have made . . . if she'd never had to see him again.

But here they were, standing before the tomb that would bring her success and revenge, and as she watched him take a towel and blot up the spots of Hardwick's blood on the stone and arrange for different shifts to guard the tomb, all she could think of was how much she wanted to keep him safe.

She was an idiot. Such an idiot.

His gaze shifted to hers. For one moment, her heart trilled as he focused on her.

Then he said, "Miss Hunnicutt, I'll need you to supervise the team up here while I open the tomb —"

In a flash, all her determination came rushing back. If he discovered what she hoped he would discover — proof of the

Varinskis' perfidy stretching back a thousand years — she *would* be by his side. She
smiled, a full-frontal assault of charm mixed
with resolve, and she said, "You'll need me
to take photos as you excavate the site. So
I'll stay with *you.*"

CHAPTER 4

Rurik knelt before the window into the tomb, removing the stones one by one, brushing away the dust of a thousand years. Concentrating on his work . . . and all the while, along the edges of his mind, he was aware of Tasya. He heard the clicking of her camera as she recorded his movements. Listened to her voice as she noted his progress. Felt the heat of her body as she knelt beside him.

He didn't want her here.

Every bit of research he'd done on Clovus the Beheader told him the warrior had been nothing better than a medieval serial killer — a cannibal, a savage, a bully who scorched a path of destruction across Europe, and took such pleasure in others' suffering, modern society would label him a psychopath.

Traps? Yes, for all that Clovus was most certainly burning in hell, and had no use for his plunder there, he would have made sure no one else would ever have a moment of pleasure from his loot.

Working here was nothing more or less than waiting for the next blow to fall . . . and if Rurik wasn't careful, Tasya would be the next one lying dead on a slab in the church.

At the same time, he rejoiced to know they worked together again. He would keep her alive, and somehow make her pay for making a fool of him. Make her pay with her lips and her body and her mind, over and over, until she hadn't the strength to walk away again.

As he eased each stone away, opening a larger and larger door into the home of the dead, he kept his attention on his work and away from the stone shelf that held the treasure chest.

He wanted to reach out and take it, but the lesson taught by Hardwick's greed couldn't be discounted. And, too, the placement of the chest was suspect — why put a treasure where it would be so easily seen by any casual grave robber? Why was there a stone wall behind it that concealed the interior of the tomb?

A thin sheet of hammered gold covered the box, and the brass lock held a key, waiting to turn. The treasure chest was a lure, and Rurik did not doubt that more traps awaited him.

"Wait a minute, Rurik." Tasya turned and handed Ashley the camera. "Step back — carefully! — and take pictures of the project as a whole. I want a wide frame of the walls, the path, and the hole we're opening here."

"Right." Ashley sounded glad to move back — she must be truly frightened.

As he placed his fingers on the next stone, Tasya laid her hand over his, and spoke softly in his ear. "Don't pull that one loose."

He turned to look in her eyes.

The bright blue had turned gray and grave; she knew something he didn't. "It doesn't feel right. Step away, and pull it with a stick or a grappling hook."

It doesn't feel right? What the hell does that mean?

"Why should I listen to you?" Why should he listen to a warning issued by a woman concerned with nothing but herself and her career?

Tasya's hand clenched on his. "It's not like I give a damn whether you live or die. But I'm not anxious to see another man dripping blood while he hangs on the tip of a sword."

"Charming."

"Right. So what have you got to lose?" Her sarcastic tone belied the intensity in her face. She was sure. So sure.

And while he wanted to dismiss her, he'd seen his mother, the most prosaic woman in the world, clutched in the jaws of a powerful prophecy. On that day less than two weeks ago, his life had broken in half . . . again.

A man learned from his experiences. Rurik would not dismiss Tasya's warning, but he would use the opportunity to discover more — about her, and about her past, the past about which she never spoke.

Moving with care, he withdrew his hand from the stone. He turned his palm within hers, and grasped her fingers. "Is there something you want to tell me?"

Tasya shrugged and looked away. "I have a feeling," she said in a low tone.

"Did you have a feeling about Hardwick?"

Tasya's pale complexion turned gray.

Apparently, even a tough reporter knew fear when brushed by the supernatural. "Yes. But I couldn't get to him in time."

She pulled her hand free, and he let her. She avoided his gaze, not wanting to give him an opening to question her about her intuition . . . as if he would, while reporters and tourists avidly watched, and Ashley stood behind them, camera in hand, recording every movement and word.

"Ashley, get the grappling hook," he called. As Ashley scurried up the path toward their storage shed, he smiled at Tasya. "Alone at last."

Her gaze flashed to his, then away. "Don't."

He relished the upper hand — she'd abandoned him, run without a word, without a note, without a call. He had awakened from a long night of making love to discover a cold bed and not a sign of the woman he'd so carefully, craftily courted and claimed.

Now here they were, face-to-face, alone, and she desperately wanted to avoid an intimate discussion . . . what sweet revenge. This was a resumption of the chase — but this time, he didn't bother with subterfuge or subtlety. This time, she knew he was in hot pursuit — and she knew he was pissed.

Naturally, being Tasya, she tried to take command of the situation. "This isn't the time or the place to discuss personal matters. We have a job to do."

"I agree. We'll discuss our personal matters . . . later." He allowed his gaze to wander from the crown of her head to the toes of her scruffy running shoes, touching all the important points in between. He smiled, the smile of a sultan approving of a new purchase. "This time, it will be difficult for you to run away."

She flushed a painful red. "I did *not* run."

"Like a scared rabbit." He spaced the words, taking care to emphasize each syllable. "Look at you. You can't even lie about it successfully." He laughed softly, with an edge of menace. "I intend to take possession of what is mine."

She leaned toward him, her chin jutting. "I am not *yours.*"

Into their battle stepped an unwitting civilian. Ashley chirped, "Here's the grappling hook, sir."

"Thank you." Without taking his gaze off Tasya, he accepted the long pole.

"I should have let the trap take you out," Tasya said fiercely.

"Would you save the world and let me go to hell?" he mocked.

"From where you're sitting, I promise, it's a short trip."

"But, Tasya, I'm taking you with me . . . everywhere I go."

They stared at each other, challenging each other with their bodies and their minds.

"Wow, these are going to be great pictures!" Ashley said.

He heard the clicking of the shutter. Saw Tasya turn and snatch her camera out of Ashley's hands. And he relaxed and grinned. "You're right, Ashley. Those are going to be great pictures."

By the time they finished two hours later, Rurik had sprung three more booby traps. With Ashley's help, Tasya had taken two hundred photos. They'd completely cleared the opening — and Rurik held the treasure chest in his hands.

If anything, the crowd around the tomb had got bigger. He didn't know where they were coming from; everyone on the island was already here. Then a helicopter went over, and he realized the newspeople were arriving any way they could. He'd been concentrating too hard to notice. Concentrating on his job. Concentrating on keeping Tasya safe. Concentrating on observing the sixth sense she'd been at such pains to hide.

She was sensitive to . . . what? Cruel intentions? The residue of evil that surrounded the long-dead Clovus and all his deeds?

Rurik didn't know, but he did know her knowledge hadn't taken her by surprise. She had been well aware of her ability, and that made him even more curious about her. When had she learned she had such a gift?

What event had triggered her instinct?

"Is there a booby trap in the chest?" he asked softly.

"No." She met his questioning gaze. "I'm sure." She glanced back at the tomb. "We're safe for now. There are more in there, but not . . . somehow, they're muted. Behind something, I think."

"Right." The sun was getting low on the western horizon. Reverently he carried the treasure chest up out of the shadows and into the rays that still beamed on the end of the stone path. He placed it on the ground, knelt before it.

As if on cue, Tasya knelt on one side and Ashley on the other.

He was well aware that they looked like ancient priests worshipping a golden god. He glanced at Tasya.

She snapped her photos reverently, yet with an animation that made it clear this find was important and thrilling. She played her part to perfection, for she served National Antiquities and their desperate need for funding.

He twisted the key in the bronze lock, never expecting it would open. Yet while the workings made a horrible grinding sound, the shaft of the key held steady. He opened the lid without visible hesitation.

Ashley gasped.

The crowd murmured.

Tasya's camera clicked as she took shot after shot.

The contents were everything an archaeologist could desire. They *glittered.*

With great ceremony, he removed each piece and placed it on the ground. A steel dagger with sapphires set in a silver hilt. A gold armband in the shape of a snake with ruby eyes. Rings of beaten gold and amber bracelets.

Each time he brought forth an artifact, the reporters spoke into microphones, took stills, and recorded video.

But when he reached the fine cedar base of the chest, he tapped it to make sure no false bottom existed and nothing hid in the depths, and he whispered, "Damn."

Each of my four sons must find one of the Varinski icons.

Rurik had always known the legend of the Varinskis. His father had told the story to him, to his brothers, Jasha and Adrik, and to his sister, Firebird.

A thousand years ago, a brutal warrior roamed the Russian steppes. Driven by his craving for power, the first Konstantine Varinski struck a terrible bargain. In return for the ability to change at will into a coldhearted predator, he promised his soul, and the souls of his descendants, to the devil. He paid with the blessed Varinski icons — and his mother's lifeblood.

Each of my four sons must find one of the Varinski icons.

Zorana had only three sons. One had vanished into the wilds of Asia. Her prophecy was impossible.

Yet less than a week after her vision, Jasha had arrived at their Washington home with his woman — and one of the Varinski icons: a traditional Russian rendering of the Madonna. She held the infant Jesus, Joseph stood at her right hand, and their halos glittered with gold leaf. Her robes were cherry red, the background was gold, and her eyes . . . her eyes were large and dark, filled with compassion.

So Rurik, who had already been searching for a way to break the pact, now *had* to find the next icon.

He had been an Air Force pilot; it went against every fiber of his being to believe in a vision and a prophecy.

But like the other men in his family, he lived every day bound to a pact with the devil. He'd be a fool to dismiss the supernatural, but truthfully, he put more faith in his research. He had believed he'd located the right warlord and the right tomb.

But the icon was not in the chest.

And in a tone of despair, Tasya whispered, "Damn."

He shot her a hard look.

This find brought National Antiquities publicity, a rich haul of artifacts, and reporters to cover it all.

What else could Tasya desire?

What was she looking for?

And why?

CHAPTER 5

In July in the north of Scotland, the sun rose at four in the morning.

Rurik rose earlier. He dressed in camouflage and combat boots, and set off for his usual morning run — except that this wasn't his usual morning run.

Now while he knew the reporters had pulled their pillows over their eyes and the locals were sleeping off hangovers, he ran up the road to the tomb.

He'd spent the previous evening in the village pub, eulogizing Hardwick, showing off the tomb discoveries, pretending modesty, and sharing credit with every one of his team. He'd had one too many ales, and watched Tasya as she made her way through the crowd, exchanging information with the reporters, answering questions for the tourists, and talking with the archaeologists and locals. Oh, and ignoring him. She did that with obvious and consummate ease.

At least he could take comfort in the fact that she bothered. Worse, much worse, would be if she treated him as casually as she treated the others.

It was midnight by the time he got to bed, and three a.m. when he got up, sleepless and itching to go back to the tomb.

He hadn't located the Varinski icon. The treasure chest might have contained it once — according to Rurik's research, *had* contained it once — but it was gone now.

Yet the tomb was large and Clovus had proved wilier and more ruthless than Rurik imagined; perhaps the icon was secreted somewhere inside. Or perhaps the tomb contained a clue as to its whereabouts. Today the archaeologists and reporters would rush to the tomb in hopes of more electrifying discoveries . . . so he ran.

The sun was at his back. The fresh air filled his lungs. He moved swiftly along the road, his long stride challenging the upward slope of the island.

Yet as he approached the mound, he met his men walking away.

What the hell . . . ? He stopped and waited until Connell and Tony reached him. "This isn't time for the guard to change."

Connell pointed. "MacNachtan's still up there with his rifle."

72

The grim villager stood on a cluster of rocks, silhouetted against the sky, and he sent Rurik a sharp salute.

"We couldn't see any sense in all of us being here." Tony's hair stood on end — he'd probably slept through his whole shift.

"All of us?" Rurik asked.

"Hunni said you'd be along soon," Connell said.

"Hunni?" Rurik stared at the grass, blowing in the ocean breeze, at the tomb, patient and menacing. "Tasya Hunnicutt is here?"

"Yeah, she said you wanted her to start photographing the entrance." Tony grinned at him, that infatuated grin of a man who a moment ago had his dreams fulfilled by a woman's smile and a few flirtatious words. "You know, boss, it's great to have her here from National Antiquities. She's got a real case of the hots for the stuff in there. She could be an archaeologist — she totally *gets* it."

"She is amazing." *In more ways than one.* Rurik watched the guys as they walked away.

The dumbshits. It never occurred to them Tasya might be lying, that she might have an ulterior motive. Using archaeologists to guard the tomb was like using puppies to protect a fire hydrant.

Of course, it had never occurred to *him*

Tasya would get up earlier than he did to check out the tomb. So who was the dumbshit now?

He walked down the stone ramp to the tomb's entrance, taking care that Tasya not hear him.

He'd always thought she knew too much, was too interested, had reasons of her own for following the excavation so closely. Now he intended to interrogate her — and he would enjoy every minute.

Light leaked from inside the tomb. She had some source of illumination set up, and he could hear her camera as she took picture after picture. Taking care not to alert her to his presence, he eased around to peer inside.

There she was, dressed in a camouflage T-shirt tucked into her glorious tight jeans.

No wonder his guys believed every word she said. The woman had a shape that made a man want to throw that football through that tire. Repeatedly.

She wore black work boots, and her khaki backpack rested on the floor beside her. One might suppose she'd come dressed for the dust in the tomb . . . or if one was suspicious, one might believe she'd worn camouflage for the same reason he had. So she wouldn't be easily seen.

She knelt at the wall behind the shelf where the treasure chest had been placed. Carvings covered the stone, and she leaned close, macro lens on her camera, to capture each panel.

How fascinating. She worked exactly the wall he intended to examine.

Why would she be interested in the carvings when the interior of the tomb might contain more gold? More jewels?

What was she looking for?

Right now, he didn't care.

Because they were alone. Just as he'd promised her, he had her cornered, and she had nowhere to run.

Deliberately, he loomed in the entrance, blocking the sunlight that reached inside, touching the wall . . . touching her.

As she swung around, she crouched into a fighting position.

"You're nervous." He ducked down and entered the tomb. "Why? Are you guilty?"

"Rurik. What are you doing here?" She looked him right in the eyes.

"According to what you told my guys, I'm supposed to meet you here."

"Yeah. Well." She put her camera around her neck and fussed with the settings.

Yep. She was guilty.

"I couldn't wait to see what's inside the

tomb," she said.

"But you're not inside. You're concentrating on the wall carvings in the entrance. Why would that be?"

"I'm the National Antiquities photographer. I need to record each piece of this tomb." Her black hair curled riotously, as if she'd done no more this morning than run her fingers through the strands.

Rurik reached out.

She tried to dodge, then consciously stood still.

Was she trying to convince him she didn't care if he touched her? *Good luck.*

He tucked a curl behind one ear.

She chewed her lip.

Smart girl. She should be apprehensive.

Sliding his hand behind her neck, he pulled her toward him.

"No." She put up her fists.

"Try and stop me." He smiled a toothy smile. "I would really like it if you fought."

"Why? What are you going to do? Force me to kiss you?" She sounded scornful as only an independent woman could sound.

"I don't have to force you to do anything." He whispered in her ear, "I'm going to get you so hot, we'll melt together, and you'll never know where I end and you begin."

The way she caught her breath did wonders for his temperament.

Turning his head, he kissed her cheek. "But later." Later, when he had toyed with her, kept her off balance, threatened hell, and promised heaven.

He couldn't make her love him, he couldn't make her stay with him, but by God, if she ran again, she would remember him.

Turning his attention to the wall, and in a tone guaranteed to annoy her, he said, "This shows Clovus getting a gift that looks very much like a . . . wait, yes, it looks invaluable. . . . It looks like the wrapping on a Hershey bar!"

Actually, it looked about the shape and size of an icon. But medieval artists didn't use realistic perspective, and stone carvers in the north of Scotland at times lacked the skills of the southern artisans. Until he'd studied the script, he couldn't be sure what gift Clovus had received, and even then, it would be tough; time had worn pieces and patches away.

"Don't be a jerk." Obviously, Tasya had never meant anything so sincerely. "It's too short and too wide to be a Hershey bar. Believe me. I know my Hershey bars." She looked in the camera's viewfinder again, and took photos from several angles.

Why Tasya was so interested he didn't know. But in the end, what did it matter? As long as he could read the writing and study the carvings, he would succeed in his part of the quest. "Did you take photos of everything?"

"I took an overview. Now I'm getting it from every angle using all kinds of light."

"Good. Still no woo-woo about the booby traps?"

"Nothing. We're safe."

"Well." He removed the flashlight from the pocket on his leg. "I'm safe. You're in deep trouble."

She stopped taking photos and turned on him in exasperation. "You don't have to be obnoxious every chance you get."

"I'm not being obnoxious. I'm being truthful." He picked his way through the rubble on the floor and around the edge of the wall, and shone the light into the ante-chamber of the tomb.

The walls were stone, dense and dark, and his head brushed the stone ceiling. Ancient tools and animal bones cluttered the floor, and before the far wall stood a stone altar. A half-opened stone sarcophagus leaned against it.

Tasya stepped inside with him. "What's in here?"

"A mixture of Bronze Age and early medieval artifacts. That confirms my suspicions — the tomb is probably four thousand years old, and Clovus removed the king buried here, and confiscated the burial ground for himself."

"That guy had no fear, did he?"

"No fear of the dead, and no respect for the past. I suspect that sarcophagus contains the first occupant of the tomb."

"I don't like this place." She shrugged uneasily. "Where's Clovus?"

"The burial chamber is in there." Rurik nodded toward a wall of smooth stones.

"Yes." She shivered. "I can feel him."

He knew nothing about her. Nothing. And here was his chance. "What do you feel? How do you know it's him? How long have you been able to tell if a man is evil?"

He didn't think she would answer, but she took his questions one at a time. "I feel as if I'm being smothered by darkness. I don't know for sure it's Clovus, but who else would it be? And I felt *them* when I was four, and I've never forgotten the sensation."

"Them?" She had his complete attention. "Who's them?"

She paid him no heed, but gradually turned her head toward the entrance and stared intently. She whispered, "Perhaps it's not Clovus I feel. Because . . . they're here."

At the same time, he heard the voices, and it didn't take her warning for him to recognize their accent, their boastful tone, their menace.

Varinskis. Son of a bitch. Varinskis. His cousins from hell had found him.

Varinskis were trained to ferret out the unwary, to assassinate their enemies, to destroy whatever it suited them to destroy. Usually, they performed their assassinations and sabotage only for their paying clients.

No one was paying them now. They hunted the Wilders for vengeance. They'd found his older brother, Jasha. Now they'd found him.

Rurik was caught here . . . between his fate and a woman who made his heart ache and his temper flare.

His death would put an end to his family's hopes, but he'd fight, and he'd get Tasya out. She didn't deserve to die because she was with him.

"Get back," he said. "Get behind the altar."

She looked at the camera in her hand. "My backpack. My backpack's there in the entrance!"

He hurried, grabbed her backpack and her

flashlight, and hustled her to the back wall. Together they knelt behind the altar. He put her behind him — and with a gasp, she vanished into the wall. A short panel of solid rock had swiveled and swallowed her.

He reached into the pitch-darkness.

She caught his hand in hers, and her hand trembled. So did her voice. "I'm here. It's a passage."

Yes. The fresh air blew in right from the sea.

He leaned in. His vision was excellent — more than excellent — and he saw a small stone chamber and a tunnel twisting away into the earth. He shoved her backpack and flashlight toward her. "Go. I need to hear what they say."

Pulling himself back into the antechamber of the tomb, he closed the wall, crouched, and waited.

There were four of them, men, of course — the Varinskis produced only sons — and Rurik realized at once they didn't suspect he was here.

He also realized that Boris, the head of the Varinskis, hadn't sent his top men on this mission. Or if he had, the Varinskis were sadly overrated. Because these guys were loud, inept, unworried about what, or who, might be hiding in the tomb. They walked

81

right in, boys without a care in the world.

One of them, a husky thirty-year-old, carried a good-sized leather bag. "So, what's the big deal here?" he asked in Russian.

"Yeah, why did we have to come to a crap little island in Scotland?" Another guy examined the stone pillar and the wall that blocked the entrance. He wore a cowboy hat and boots, and looked like a Cossack imitating a Texan.

Rurik slid around, staying behind the altar, watching.

The leader was maybe forty, and he stood in the middle of the tomb with his hands on his hips. "Apparently one of the old boys had a vision. I don't know what it was, but man, did it scare Boris."

"I was there when it happened," the youngest boy said.

The other three turned on him.

"You were not." The leader plainly didn't believe him.

"Yes, I was," the kid insisted. "Freaky Uncle Ivan, the blind guy with the white film over his eyes, called Boris over like he could see him, grabbed him by the throat, and in this voice that sounded like . . . like . . ." The kid shivered. "It sounded deep and strong and spooky."

"Uncle Ivan never has liked Boris," the

leader said. "He's baiting him."

The kid shrugged uneasily. "Yeah. I wish I believed that."

"So what did he say?" one of the other guys asked.

"Uncle Ivan told Boris the deal with the devil is breaking apart, that unless the Varinskis get their shit together and kill that guy who married the Gypsy —"

"Konstantine," the leader said.

"Yeah, Konstantine. If the Varinskis didn't kill Konstantine and his whelps and the bitch he married, the Varinskis would become a laughingstock and the pact would be broken. The whole thing gave me the creeps."

The story gave Rurik the creeps, too. He'd assumed his mother's vision was an isolated incident, and without considering it, he'd figured some benevolent force had worked through her. The vision had warned his family of trouble, instructed them about how to break the pact with the devil.

Now it sounded as if one of the Varinskis had had a similar vision telling Boris to destroy Konstantine and his family — or else.

Shit.

"So what has this place got to do with it?" The guy with the bag pulled it open. He

83

tossed a round metal disk to each of the others.

"Uncle Ivan said there was an icon, some kind of holy thing, that we had to find." The kid caught a disk and attached it to a pillar. "I guess the icon's here, and we're going to blast it to smithereens."

Rurik, who'd been concentrating on eaves-dropping, realized that his killer cousins . . . were the demolition team.

No wonder they didn't care if someone hid in here. They were going to blow the tomb, and possibly destroy the icon, his father's chance for salvation, and . . . oh, God, would Tasya survive?

"You knew Konstantine, didn't you, Kaspar?" the kid asked.

"I knew him," the leader said.

"Is it true he was the biggest, best boss we ever had, and Boris was afraid of him?" The three subordinates turned to Kaspar and waited for the answer.

"He wasn't the biggest, but he was smart. Wily. When he fought, he always won. He had great strategies, and when he was in charge, the Varinskis were the greatest power in the world." Kaspar spit on the ground. "Not like now."

The team was quiet, setting the charges.

Rurik didn't dare move. The icon . . . and

Tasya. Would he lose them both?

The kid said, "Boris better do something soon, or he's going down."

"Did you overhear that, too?" Kaspar mocked.

"Boris is my father, but Vadim is my brother. Vadim has my loyalty, and I promise, he's the next boss." The kid smiled, and turned his head toward the sunlight.

Rurik jumped.

His lips were colored red; his cheeks were equally bright; his eyes were slanted. Maybe he wore makeup so he could look like that, but Rurik didn't think so. That kid was a natural freak.

"Don't be a fool," Kaspar said sharply. "Vadim's too young."

The kid hissed at Kaspar. He swayed, and Rurik had a sudden vision of what the kid could become. . . . The pupils in his eyes were pointed from top to bottom, his smooth skin gleamed as if covered by nail polish, and the teeth in that red mouth were pointed like a vampire's . . . or a rattlesnake's.

Kaspar snapped his fingers at the kid. "Stop it! Alek, we don't have time for that shit. We've got to get this done before someone comes to check the tomb."

Alek stopped swaying.

"If anybody catches us, it'll be a damned mess," Kaspar added.

"Okay. But don't jeer at my brother, or he'll get you." Alek took his charge and leaned down to set it.

When Kaspar was sure Alek paid him no heed, he turned his back and used his handkerchief to wipe his forehead.

Rurik felt like doing the same thing. Varinskis were birds of prey or wolves or panthers. Never snakes. Never something that slithered on the ground and killed by poison. What had happened? When had this change occurred?

When Alek straightened up, Kaspar asked, "Charges in place? Timers set?" When everybody nodded, he said, "Then let's get the hell out of here."

The Varinskis hustled out at a speed that expressed only too clearly the power of the blast. Rurik dived through the wall and into the tunnel — and ran into Tasya.

"What did you find out?" she whispered.

"What the hell are you doing here? Run. Run!" He shoved her forward.

Smart girl. She didn't ask for details. She responded to his agitation and sprinted into the darkness.

He raced with her, his hand on her back.

The light faded behind them. The tunnel

got narrower and shorter. They ran through dirt now, with a few rocks . . . but the scent of the sea lured Rurik on.

Darkness surrounded them. Tasya stumbled on the rubble on the floor.

He kept her on her feet. "Bend down. The ceiling is dropping. We're going to have to crawl — now." He shoved her to her knees and pushed her ahead of him. The tunnel narrowed more, but ahead and around a corner, he could see light. "We're almost there."

"It's getting so tight." She was panting from exertion, but more than that — she was panicked.

Claustrophobia. What a hell of a time to find that out. "Let me get in front. If I can get through, you can."

"Yeah. Okay." The thought seemed to make her feel better.

Maybe it wasn't a good idea to add to her terror, but from what he knew of Tasya's character, she would rise to the occasion. As he squeezed past her, he said, "Keep up. The tomb is going to blow."

She kept up.

They rounded the corner. He could see the sunlight ahead. It was a small hole, but they could make it out. They were crawling, moving fast. The tunnel narrowed more, decaying to a mere burrow, and he found himself wiggling along on his belly. "A few more yards. A few more!"

At first, the vibration was a hum in the earth. It grew to a rumble. The tremor came from behind, caught them. The ground lifted once, a huge shock. His hand grasped a stone on the wall outside.

Tasya screamed.

And in the violent shaking, the tunnel collapsed, burying them in the earth.

CHAPTER 6

Tasya couldn't breathe. She couldn't breathe. There wasn't air. It was dark. The earth weighed her down. She had dirt in her mouth, in her lungs.

All her life, this had been her nightmare.

She was buried alive.

She flailed helplessly, disoriented, not knowing which way was *out.*

Then some *thing* grabbed her. Pulled her by her shoulders. She fought, trying to help. Trying to get away.

She hit something hard with her head. Felt something frantically slither past her. Grabbed a metal rod and used it as an oar. Tried to scream, but she couldn't *breathe.*

Oh, God. She was going to die. In the darkness. She was going to suffocate in the darkness.

And suddenly, her head was out. Out, in the open. She couldn't see; her eyes were caked with dirt. She couldn't breathe. Dirt filled her mouth and nose. But the weight was gone from her head. She could feel the air, and savored the impression of sunshine.

Some *thing* pulled her harder. Pulled her all the way out of the tunnel that had been her grave, and flung her on the ground.

Frantically, she brushed at her face, spit earth, still couldn't breathe. Her head was buzzing.

She was dying.

"Stop." *Rurik. Rurik is here.* "I'll help you."

He put his mouth to hers and gave her his breath.

Her lungs expanded. When he pulled away, she coughed. Coughed and coughed, spewing dirt, getting air, blowing her nose . . . she was alive. She felt like hell, but she was alive.

When she could open her eyes, she found herself propped up on a narrow rock ledge on the cliff over the sea. They were about ten feet below the level of the ground above, and about ninety feet above the ocean.

Rurik sat beside her, his arms resting on his upraised knees, his hands dangling. He stared out to sea. Dirt caked his hair, his eyebrows, his clothes, his skin. Dirt was in his ear. A cut on his forehead oozed blood.

He gave her an idea how horrible she must look.

She didn't care. She was alive.

She leaned her head back against the stone. The air smelled good, like the ocean . . . and the earth. The rocks dug into her back, and the discomfort told her she was alive. Dirt filled her boots, and pebbles had worked their way between her toes, and that was good, too.

"You afraid of heights?" Rurik asked.

"Nope." Far below, the waves pounded the rocks. "Just the dark."

He nodded. "I can't believe you made it out with that backpack."

She looked down. While she'd waited for Rurik at the entrance of the tunnel, she'd placed the backpack on her front, tightened the straps as much as she could. "Camera," she said.

He chuckled a little. "Figures." And, "Is it okay?"

She unzipped the main flap, pulled out the Nikon, and examined it. Her water-proof, dirt-proof, ripstop, padded backpack had come through. "Looks good."

"Good girl." He chuckled again.

Tenderly, she put her beloved camera back away.

Pulling his cell phone out of his pocket, he opened it. Dirt showered out. "Shit." The screen was cracked.

He shook it, pushed TALK, put it to his ear. "Shit," he said again. "It wasn't built for a cave-in." He put it back in his pocket. "Have you got one?"

"In my backpack," she said vaguely. "It's off, though. Who's going to call me?"

"I don't know. Your mother? Your father?"

She gazed across the ocean. A thin, pale gray line crept up from the horizon, swallowing the blue sky. "My parents are dead."

"Your other lover?"

"He's busy," she said without missing a beat.

"Are you trying to make me jealous?"

"No."

"No. Of course not. To do that, you would have to care."

Do you really want to talk about this now? But she didn't ask. He did want to talk, anytime, anywhere. And she wanted to avoid that confrontation at all costs. She started to unzip the backpack. "Do you want to call your family? Because when news of the explosion hits, they're going to worry."

He placed his hand over hers to stop her. "They won't worry, not for a few days, anyway. I have a way of landing smoothly. No, keep your phone off for now."

She knew why. Pointing up at the top of the cliff, she asked, "Are we in danger here?"

"No. Those boys never knew we were in the tomb. They certainly don't know we escaped."

"I knew the legend was overrated," she said with satisfaction.

He rolled his head toward her. "What legend?"

"I'll tell you when we're off this island."

His eyes narrowed. He started to speak. Changed his mind. Spoke anyway. "What are you holding?"

She would bet that wasn't what he'd been about to say.

She looked down at her hand. She gripped a piece of dirty, rust-encrusted metal about eight inches long and narrow as a blade. "I don't know. A knife of some kind. It sort of found me while you were pulling me out."

"Keep it. We'll examine it later."

She unzipped the pocket in her backpack, the one on the outside for the water bottle she never carried, and dropped the ancient thing inside.

Rurik watched her, and disappointment turned his mouth into a thin line. "That knife may be the only thing left from the excavation."

"I'm sorry." She put her hand on his arm. "I know what that tomb meant to you."

He considered her hand. Looked up at

her. And his eyes were savage. Almost . . . frightening, with a red flame deep inside.

She caught her breath. She yanked her hand away.

"As long as you're alive, the tomb is nothing."

She'd expected him to hit on her, grab her, kiss her. Not say *that.* And to say it in such a serious tone . . . "I've been in danger before."

"Not like this. Not because of me."

He could be so irritating — and powerful, and seductive. He made her put up all her defenses, because he made her feel safe from the world — and in peril from him. If she gave in to him, leaned on him, trusted him, she would be the biggest fool in the history of the world. She kept her voice brisk and unwelcoming. "You give yourself too much credit. I'm afraid I'm the one who's put you in danger."

At first he started to deny it. Then he chuckled. "Yes. You could infuriate a saint. But no matter whose fault this is, I'm going to do everything in my power to keep you alive." He stood and extended his hand.

She let him pull her to her feet.

Sliding his arm around her waist, he pulled her close and leaned his forehead against hers. "I can't predict the future, but

I know this has just begun."

His eyelashes were grainy with dirt, but his brown eyes were somber, calm, thoughtful — and he wasn't talking about the tomb or the explosion; he was talking about *them.*

Scary. Rurik was scary when he was like this.

Not physically scary. She never thought he would hurt her. But relentless scary.

He wanted her, and he intended to have her. Maybe she could explain why that was impossible. Maybe she could confess her past, and explain the danger of being with her, and frighten him away.

But Rurik didn't seem to frighten easily, and if she talked about the ghosts that haunted her — he'd know. He'd know the brave-reporter facade was a sham, that she was a frightened little girl who shivered in the night. He'd shine a light into the dark corners of her soul, and she'd be forced to face the memories and the fears.

Then . . . what if he hated what he saw? What if he laughed and told her to grow up? What if he used her fears to manipulate her?

What if he walked away?

No, she was better off keeping him at arm's length.

How's that going, Tasya?

Not too good, since he's holding me pressed against his body and looking into my eyes like he understands way, way too much.

Moving with slow deliberation, she untangled herself. "Look, we need to get back to the reporters and the archaeologists so I can upload the photos I took yesterday and today, and send them to my boss at National Antiquities. I'm not too happy about carrying around the only real record of your findings, and they'll be safe on the National Antiquities computer."

Rurik kept one hand on her as she stepped away. Maybe because the rock shelf where they stood was only three feet wide. Maybe because he didn't want to let her go. "I listened to the guys who blew up the tomb. Someone back there wants *all* the information erased. These are well-funded, desperate men, possibly ecoterrorists, and as witnesses, we need to lie low and not be recognized until we can talk to the authorities."

She almost told him then. It would have been such an easy segue from his speech to an explanation of who those men were, and the real reason why they'd set their explosives.

But then she'd have to tell Rurik what she'd been up to, and that she had put him, and his beloved excavation, in danger.

She looked over the edge of the shelf.

It was a long drop to the ocean.

She'd tell him afterward.

CHAPTER 7

Rurik kept an eye on Tasya as she climbed the cliff behind him.

She wasn't lying. She had no fear of heights. No fear of anything that he could see — except the dark.

He'd love to know why, but now was not the time. Now they had to run. Run far and fast, protect those photos of the wall carvings, study them, and maybe, just maybe, find a way to save not only his father's life but also his father's soul.

"Here's the situation." Rurik reached the top of the cliff. He flopped onto the flat ground, and belly crawled away from the edge. "We've got to get off this island without being spotted, and I've prepared for such an eventuality."

On a cliff a hundred feet over the ocean, Tasya stopped climbing. She ignored his hand, wiggling for her to grasp it, and looked at him as if he was nuts.

He didn't give her the chance to ask. "I've stashed survival gear not far from here."

"Sure you did." Tasya finished her climb, and flopped on the flat ground, too.

They'd come a long way in the tunnel, and now a rise concealed them from Clovus's tomb. The bare, treeless island left them little in the way of cover; he would have to use the contours of the earth to keep them out of sight.

Not that any of that mattered. If the Varinskis came looking for them, they would be found. He knew them by reputation. He recognized them in his blood.

From the day he was born, his father had trained him to expect trouble, to be prepared for trouble, to walk unseen and hear every sound. Konstantine had trained his sons — and his daughter — for the Varinskis' inevitable appearance. Rurik wasn't surprised that they'd arrived now; he was surprised only that it had taken them so long to find him.

"No one will ever spot us." Tasya brushed at her clothes and ran her fingers through her hair. Dirt showered everywhere. "We're part of the earth."

He marveled at her naïveté.

She glanced up and caught him staring at

her. "What? Why do you look at me that way?"

"Come on." He drew Tasya away from the tomb, leading her swiftly across the Isle of Roi, hoping they could escape before they were spotted. Perhaps he could commandeer a fishing boat? . . . Or the ferry?

"I've been thinking about how to get off the island." She followed close on his heels. "My ultralight is here."

"An *ultralight*?" He stopped so suddenly she almost ran into him, and swung around to face her. "What do you mean, an ultralight?"

"You know — small, fixed-wing airplane designed to fly short distances at a slow speed?"

"I know what an ultralight is," he said in irritation. "*Why* is it here?"

"I like to fly. It's beautiful here, and the skies aren't crowded." But she glanced aside.

She didn't want him to look into her eyes. Why not? "When did you bring it?"

"While you were gone."

"When did you start flying?"

"I took lessons last time I was in the States."

Lessons. Last time she was in the States. "Why now?"

"Why wait?"

"Where did you land?" An ultralight. The damned things were notoriously unstable. A person could get killed —

"I've got the plane," he shouted as he grabbed the controls.

A stark mountain face loomed before them.

The missile was almost on them.

He drove the plane up and to the side.

They weren't going to make it —

"There's lots of flat ground here to use as a runway." She was getting annoyed.

Good. "Again — *why* did you bring an ultralight to Scotland?"

"What is it with the interrogation?" she burst out. "What's wrong with having an ultralight? Lots of people enjoy them. You know, hobbies and stuff!"

A hobby. She thought flying was a *hobby.* "Lots of people enjoy their ultralights when they're home. But on an island in the North Atlantic? Where you visit only occasionally? Where the wind currents are treacherous and a good storm off the ocean will push that ultralight into the drink?"

Rurik drove the plane up and to the side.

They weren't going to make it —

He breathed hard, trying to throw off the memories. "It is very *convenient* that you brought it just when we have trouble. I don't trust *convenient.*"

"All right. Maybe I suspected there might be trouble because of the book I've written about the Varinski family and specifically nailing the Varinski Twins."

The Varinskis.

He forgot the plane. He forgot the ultralight.

The Varinskis.

He felt exactly as he had when the tunnel collapsed. Stunned, winded, unable to grasp the magnitude of the disaster.

She stood and looked up at him, his mouth agape. "Great teeth."

He snapped his jaw shut. "Give me more information."

"My publishers have me set up for an interview on *GMA* as soon as I lay my hands on some proof of their legend. I'm pretty sure having them blow the tomb that I happen to be exploring will put me and my story on the front page."

"I'm pretty sure you're right. Tell me all about it when we're off the island." Grabbing her arm, he marched her toward his hiding place.

"Besides, *you've* got survival gear hidden on the island. That's convenient, too." She was panting, but she snapped as briskly as ever.

"My father taught his children always to anticipate every threat, then be thankful if danger doesn't rear its ugly head."

"Your dad's a survivalist?"

"You could say that."

"Is that why you live in the mountains in Washington? I always heard they were full of —" She caught herself in time.

"Head cases? I know a lot of them." He knew a lot of Varinskis, too — only their last names were Wilder.

She looked sorry she'd asked.

"But actually, my parents moved to Washington to avoid their families. The families didn't want them to marry, so my folks ran away." *Don't tell Tasya the truth. At least — not all of it.*

"A love match."

"For sure. They're the reason I believe in love."

Now Tasya looked as if she wanted to sprint away.

Yeah, honey, I can talk about love, and that scares you to death — and I'm going to find out why.

They reached the headspring of the stream that ran across the island. The ancients had worshipped here, too, piling stones around the spring, planting a single tree. It was dead now, except for one branch, warped by the winds that constantly blew off the ocean.

Rurik stripped off his boots and his belt. "What about your parents? You said they were dead, but were they a love match?"

"I don't think so. I think it was an arranged marriage." She clamped her mouth shut.

"An arranged marriage? In this day and age?" Taking his dead cell phone out of his pocket, he dropped it into one boot.

"They weren't born in the United States."

Tasya really clamped the lid on her private info.

Luckily for him, he was good at prying. "But did they love each other?" He stepped into the stream.

"I don't remember. They died a long time ago." She watched him, frowning.

Without hesitation, he reclined. The clear, cold water flowed over him, stripping away the dirt that had worked its way into every crevice. It cleansed his scent, too — if the Varinski bomb squad got smart enough to look for him, they wouldn't easily track him.

When he came up out of the water, he shook his head like a dog, spraying water everywhere.

"What did you do that for?" Tasya asked in a tone that clearly told him she'd already asked several times.

He looked up at her. "The question isn't, what did I do that for? It's, why aren't you doing it?" He stood and stepped out, wiping the water from his face, squeezing the worst from his clothes.

She glanced up at the sky.

The line of thin gray had overtaken the blue, and the sun faded. The breeze kicked up; they hadn't much time before the Scottish summer storm stole the warmth.

Kneeling, she thrust her hand in the water, and grimaced at the cold. She looked at him again.

He pointed to himself. "Clean."

She removed her boots and her belt, and with great care set her backpack aside. "All right." Taking a deep breath, she immersed herself.

She was exactly like him. She probably tore off her bandages in one swift yank, too.

While she writhed in the stream like a beached salmon, he lifted two carefully balanced rocks from the primitive monument and recovered his survival gear.

Tasya wasn't the only one with a backpack that could outlast a nuclear blast. He had a change of socks in there. One passport identifying him as John Telford, and one identifying him as Cary Gilroy. A flashlight.

A compass. A signal mirror. Matches in a waterproof cylinder. Fishing line. First aid kit. Iodine tablets. Freeze-dried rations. Space blanket. Three knives, a small pistol and ammo, sunglasses, a hat — and a razor.

He waited until Tasya came out of the water, sputtering with cold. "You look good." The dirt had washed downstream, leaving her pale skin damp and vibrantly pink. Her short, curly, black hair sprang up in every direction, and . . . oh, damn, he could see her nipples poking through her shirt.

He didn't want to see the outline of her nipples right now. He didn't want to think about her breasts, or the curve of her waist, or her tiny clit, or the way she made him feel when he pressed into her and she moaned and came. . . .

They were trapped on a Scottish island. They needed to get off before his cousins caught up with them. The best way off was an ultralight that Tasya had brought over for some nefarious reason.

And he'd sworn never to fly. Not like that. Not with the wind in his face.

Death had come too close today; the cave-in had closed his eyes and his ears, the earth had weighed too much, and for a few horrified minutes, he'd thought they'd both

breathed their last. He'd thought the Varinskis had won.

Then he'd fought his way out to stand on
the ledge, dirt cascading off him — and the
damned tunnel had collapsed behind him.

He'd had to go back in. Into the airless
darkness to rescue Tasya — or die with her.

He'd served as midwife and pulled her
free, and now, whether she liked it or not,
the strength of that portent bonded them
together.

Foolish woman. She didn't understand.

But he walked the sidewalk of legend
every day, and lived with the proof of evil.
In his mother's prophecy, he had seen the
evidence of God.

Now with death's cold stench still in his
nostrils, two great wants tore at him —
wanting to fly, wanting her. Both needs
heated his blood, and all the frigid water in
the world couldn't wash them away.

And Tasya offered one while withholding
the other.

She didn't understand . . . anything.

He thrust the razor at her. "Shave my
head."

"Shave your —"

"There's no faster way to change my
looks. I need to be unrecognizable."

She half grinned, and dropped into her

best Mae West imitation. "I don't know how to break it to you, big boy, but a guy who's six foot four is recognizable anywhere."

He didn't grin back. "The gold at the site is big news. The explosion is even bigger news, and the newspeople are here to cover it. Our disappearance will lead to speculation — first, that we're buried in the tomb, then when our bodies aren't found, that we set the charges."

She blinked, startled. "That sucks."

"Yeah. But it's reality. If you want to get somewhere safe and upload those photographs, shave my head."

She got serious. "Everyone's going to look at you."

"Honey, everyone expects big-ass guys to look tough, and the meaner I look, the less anyone wants to look directly at me, or talk about me, or think about me."

"Yeah." She stared at his brown hair, dark and wet, then at the razor in her hand.

During the night they'd spent together, she'd touched his hair, over and over, running her fingers along his scalp, stroking the strands.

In her eyes, he saw the memories.

For sure, she didn't want to shave his head. But she gave a jerky nod, and pointed to the ground.

He sat, cross-legged in front of her, and took care not to flinch as she slid the razor carefully along his scalp.

"What are we going to do about me?" The razor was new and sharp, but with only the water to ease the passage, she still removed the very top layer of skin.

"You're going to wear my hat and sunglasses, and as soon as we can find you different clothes, you're changing your style."

"Do you always think this fast?" She was getting the hang of it, the razor sliding more smoothly.

"It's part of my training."

"Air Force training, you mean."

So. She'd researched him. But there was no way for her to research his family. Konstantine had covered their tracks so well, no reporter could trace their background. "The Air Force taught me a little, but mostly it was my father. A survivalist, remember?"

She lifted the razor away from his scalp. "Are you making fun of me?"

He stoically stared straight ahead. "No."

"Smart. I'm already scraping you raw. I wouldn't want to slip and cut you."

For the first time since arriving on the island yesterday, he grinned and relaxed. They teetered on the edge of disaster, and she threatened him. Not because she didn't comprehend the danger — she most definitely did — but because no matter what the circumstances, she didn't take shit off anybody.

She stirred his body to madness, yes, but even if she hadn't, he would still adore her. "Don't worry about scraping me. Or cutting me. I heal quickly." *Very quickly.* "Tell me about the ultralight." Because the damned thing was the best, fastest way off the island, and he might be able to get himself away without being detected, but the two of them?

No. She was right. They would have to fly.

"It's a two-seater, a little heavier than normal. I can get us to the mainland."

While he broke the oath he'd made as he'd stared at Jedi's broken, tortured body. The brightest young pilot he'd ever flown with . . .

He rubbed his chest, the spot over his sorrowful heart.

But maybe it wasn't so bad. Every day he ached to fly, and if he refrained from taking the controls, if he held back from the ecstasy of being the pilot, perhaps he still embraced the essence of his vow.

"There." She brushed the loose hair off his shoulders, stood back, and inspected him. "I did an okay job, although you sort of look like —" She searched her mind.

"A pecker head?" He ran his hands over his scalp, wincing at the abrasions, but pleased to find it mostly smooth.

"Well . . . yeah." She shivered as the wind kicked up.

Off in the distance, he heard the roar of an airplane. He glanced up; it was a seaplane, landing on the ocean, loaded with reporters or curiosity seekers or the police. Yes, the report of the explosion had gone out.

"Get ready to go." He put on his dry socks, loaded his backpack, donned his belt.

She did the same. "After we land, we'll have to walk a little to rent a car —"

"No. I've scouted out a bed-and-breakfast. Out of the way. We'll stay there tonight."

"But if we drive all night, we can get to Aberdeen by morning —"

"We don't want to drive at night. We don't need headlights on a winding, empty road at night in the middle of Scotland. It's darker than the ace of clubs out there, everyone's going to be hunting us, and the first guy that finds us will either kill us or interview us repeatedly." When she would have objected, he held out his hand. "You get us off the island. I'll get us out of

Scotland alive."

She looked at his palm, reluctance clear on her face.

She didn't want to be with him any longer than required. Yet she knew he was right.

"I'll hold you to that." She tried to make this a business deal. She tried to shake his hand.

Instead, he captured her, opened her fingers, stared at her palm. At the pale, sensitive skin and the lines experience and fate had carved there. "Do you realize what happened today?"

"What?" She watched him suspiciously.

"You and I were reborn from Mother Earth, clawing our way out of the birth canal and into precarious life." Rurik stared down at her. "Together."

He could almost see Tasya's hackles rise. "What does *that* mean?"

"I don't know, but lately I've learned one thing — omens are not to be ignored." Tenderly, he brought her palm to his lips, and kissed the pad beneath her thumb. "I suspect that, soon enough, we'll find out what it means."

CHAPTER 8

Tasya waited until they were airborne and over the ocean before calling back, "You never fly anymore."

Rurik didn't answer. He sat directly behind her on the tiny seat, his body warm against her backbone. During preflight and takeoff, he'd been tense and uncommunicative, and she remembered all too clearly that her research had turned up Rurik's resignation from the Air Force following the accidental death of his copilot.

She hadn't been able to get more information than that; her inquiries had made the Air Force tight-lipped and suspicious, so she'd dropped the matter. She couldn't afford to make them mad; a woman who traveled the world taking photographs never knew when she might need military assistance.

But obviously Rurik had suffered some trauma because, except for taking commercial airlines, he hadn't flown since.

The motor — small, compact — hummed loudly, but the breeze blew the sound away. His weight made the ultralight handle differently. His silence made her want to help him relax. She chatted, "My instructor told me I have a real sense for flying. I don't know if he was bullshitting me, but I love this. I love the wind in my hair. I love the feeling of freedom."

No response.

"When I'm up here, I wish I could do this forever. I wish I could climb to the clouds, and skim the tops of the trees. But I won't." She chuckled. "Am I making you nervous?"

No response.

"Did you feel like that when you flew?"

Still no response.

She didn't know if he was petrified or catching a nap. As soon as they were over the mainland and the winds stabilized enough for her to glance away, she twisted around and looked at him.

His eyes were closed.

But he wasn't afraid.

He wasn't asleep.

He wore an expression of bliss unlike any she'd seen . . . except once, when she'd held him in her arms, in her body, and felt him shudder in ecstasy.

She faced forward again, and wondered what the story behind his flying might be — and desperately wished she didn't care.

CHAPTER 9

Rurik stood on the mat in the entry of the small bed-and-breakfast. He was dripping from the rain that had been falling for the last four hours, and Mrs. Reddenhurst wouldn't let him walk any farther into the warmth.

Instead, she stood with her hands on her ample hips, and impatiently listened to him beg.

"Please, my wife and I need a room." He wiped his face with the kitchen towel she handed him. "We decided to hike the Highlands for our honeymoon. Because we both have, you know, Scottish ancestry. And we really liked *Braveheart.* We were supposed to stay in Cameron Village tonight, but then the rain started falling —"

"A wee mist." Mrs. Reddenhurst was tall, stout, and brisk, with a strong accent. "It does that here."

"Yes, I guess it does. We brought slickers."

He lifted the edge of his poncho and showed her the camouflage waterproof nylon. "But we took the wrong turn. We're cold and we're hungry. Please, please, if you have any compassion in your heart —"

This place was perfect. Small, out-of-the-way, a private home that catered to tourists, but not well-known.

"Mr. Telford, I told ye. We dunna' have any rooms left."

"A closet. An attic. Someplace we can bed down for the night. We'll leave first thing in the morning." He gestured out the door. "I promised Jennifer I'd come ahead and get us a room. Please. We're newlyweds and I don't want her to realize . . ." He shuffled his feet. "She thinks I can do anything and I wish . . ." He took Mrs. Reddenhurst's reddened hand, and looked soulful and pitiful. "Please, don't mess me up now."

He had her. Mrs. Reddenhurst sighed hugely, but she said, "Ye remind me of my husband. A big doofus with more hair than brains." Taking her hand away, she wiped it on her apron. "All I've got is the attic."

"We'll take it."

"I call it the honeymoon suite."

"That's perfect!"

"I call it the honeymoon suite because the bed is awful, and ye'll both roll to the middle."

"Oh. That's even better." He'd never spoken with more sincerity in his life.

"Ye'll have to share my bathroom. That's down the attic stairs, first door to the left."

"Here's my credit card." He dragged his wallet out of the backpack. When the charge came through the Telford account, Jasha would notice at once. It was a smarter and safer way than a cell phone call to let the family know he was alive and safe.

"Ye'll have to make do with steak and eggs for dinner. I havena' got salmon or lamb for ye!"

"Whatever you're making smells good." It did, and he was starving. "Do you need to see my ID?"

"I'm not waiting on ye." She shook her finger at him. "Ye'll have to fend for yerselves!"

"We can do that."

"When will yer wifey get here?" Mrs. Reddenhurst peered out the door into the mist.

"I left her back about a mile ago. I'll run up and bring her back." He did his best imitation of a bashful American. "We haven't seen anything but sheep all day, and she's sort of embarrassed by the way she looks. So if you don't mind, she'll stop in and say hello to you, then skedaddle up the stairs to the attic."

"I'm fixing supper, so take her to the attic and let her get cleaned up." Obviously, it never occurred to Mrs. Reddenhurst that he might be lying.

"The other guests aren't here?" He peered down the long corridor behind her. There were wide openings on either side — public rooms of some kind, he would guess.

"One couple is up in their room, changing for supper. The other drove to Loch MacIlvernock. Ye Americans are always so energetic!" She shook her head as if she didn't understand.

Rurik and Tasya had arrived at precisely the right moment.

As he dashed out the door, she called, "Ye'll have to eat in the kitchen."

He waved back at her, waited until she was out of sight, then walked to the shed in the yard, and found Tasya standing under the overhang, her arms crossed, her lips blue.

Her clothes had been damp while they flew over the sea, and by the time they'd set down on a flat piece of ground, she'd been shivering. They'd started across the hiking paths toward the B and B, and within an hour, the rain had started to fall. They'd both donned their slickers, but while the

119

exertion made Rurik warm up, Tasya couldn't shake the chill.

Being Tasya, she complained heartily, pointing out that they could have reached the town and the car-rental counter within an hour, but she trudged on after him. She'd pledged to trust him, and she wouldn't break her promise because of some lousy weather.

"Come on. We can go right up to the room, so let's try to avoid being spotted." He took her hand, and for once, she was too tired and cold to wrestle it away.

They ran for the house and up the stairs to the second floor. He located the door to the attic, and when he opened it, a cold draft whipped down the narrow stairs. "The Scots and their obsession with fresh air could be the death of us," he said.

Tasya shuddered. "I'm going to the bathroom, take a shower and change, and see what I can do to make myself look different." She clutched her backpack and tried to smile. "Shaving my head may be my best bet."

He wanted to forbid her. He wanted it so badly. But looking into her eyes, he saw the mixture of mischief and challenge, and he did what he did well and she did abysmally — he picked his battle. As mildly as any henpecked husband, he said, "We want to change your appearance, not make you a terrorist suspect."

Tasya looked crestfallen that he'd refused her challenge. "I hope the owner has some makeup or some hair product I can sneak." She headed for the bathroom.

"Yeah, me, too," he muttered. Recalling Mrs. Reddenhurst's iron gray hair and thin mouth, he wouldn't bet on it.

With Tasya's pale, clear skin, her electric blue eyes, and that sooty black hair, she was far too recognizable — and far too appealing to him.

He ran up the stairs and looked around — and if Tasya had seen his wicked grin, she would have sprinted in the opposite direction and not stopped running until she reached the English border.

How many weeks had it been since he'd laid claim to her? How many weeks had he been waking every night in a roaring fury that she'd left, and he'd spent every day brewing in a red lust for her?

Now Rurik and Tasya would spend the night in a B and B in the middle of nowhere, in a cold, tiny attic, huddled together in a double bed piled high with comforters, with a mattress that sagged in the middle.

Tasya Hunnicutt was in such trouble —

and she didn't even know it.

Tasya was in such trouble, and she knew it. She leaned against the chipped white porcelain sink and stared in the mirror into her own darkly circled eyes.

This morning, Rurik's determination to stay at a B and B made sense. But then, this morning she'd barely made it out of an explosion and a cave-in. This morning had been a miracle of life. This morning, she had felt she could handle anything, even Rurik at his most ruthless.

Now she'd been cold for hours, she was starving, and she had to play the role of a bride . . . to Frankenstein.

Okay, Rurik didn't look like Frankenstein, but he was big enough to be the monster. In fact, the first time they'd made love and he'd pushed inside her, she'd had second thoughts.

That night, if she'd been thinking, his reaction to her panicked gasp would have scared her more than his size. They'd been sprawled on the bed, fully naked, and at a time when most guys would have been full steam ahead, he had noted her apprehension. He had stopped, actually stopped himself. He'd taken the moment, adjusted her legs, kissed her lips, swept his fingertips across her nipples, then down her belly. . . . When it came to figuring out what worked for a woman, he was the master. When he touched her clit . . . well, by the time she had finished coming, he was all the way inside and teaching her the meaning of *multiple orgasm.*

He was big, he was determined, he was ruthless, and he wanted her. *Oh, and, Tasya, let's not forget that he's pissed because you walked out on him.*

Walked out because she'd given far too much of herself, and Tasya Hunnicutt never did that.

Worse, she wanted him so much that when he got close, whether she knew he was there or not, every nerve went on alert and she got this low-level adrenaline rush going.

She turned on the faucet and splashed a little cold water on her face. Taking the hand towel, she dabbed it on her face, and looked at herself again.

She still looked like hell.

Because she had to tell him the truth soon.

Well, not all the truth. She never told anybody all the truth. But enough truth to make him realize that the responsibility for the explosion rested on her shoulders, and that if he was smart, he'd get the hell away from her.

She lifted her chin at herself.

She would probably be killed before this was all over, but if she succeeded in getting damning information on the Varinskis, justice would have to be served; in Sereminia, Yerik and Fdoror Varinski would be convicted of racketeering and murder, and executed. Tasya might die, but she would die with the satisfaction of knowing the Varinskis would be shattered, their thousand-year reign of terror over — and she had her revenge.

She looked down at her backpack. Her camera was in there. The photos were in the memory.

A sense of urgency prodded at her. If only she could see exactly what evidence she had collected!

She glanced at the door, wondering if Mrs. Reddenhurst would let her use a computer.

Still, having the pictures wouldn't matter if she didn't live long enough to get out of Scotland.

Somehow, she had to disguise herself.

Opening Mrs. Reddenhurst's medicine chest, Tasya hopelessly dug through the tubes of ChapStick, the ointment for bunions and the one for hemorrhoids, the hand lotions, the tweezers, the Band-Aids. . . .

Mrs. Reddenhurst must be the most boring woman in the history of the world.

Then, back in the bottom corner, Tasya found what she wanted. She looked at the battered box, at the expiration date long past, and realized — this was perfect. Absolutely perfect.

Not only could she change her appearance, but she could almost guarantee Rurik was going to loathe this makeover. Loathe it, despise it . . . and have to live with it for the rest of this trip.

Rurik stood in front of the old-fashioned kitchen stove, warming his rear end, watching Mrs. Reddenhurst cook.

On the counter, the small-screen television blared with reruns of BBC sitcoms. One pot on the stove popped its lid every time it bubbled. The earthenware plates in the oven turned dark as they grew warm. All the while, Mrs. Reddenhurst talked about her big, dumb husband in tones of affection and exasperation. It was obvious she missed him; Rurik had gathered from her conversation that the loss of his income was the reason she'd had to turn her tiny home into a bed-and-breakfast.

Mrs. Reddenhurst reminded him of his mother — tough-talking on the outside, soft and sweet inside. Mrs. Reddenhurst had sworn she wasn't going to put herself out for her unexpected guests, yet in the space of a half hour, she had agreed to let him use her computer to look at his "vacation" photos. She had offered to wash and dry his clothes for him, and have them ready by daybreak. She'd arrange for them to ride to Edinburgh with one of the other couples staying at the B and B. Most important, she'd scrounged up this morning's oat scones for him to snack on while he waited for Tasya.

Which was good, because Tasya had been in that bathroom for over an hour.

"Young ladies like to take their time over their toilette, especially when they've got a young man to impress." Mrs. Reddenhurst moved him over to the counter and got the lamb out of the oven. "You'll see. When yer missus steps into that doorway, ye'll be bowled over."

"That's what I'm afraid of," he muttered.

But really, what mischief could Tasya get into in Mrs. Reddenhurst's bathroom?

Mrs. Reddenhurst looked up from arranging the serving plates and said, "Here's the young lady now!"

Rurik looked toward the door — and did a horrified double take.

Somehow, Tasya had got peroxide and now the tips of her hair were brilliant white. As if that weren't enough, she'd found styling gel and worked all the curl out of her hair. Spikes stuck out in every direction. She looked like a frightened, aging porcupine.

He was going to kill her.

He took one step in her direction — and almost ran into Mrs. Reddenhurst as she bustled around, setting the wooden table.

"Aren't you a pretty thing!" Mrs. Reddenhurst looked disapprovingly at him. "I didn't realize you'd taken a child bride, Mr. Telford."

Oh, God. Mrs. Reddenhurst was right. The hair made Tasya look like jailbait.

Why? he wanted to say to her. *Why? Why? Why?*

But he knew the answer — because he'd said they needed to change her appearance, because she'd somehow found some bleach, and because she loved to irritate the shit out of him.

She'd done a good job this time.

"Those clothes are perfect for a casual evening." Mrs. Reddenhurst approved Tasya's easy-care khaki pants, loose-fitting black T-shirt, and close-fitting khaki jacket. "Come on in and sit down. Don't be shy."

"I'm so glad to meet you, Mrs. Reddenhurst." Tasya marched in and, with a smile, extended her hand. "Thank you so much for taking us in, and I hope we're not too much trouble."

Rurik wasn't the only one who had charm in abundance. He saw the proof now as Mrs. Reddenhurst beamed and responded, "No trouble at all."

"Mr. Telford got us lost, but you've saved our lives." Tasya slipped an arm around Rurik's waist and hugged him with phony affection.

Rurik hugged her back, a little too hard, and held her closely enough for her to intuit his ire. "Now, darling, if you start telling Mrs. Reddenhurst all our exploits up in her beautiful mountains, someone's going to blush."

Right on cue, the color sprang to Tasya's cheeks.

"I guess it's you." He leaned down and kissed her on the mouth, and for all he was doing it as retaliation for her smart-ass comments, his lips still lingered . . . and returned. She was warm from the shower, damp, and fresh smelling, an aphrodisiac in his arms. Lifting his head, he looked down at her face: her closed eyes, those ridiculously long eyelashes, the way her lips blushed to match her cheeks. . . .

The sound of a distant bell pulled them apart.

"I guess the others are wanting their main course. Good thing — 'tis getting warm in here." Mrs. Reddenhurst smirked as she took the plates and hustled into the tiny dining room, leaving them alone.

Rurik leaned to kiss Tasya again.

She put her hand on his mouth. "Let me go. I'm starving."

She'd aggravated him today; he held her captive just for fun. "I ought to spank you for that hair."

"You told me to change my looks." She had that cocky air about her that clearly told him she delighted in his reaction.

"Then I ought to spank you for fun."

She almost laughed. Almost.

He wouldn't have thought she would. She seemed like the kind of woman who took a threat, any threat, no matter how rooted in sexuality it might be, too seriously. "Do you think I wouldn't do it?"

Now she did chuckle. "I think if you did, you'd enjoy yourself too much."

"I think you'd enjoy it, too." He leaned back against the counter, and adjusted her so all her body parts rested against all his body parts. "You'd especially enjoy the part where I held you facedown in my lap afterward, and spread your legs, and touched you."

Tasya's laughter faded.

"Pretty soon you'd be begging me. You'd use that breathless tone you have when the need is driving you."

Her blue eyes turned a smoky gray.

"I heard it several times that night in Edinburgh." He drawled, "You do remember that night, don't you?"

"Let me go." She squirmed against him.

The best damned torture he'd ever suffered. "That night, I learned a lot about what you like. That's why I know that after I spanked you, I could touch you here." He slid a hand between their bodies and pressed where it would do the most good. "Then I'd slip a finger inside you, and you'd come right on my lap."

She pulled out of his grasp.

He let her, then stalked her as she fled to the kitchen table. "By the time I pushed that second finger inside you, you'd be so ready, I'd have to hold you down with the other hand so you wouldn't bounce right onto the floor."

"Stop it!" She watched him with haunted eyes.

"Make me." He sat down at the table, his

hands palm down on the surface.

Tasya stood facing him, her hands in fists before her chest.

"Break and run, Tasya," he taunted, "so I can chase you down."

"I wouldn't give you the satisfaction."

"Oh, yes, you will. I promise you'll give me exactly the satisfaction I demand."

A slight cough made them both whirl to face their hostess.

In a tone both horrified and delighted, Mrs. Reddenhurst asked, "Do ye two want yer steak and eggs now, or yer salad first? Or would you rather I put yer supper back a bit while ye finish yer fight upstairs?"

CHAPTER 10

Boris Varinski sprawled in the biggest recliner in the Varinskis' family room in the Ukraine, remote control in hand, watching CNN news on the fifty-eight-inch plasma flat-screen TV. The sound was blaring. All around him, Varinskis were pounding fists on one another's backs and hooting with laughter.

He wasn't laughing.

He had been; when news of the explosion at the Scottish excavation broke, he'd gladly received congratulations from his men. He'd basked in their renewed respect.

Then the reporters came on and announced that the administrator of the dig, Rurik Wilder, and the National Antiquities photographer, Tasya Hunnicutt, had vanished and were believed dead in the explosion. They'd flashed pictures of them, and right away, Boris knew everything had gone to hell — and he was the only Varinski smart enough to know it.

That man in the picture was Konstantine's whelp.

Boris had spent one whole long day in Kiev, closeted with Mykhailo Khmelnytsky, the respected historian, while Mykhailo researched the Varinski family icons and where they could be now. Occasionally, Boris had urged him to hurry, and as incentive, he cut little pieces off Mykhailo — the tip of a finger, his little toe. In the end, Mykhailo had come through, identifying the tomb in Scotland as a place one of the icons was hidden. Boris had sent the demolition team, they'd blown up the site, and in the celebration that followed, he had had a few moments of hope that he'd saved his own ass.

But if Konstantine's son directed the excavation at the same site, Boris could bet the boy was looking for the same damned icon Boris had been instructed to find — and not for a good reason.

Worse, he would not die as easily as the reporters imagined, and if he had the icon in his possession . . .

Boris glanced around.

At least, Uncle Ivan had stumbled off, drunk again, and now should be lying somewhere in the big, rambling house, his white eyes rolled up in his head. Uncle Ivan slurped more vodka than any one liver could bear, trying to cure his grief that he was the first Varinski in a thousand years to go blind, and Boris gladly sent the bottles over. Because when Uncle Ivan had drowned his sorrows, Boris knew he was safe from Uncle Ivan and the being that possessed him. The thing that knew about the icon, that used Uncle Ivan's body to grab Boris and threaten him.

If Boris was lucky, his demolition team would find Rurik, find him fast, eliminate him, and grab the icon. Boris would give them the girl. She would be a reward for them, and that would be a lesson for her.

"Give me a phone," Boris said.

No one paid any attention to him.

He came to his feet. Pain streaked through his bad hip, and the pain made him louder and more belligerent. "Give me a phone!"

Abruptly, the celebration died. The boys stood and stared at him, and he stared back.

Blin! Half of the young ones were idiots, drooling, staring blankly, understanding nothing. They had all the intelligence of chimpanzees.

Some of them, the youngest ones, changed into repulsive beasts — weasels, or snakes, or vultures. Predators, but not noble predators — predators that preyed on carrion. Predators that slithered or scampered or scuttled.

And there was Vadim. Boris's own son. Vadim was smart, mean, big, and not quite twenty. Since the time he could crawl, he had ruled his generation. That little *govno-sos* eyed Boris like a tiger eyed an aging antelope that would soon be brought down. Vadim watched, and he waited, smug in the belief that soon Boris would fall and he could step into his shoes.

That was crap. Sure, after Konstantine abandoned them, Boris had had to fight to be declared leader of the Varinski clan, but he'd held power for over thirty years. He'd been the one who decided to abandon the search for Konstantine and his bitch wife. He'd been the one who brought the Varinskis into the modern era with tracking devices and modern explosives and a really good website that stated their goal and had a great corporate logo.

Varinski — When You Want the Job Done, and Done Right.

Boris had made it up himself, and the slogan said it all. Business had been up since he'd started advertising. The Varinskis were raking in the gold — and it *was* gold. When a dictator came and wanted someone put down, he paid in gold. When an oil corporation wanted to start a small war, they paid in gold. And when Boris blackmailed the dictator and the oil company to keep the information quiet, they paid in a lot of gold.

Hell, Boris had an investment counselor, and the guy had real incentive to make sure the investments were sound. He knew if he didn't, Boris would kill him with his bare hands.

Just when he got the whole Varinski family arranged to his liking — stuff happened.

Some of the guys got sick.

Varinskis didn't get sick.

Some of the old guys died in their eighties.

Varinskis lived well into their hundreds.

Some victims of the Varinskis started fighting back; women who had been raped brought charges against them.

They got nowhere — the Varinskis held the Ukrainian justice system in a tight grip — but that the women had so little respect for custom boded ill for future Varinski generations.

Yerik and Fdoror had been captured and awaited trial for racketeering and murder. Like that hadn't happened before!

But this time, nothing Boris did, no pressure he brought to bear on the Sereminian government, no bribes he offered, no threats he made to the Sereminian officials, could get them released.

The world and everything in it plotted a conspiracy to bring Boris down.

"Here's a phone, brother." One of his brothers, one of his own generation, handed him a cordless.

Boris looked down at it, clutched in his shaking hands, and realized he couldn't talk here. His agitation had already betrayed too much. "I'm going to my office."

"Uncle, before you go make your phone call to try and fix this mess, give me the TV remote." Vadim lounged on the couch, smiling that repellent, mocking smile.

Boris stared at the wide-eyed young idiots, at the critical mature men, and at the decrepit old guys. He tossed the remote to Uncle Shaman.

Vadim snapped his fingers, and Shaman tossed it to him.

His own uncle betrayed Boris! Betrayed and stared at him accusingly.

"Hey, thanks!" Vadim laughed and changed the channel.

Boris lunged toward Vadim.

Vadim never moved. But the other boys did, stepping in front of him as if they would willingly sacrifice their lives for him — and some of them were Boris's sons.

His sons! His uncles! All disloyal. All!

Boris stopped. He sneered, "You're not worth my spit." He turned to go — after all, what choice had he?

Vadim called, "You're limping, Uncle. Can I help you to your office?"

"You dumb little fuck," Boris muttered. He left the TV room, walking without a hitch. Stopping just outside, he leaned his hand against the wall, shook his leg, trying to move the joint into a more comfortable position. Then he limped down the darkened hall toward his office.

His hip hurt. The stupid doctor had said it was the arthritis.

So Boris had killed him. Boris needed no witnesses to his weakness.

But he couldn't kill the witness that ground his bones and ate at his nerves, night after night, day after day. The disease was there, and getting worse.

He needed his medicine. He stepped more quickly — when out of the dark, something grabbed his ankle.

He stumbled. His leg gave way. He fell on one knee, caught himself on one hand — and found himself on the floor with Uncle Ivan.

Uncle Ivan, with his eyes glowing blue in

the dark. Uncle Ivan, who moved with a speed and a strength far above the old warrior's capacities. "I warned you." His voice was deep, cruel, cold enough to freeze the marrow in Boris's bones.

This wasn't Uncle Ivan. It was . . . it was the Other.

"It's not my fault," Boris said. "I didn't know Konstantine's whelp was director of the excavation. I didn't know —"

In a flash, Uncle Ivan changed his grip from Boris's ankle to his throat. The twisted old fingers squeezed Boris's windpipe, cutting off his breath. "Fault? Who talks of fault? I care only about results."

The pressure eased a little, just enough so Boris could speak. "I know. I'm going to fix —"

"I told you to find the icons."

"I did. I found one. I tried to destroy —"

"You can't destroy the icons. No man can."

"The explosion —"

"Did nothing. Don't you understand?" The hand tightened. And tightened. "The Varinski mother gave her life to protect the Madonna. Her blood made the icons indestructible."

The last thing Boris remembered was clawing at the enfeebled arm, and realizing that something gave Uncle Ivan strength. . . .

When Boris returned to consciousness, the Other leaned over him, remorseless, old, evil in a way Boris had only begun to fathom.

The blue flame glowed within Uncle Ivan's eyes, and he whispered, "Bring the icons to me. All of them. And find the women."

Boris desperately wanted to shut his eyes — and he didn't dare. "Yes."

"The women the Wilders love are linked to the icons. Find the women. Find the icons. Find them, bring them to me."

"Yes," Boris said hoarsely.

"Succeed, Boris." The smell of brimstone tainted the old man's breath. "Boris, you will succeed, or you'll see hell in all its glory, and much, much sooner than you ever imagined."

CHAPTER 11

"She heard you." In a fury of embarrassment, Tasya strode down the dimly lit corridor toward the miniature library. "Mrs. Reddenhurst heard every word!"

"And enjoyed it, too." Rurik strolled behind Tasya, his long legs easily keeping up. "I'll bet she goes to bed tonight and hugs her pillow."

"Only if her pillow contains two D-sized batteries." Tasya had never been so mortified in her life.

He hadn't been bothered. Obviously. He'd simply smiled and eaten his steak and eggs with gusto.

And that bugged Tasya all the more. "I mean, I'm no prude —"

"Just inexperienced."

She stopped. Turned. Found her nose almost buried in his chest. "I am not!"

"Inexperienced and flustered." He walked around her, past the front room where Mrs.

Reddenhurst sat with two of her guests, television blaring, and into the empty library. Mrs. Reddenhurst's computer sat on the desk, a four-year-old Mac with a twelve-inch monitor. He turned it on, examined the connections, and extended his hand. "We can do it. Where's the memory?"

Tasya slid into the chair. "Right here." She pulled the memory out of her pocket and stuck it into the reader.

She halfway expected Rurik to try to evict her from her seat, but he pulled up a chair and sat by her left shoulder. "Are the pictures there?"

She loaded the photos in the program, brought them up, and gave a sigh of relief. "It looks as if there's no problem."

Yesterday she had taken hundreds of photos of the site, the treasure chest, and all its contents, but she zipped past those to get to ones she'd taken this morning.

She winced when she saw the number — only a few dozen of a panel three feet long and densely covered with figures, symbols, and writing. She squinted. The monitor wasn't good; everything was tinted green, and the resolution was lousy. "How's your Old English?" she asked.

"Not good, but luckily this carving was

made only a few years before the Norman invasion, so we're getting close to Middle English. Plus most of the story is told in pictures." He pointed to the first photo. "Can you enlarge that?"

She did, and the two of them studied her view of the wall.

She pointed to the figure on the left. "Clovus is a warlord — he beheads his enemies until they're a great pile of bodies beneath his feet, and the other warriors cower before him."

"I've found the proof of that," Rurik agreed.

"He cuts a swath of destruction through Europe, and the only one who can stand against him is this guy." She pointed at the stick figure, crudely drawn, of a crowned figure with one eye and a melted face. "Makes you wonder what the king was like if he managed to outdo Clovus the Beheader."

"There were a lot of charmers in those days."

She brought up the next photo, and realized it helped if she sat back and looked at the overall picture rather than trying to decipher every line. "Clovus took a boat." She knew it was Clovus, since he'd brought along a dripping souvenir head. "So I'm guessing he crossed the channel to England."

Rurik pointed to some script. "That's what it says here."

She squinted at the monitor. "Really? That's what that says? I should have studied more *Beowulf*."

"I'm glad to discover a reason I did." Rurik put his hand on the back of her neck and used his fingers to massage away the knot there.

If she was smart, she'd tell him to knock it off. But he used his hands with real talent, and she'd had a long day. A very long, very tense day. "Okay. So this time, Clovus cut a swath through the English countryside, right up until the time he met —" She enlarged the picture. "He met the devil?" This kept getting better and better.

"Cloven hooves. Tail. Yep, that's the devil." Rurik sounded prosaic.

"Clovus really hung around with the wrong crowd." She controlled her excitement and brought up the next photo. "The devil gave him a wonderful present."

"The Hershey bar." Rurik pointed at the square that was changing hands.

"Oh, bite me." But she was concentrating too hard and his massage was too good for her to put much vitriol behind her insult.

"What do you think it is?"

"I don't know."

"See that glow around it? I think it must be a gold tablet."

"You might be right."

She twisted to look at him. "What's wrong?"

"What do you mean?"

"You sound so . . . neutral. And you look —" He looked funny. Sort of knowing, and filled with suppressed excitement. "You're the archaeologist. I'm only the amateur. Am I reading this wrong?"

"You're reading it exactly as I would. Except . . . I don't think that's gold." He pointed at the screen, at the object the devil gave Clovus.

"What do you think it is?"

"I think it's a holy object."

"Because of the halo." That shot her theory about the Varinski treasure all to hell. "But what is the devil doing with a holy object?"

"Nothing good, I'll bet."

"No." She tapped the desk.

"You're disappointed."

"I don't know." She thought about the details of the Varinski mythology. "There's the part about the icon —"

"Icon?" Rurik was instantly alert.

145

"Nothing. I just . . . nothing." She did not need to go into that right now. Turning back to the screen, she said, "Look. Clovus is sick." The stone carver had rendered the picture of Clovus's various bodily disorders with disgusting completeness.

"And he blames the object, whatever it is, and sends it to the king with one eye." Rurik leaned back in the chair and pressed the heels of his hands to his forehead. "That would be perfect!"

"Perfect?" She could hardly contain her disappointment. "If the Hershey bar were in Europe somewhere? Why?"

"Because otherwise, this object was blown sky-high in the tomb, and even if it wasn't destroyed, it's going to take ten years to sift through the wreckage and catalog every piece, and who the hell has ten years?"

"Right," she said sarcastically. "Now all we have to do is figure out which one-eyed, mean son-of-a-bitch eleventh-century European ruler he sent it to."

In the end, for all his disclaimers, Rurik deciphered enough of the Old English to figure out the one-eyed king had lived and pillaged in Lorraine, now a province on the far eastern edge of France. They would start there.

His scholarship impressed Tasya. That and

the heat he provided by sitting close, and his fingers rubbing at the base of her neck . . . she liked sitting here with him, deciphering the carvings, talking about their next move. They were comfortable with each other, two people who had a lot in common. Almost . . . friends.

Friends, except for the fact that she hadn't been completely frank with him — to say the least — and there was that sex thing that they did so well and which made her want to run so far away.

Because Rurik Wilder would never be threatened by her career and her independence, and scamper away. Rurik Wilder wasn't threatened by anything. He wanted a relationship with her — what kind and how long, she didn't dare ask — and that terrified her. Terrified her because of the people who chased her. Terrified her because he could get hurt. And that wouldn't be fair to him.

While she pulled the card, replaced it in her camera, and stashed her camera safely away, he cleaned the remnants of the photos from Mrs. Reddenhurst's computer. Tasya watched with a sense of satisfaction; they'd done a good night's work. They made a good team.

He switched the computer off, then

turned, and so swiftly she didn't have time to back up, he caught her hand in his. "Now, tell me about you and the Varinskis."

The reckoning had come sooner than she'd thought.

CHAPTER 12

"I don't know where to start." Tasya tried to run her fingers through her hair, and at once the rigid spikes reminded her what she had done to change her looks, and why.

"Start at the beginning." Rurik used his toe to pull the chair right in front of him, and pointed.

She might not like his attitude, but she sat. After all, she owed him. She'd got him involved in something so far above his head, he could never handle it.

Although perhaps she was kidding herself. Because as this day had worn on, she'd become more and more impressed with his competence. The guy had a way about him: He'd dug her out of the tunnel, hidden that backpack full of survival supplies, scouted out the B and B — all actions that revealed his character. This was a man who expected danger and prepared for trouble.

Still, she'd brought the trouble, so she

leaned forward. "You know who the Varinski Twins are?"

"Two experienced assassins from a legendary Russian — well, now Ukrainian — crime family who were caught in Sereminia committing murder for hire and are now in prison awaiting trial."

"Exactly. They're not the first members of the family to be caught, but they are the first ones who haven't managed to 'escape' " — she used air quotes — "before their trial. The Varinskis have been hiring themselves out as mercenaries for a thousand years, committing horrible misdeeds, and they've never been convicted of a single crime." She leaned farther forward, enthusiasm for her subject warming her. "Can you imagine that? A thousand years."

"Incredible." He sat completely still, listening as if she were the most scintillating speaker in the world. "Why do you know so much about them?"

"I've done my research."

"What kind of research?"

"Every kind. At the library, online, I've done interviews." That wasn't all, but she suspected he wouldn't approve of the rest.

She was probably saying too much. But she never got to talk about this stuff. Not with anybody who hated the Varinskis like she did. Here was Rurik, his archaeological site blown sky-high, his life's work ruined — he would understand. "I've documented the Varinskis' history, their legend, and their crimes. Do you know the oldest Russian mention I could find is almost eight hundred years old, an illuminated manuscript that spoke of a treasure of great worth which the first Konstantine Varinski had given 'to the devil' to receive his supernatural abilities."

"What supernatural abilities would those be?" Rurik sounded polite, like someone who thought his leg was being pulled.

Tasya didn't blame him a bit. "I know — I can't believe the Varinskis got away with this bullshit, either. Supposedly, these guys are shape-shifters, and change into predators whenever they want to. The monks were afraid of them, and said this deal with the devil turned the Varinskis from humans into demons. Every Russian document I found after that said the same thing, and claimed that that is why they're such good trackers and why nobody can escape them. Is that not the best PR you've ever heard?"

"Amazing." Rurik leaned back, arms crossed over his chest, his face just out of the light. "What do you think the truth is?"

"I discovered that Konstantine had paid

somebody, some powerful man, probably a representative of the czar, a whole bunch of money to do as he wished without interference on the Ukrainian steppes. Once Konstantine received that permission, he proceeded to make quite a name for himself as a brutal warrior." She wouldn't talk about the stuff Konstantine had done, since Konstantine made Clovus seem mild by comparison. "He raised more brutal warriors, and they raised more, continuing the family tradition as men who hire themselves out as trackers and assassins, men who fight as mercenaries in any army. They don't marry, they go out and rape women, and if the women know what's good for them, they give over their babies. Supposedly, the Varinskis have only sons —"

"That is possible, since it's the male who determines the gender," Rurik interposed.

"Yes, but with these guys, I'd suspect they're leaving the girls out to die."

Rurik almost spoke, then returned to watchfulness.

"All of the Varinskis are trained to be soldiers of breathtaking viciousness."

"So you don't believe the supernatural part?"

"Oh, please."

"You don't believe in the supernatural."

"No. I believe in what I can see and taste and touch." She didn't even believe in God. She'd lost that faith the same night she'd lost her parents. "I tracked down what I believe to be the piece of the Varinski family treasure —"

"The treasure Konstantine gave to the devil?" With Rurik's face in shadow, she could see only his eyes, and they were alive and watching. "Why doesn't the devil have it?"

"According to the Varinski myth, the devil divided the treasure into four parts and flung the pieces to the four winds."

Rurik shook his head. "He flung them to the four corners of the earth."

"That's right. You do know your stuff!" She gave him points for that one. "The devil flung the pieces to the four corners of the earth. The accounts disagreed about the treasure and what it was. Some said gold. Some said silver. Some said it was a holy icon of the kind all Russian families keep in their household shrine."

Rurik's gaze flicked to the computer, and he nodded.

"I thought if it was that valuable, it was probably gold, and the etching and illuminations all showed photos like the ones on the stone panel." She tapped the memory

153

chip in her shirt pocket. "I deduced that the agreement giving Konstantine his rights as a son of a bitch must be etched on the treasure somehow."

"Okay," Rurik said slowly, frowning. "That's a big leap."

"If Konstantine Varinski was so worried about the, um, Hershey bar that he made up the story about the devil flinging it to the four corners of the earth, then there's *something* incriminating on it."

"If everything you say is true — the Varinski legend is bogus, they don't change into beasts of prey, and they merely use the myth to scare people to death — then yes, that would seem logical. But what if —"

"What if they really change into animals?" She laughed lightly.

In one swift move, he sat up straight, into the light. His face was alive with exasperation, and she would have sworn he was going to do something rash, although what, she didn't know. He subsided back into his chair, but she sensed a vigilance and an impatience, like the attitude of a hawk waiting for a mouse to bolt from its hole.

"It truly is a great myth. They're not werewolves, controlled by the moon, or vampires who can't go out at night. They can go anywhere anytime as men or as beasts. That makes them so much more dangerous, doesn't it?" She laughed again. "Talk about PR!"

"Incredible." He seemed to pick his words carefully. "What if the Hershey bar is merely a Russian family icon, and you've gone to all the trouble of tracing the Varinski treasure to Clovus's tomb on the Isle of Roi?"

"But don't you see? The Varinskis are *the* international, high-tech, successful trackers and assassins in the business. They blew up the tomb." She put her hand on his knee. "They're trying to hide something."

"So you're convinced it was the Varinskis who blew up the tomb." His leg was taut as steel beneath her grip.

"Of course I am. And if you think about it, so will you be." She tightened her fingers, then let go. "You said you didn't believe in coincidence."

"Then, likely, they wanted to kill you. The Varinskis don't like people poking around, exposing their secrets."

Rurik knew more about the Varinskis than she had imagined. "That's possible."

"You're taking your possible death very calmly."

She thought of several answers, and discarded them — they all sounded so melodramatic. "That treasure chest was such a disappointment. When you got to the bottom and the tablet wasn't there, I almost cried."

"I'm almost crying right now." He did look a little flushed. "As much as I hate to ask . . . what are you doing with all this information?"

"I wrote a book."

"You wrote a book about the Varinskis?" Rurik's voice rose.

So did her eyebrows. "It's good!"

"Do me a favor. Let's not find out."

"My *editor* says it's good."

In tones of horror, he asked, "You have an editor?"

"It's going to be published in two months. In hardcover!" She'd used all her skills as a writer to knit the facts and fantasies together into a compelling read. She was proud of herself — and he was puncturing her exhilaration. "Do you know anything about publishing?"

"I know most books fail. Maybe no one will notice yours." He sounded positively hopeful.

"Actually, presales are excellent," she said with chilly courtesy. "My publisher is talking *New York Times* best seller."

"Doesn't that just figure?"

She wanted to squash him like a bug —

him and his flat lack of enthusiasm. "I've documented all my research, but if I can produce a real live piece of Varinski history — that will excite the press and give me the exposure I need. So although some kind of written record of Konstantine's corruption would be good, I can run with the icon, too, if that's what it is. It's all about publicity."

"All about publicity," he repeated. "When we started this conversation, I told you to start at the beginning, but I don't think you did. Who are the Varinskis to you?" He carefully spaced each word.

"What do you mean? Are you asking if they're relatives?" Her cheeks heated. "Because I am not related to those monsters. And I never slept with one!"

He looked away, a quick flick of the eyes, then back. "No. That's not what I'm asking. There are a lot of injustices in this world, Tasya Hunnicutt. You know them. You've seen them. Why did you choose to try and destroy this evil?"

"Because it's the right thing to do." Lame answer. "Because that's what I do."

"No. With the other evils, you take pictures. You write a story. You move on to relative safety. With the Varinskis, once you declare yourself their enemy, there will be no safety ever again. And you know that. So again, I ask — why the Varinskis?"

"I'll have you know there are a few governments in this world who hate me for my stories." She hadn't thought Rurik would wonder about her motivation, or that he'd be so astute with his questioning. Most men were oblivious to everything except food, drink, and sex. Why did she have to get stuck with Mr. Interrogation?

"You *do* sense evil." He watched her emotionlessly.

She squirmed in her chair. She knew where he was going.

"You sensed Clovus and his traps. You knew the Varinskis were out there."

"When they're close, I feel . . . there's a sickening buzz in my ears, and I get this hot flash that makes me see flames." *Too close, Tasya! You're skating too close to the truth!*

"Are there any other times you've felt that?"

She actually felt funny when he was around, but she put that down to a constant, low-level lust that afflicted her, and the way she forgot to breathe when she stared at him.

She *liked* to stare at him, at the golden brown eyes, the strong, harsh face, the muscled body that looked so good in clothes — and so much better out of them. She liked his scent, and she liked the way she felt when he touched her . . . like she was going to live forever. Forever, in a moment.

"Are there any other times you've felt that?" he repeated.

He wasn't going to let this one go.

And she wasn't going to talk about it — about that night so long ago, about the flames on the horizon, and how she'd screamed for her mommy because when those scary men were close, she was sick, so sick. "I am sorry, Rurik. It's partially my fault they bombed the site, but I swear, it never occurred to me they would."

"So you have felt it before." He was like a dog with a bone. "And still you have the nerve to say you don't believe in the supernatural."

Her temper had been wavering back and forth, and now it snapped. "That's not the supernatural. That's just a feeling!"

"A very useful one." He stood.

"Do *you* believe in the supernatural?"

"Very much so."

She couldn't tell if he was kidding or not. "An Air Force pilot who believes in ghoulies and ghosties?"

"An ex–Air Force pilot. Perhaps the ghoulies and ghosties are the reason I quit."

He wasn't making sense to her. She stood,

too. "What do you think of what I'm doing?"

"I think you're going to get killed."

"But if I bring down a legacy of cruelty, won't that be worth it?"

"No. For I can't bear to think of a world without you in it." Before she suspected his intentions, he had her in his arms, pressed against his body. He was hard and hot, just the way she remembered, but less gentle. . . . He wanted to kiss her, and he no longer had the patience for seduction. This was a kiss as violent as a storm, as complete as a climax. He used his tongue in her mouth, his teeth on her lower lip. He held her with one arm across her back while the other cupped her rear and massaged so deeply she shuddered, halfway to yielding.

Then he let her go. Let her go and stepped back. And walked out the door.

She touched her fingertips to her bruised lips, and closed her eyes. She had thought no one would mourn her if she died, and yet — Rurik might appear to be calm and stoic, but the man hid depths of passion and anguish that raised her temperature and made her want to live, all at the same time.

In a sudden hurry, she raced into the corridor, intent on catching him.

He stood in the archway of the living

room, where the television was blaring, and stared over the heads of Mrs. Reddenhurst and two of her guests.

Tasya stopped beside him.

A reporter stood in the rain before the collapsed mound on the Isle of Roi. Behind her, people worked under spotlights, digging frantically, as she said, "We don't know who bombed the site. The speculation is, of course, terrorists, but we do know two people are missing and presumed dead. But until their bodies are recovered, they're suspects in the blast."

And photos of Rurik and Tasya popped up on the screen.

CHAPTER 13

Tasya looked guilty and like she wanted to bolt, but Rurik needed to know if their masquerades were sufficient. "Mrs. Reddenhurst, my wife and I are going up now."

Mrs. Reddenhurst twisted in her wing chair. "Come in, come in. Meet the kind folk who've agreed to share their car with ye in the morning."

Rurik took Tasya's hand and led her into the small room. "We appreciate you letting us ride along with you, Mr. and Mrs. Kelly."

"Serena and Hamlin," Mr. Kelly said, and extended his hand. He was short, aging, with a round belly that overhung his belt, and a white beard. His wife matched him in height and girth, and both of them beamed enthusiastically.

Apparently in the summer Santa Claus and his wife vacationed in the north of Scotland.

"Glad for the company, especially since

you're sharing the petrol." He cocked his head. "I recognize you."

Shit.

"Or at least I recognize your accent. You're Yanks," he continued.

"We're from just north of you," Serena said, "from Canada. It's always good to see neighbors when we travel."

Tasya leaned against Rurik as if she needed the support.

"Remember that time we saw Fred and Carol in Florida?" Hamlin said. "That was wild. Wasn't that wild?"

"Fred and Carol Browning were our real neighbors, from our neighborhood, and our kids grew up together," Serena explained.

"And we saw them in Florida in February. Imagine that." Hamlin tucked his thumbs into his suspenders.

"Imagine," Tasya said weakly.

Before the Kellys could draw breath again, Rurik said, "Mrs. Reddenhurst, we want to thank you for the loan of your computer, and thank you for giving us shelter."

"Yes, thank you." Tasya took her hand.

"Ye're welcome, both of ye." Mrs. Reddenhurst looked pleased by their courtesies. "You'll go up now?"

"Of course they will!" Hamlin said in hearty amusement. "They're newlyweds!"

163

Serena gave a laugh to match his. "Tomorrow the car windows will be steamed up all the way!"

It was going to be a long ride to Edinburgh.

Rurik pushed Tasya toward the corridor and up the stairs.

"None of them recognize us from the pictures on TV," she said in a low voice.

"We've got a chance of getting to France incognito, then." He followed close on her heels as she climbed the stairs to the second floor.

She stopped on the landing. "You don't have to go to France with me."

"Believe me. I do."

"No, really. I've put you in danger."

He laughed briefly and bitterly. He'd already been in danger, but she'd definitely added to the mix. "I have a better idea. Why don't I send you to safety while I go to France after the Varinski treasure?"

"No." He answered himself at the same time she answered him.

"I need to find the treasure for myself." Her eyes were big and blue and earnest.

"Because that's better for the PR?" He could barely contain his irritation.

When he thought about her plan — write a book about the Varinskis, and do a good enough job to make it a blockbuster — he wanted to shout at her. Tasya Hunnicutt, the most savvy world traveler he'd ever met, imagined that she could take on the longest-lived, most deadly cartel in the world, and win.

The Varinskis made the Mafia look like altar boys, and why?

Because old Konstantine *had* made a deal with the devil, and the devil knew his stuff.

So what if Tasya didn't believe in demons and shape-shifters?

Rurik lived with the proof — and the consequences — every day.

So he *was* going to France with her, and when they located the icon . . . he would take it from her.

Because they were chasing the icon that could save his father's life, and more important — his soul.

Tasya would be angry, but Tasya would have to learn to live with it, because Rurik intended to keep her.

"You should go back to the dig," she said. "Leave me to track down the Varinski treasure."

His temper wavered between hot frustration and cold intent. Putting his fingers over her lips, he said, "Don't even suggest that.

I'm not leaving you to face the Varinskis alone."

Her eyes filled with tears. She looked down, snuffled, said, "I'm sorry, I must be really tired."

She thought he was a good guy, a human guy, and her willful foolishness, not to mention the coming confrontation, made him more furious. "We both are. I'm going to take a shower. Mrs. Reddenhurst said she would loan you one of her nightgowns. Don't wait up."

"I won't." She looked up. "Rurik, I really am sorry I got your excavation blown up."

She thought he was angry because of the site. Could she be any more wrong?

Without waiting for an answer, she sprinted up the stairs.

He watched her and said softly, "Don't worry. You're going to pay — in more ways than one."

Tasya slept a long time, the absolute blackout of exhaustion, then slowly bobbed up toward consciousness.

She was cocooned in warmth . . . except for that one foot dangling off the bed. It hung out of the covers, and her toes were cold.

But the rest of her was so warm . . . so

relaxed. . . . The dream was the best she'd ever had.

Of Rurik turning her onto her back. Of Rurik lifting Mrs. Reddenhurst's ridiculous, voluminous flannel nightgown. Of Rurik sliding his fingers into her panties and stroking her just above her clit . . . building sensation slowly, letting her rest, building again. . . . The cold air in the attic pinched at her face, chapped her lips . . . and Rurik held himself above her, a large, dark, predatory shadow in the predawn light.

All she needed was for him to touch her a little more often, with a little more intimacy, and maybe a little pressure. . . .

She rolled her hips, a voluptuous invitation to invade rather than loiter.

A laugh rumbled out of him, and he slid his bare leg between hers. "No, this one's not going to be easy."

And she woke with a start. "What?"

She was too sleepy and confused to comprehend what he said, or even exactly what was happening.

Because if he'd decided to take matters into his own hands and screw her senseless — and although she knew she had very important, very reasonable objections to that idea, right now she didn't oppose having the decision made for her — then why was he arousing her but not mounting her? Why wasn't he sweeping her along with the force of his passion?

Why the *hell* wasn't he inside her yet?

She gave a soft, incoherent murmur, one that couldn't be interpreted as encouragement, but was.

He kissed her; then his lips slid along her jawline to the lobe of her ear. He sucked that, which she found mildly interesting, then bit it, a swift, slight punch of pain.

She arched off the bed.

He laughed again.

She did *not* understand what he thought was so funny.

His hand brushed her bare throat, then a little lower, then a little lower. . . . Mrs. Reddenhurst's nightgown swamped Tasya in lavender-scented flannel. It was so large and so ridiculous, and the attic was so freaking cold, Tasya had felt safe in wearing it.

Apparently Rurik had managed to overlook its absurdity and find its weaknesses, for she realized he was unbuttoning the four buttons down the front. Only four buttons near her throat — yet the gown was so big, what might have been protection for Mrs. Reddenhurst provided easy access for Rurik.

His hand slid inside, allowing in wisps of cold air to whisper along her tender skin.

Spreading the gaping nightgown, he found Tasya's breast, and plumped it in his cupped palm. He lifted it, and his mouth closed over her nipple, sucking hard, pulling it to the roof of his mouth, massaging it with his tongue.

The wave of passion hit, and Tasya went under with only a long moan.

It had been so long . . . weeks since she'd had him. Weeks of sleeplessness, of fruitless wanting, of waking from erotic dreams with her body shuddering in the grips of orgasm.

Now he was here, and he took her to the edge of climax . . . to the edge of climax . . . and left her trembling and bereft.

She caught her breath. Opened her eyes.

The sun would rise in probably a half hour. She could see Rurik leaning on one elbow, watching her. His massive shoulders were nude, with taut skin stretched over every muscle.

He was gorgeous, big, clean, and male. And she wanted him.

"Please," she whispered.

He shook his head. "No, honey. I want you right where you are."

"What are you talking about?"

"While we're traveling, I want to know that you're wanting me. While we're looking for the treasure, I want your desire to be a low hum in the background, the thing you're aware of every minute while you go on with life." His voice was low, deep, layered with smoky intent.

"You're crazy." She meant it, too.

"I'm obsessed." He leaned close enough that his breath caressed her cheek right in front of her ear. "And I want you to be obsessed, too."

He *was* crazy.

So was she, because she was half-flattered by his intentions — half-flattered, and thoroughly pissed.

"It's not like I don't know how to take care of myself." She slipped her hand down her belly ready to touch herself.

He caught her wrists and lifted them above her head. "And I know how to stop you." His leg stirred between hers, bringing her right to the edge again.

She fought against his grip.

He held her easily.

She was in great shape, yet while she thrashed beneath him, using every self-defense move she'd ever learned, the bastard never broke a sweat.

Finally she tired.

When she lay there, panting in rage and frustration, he kissed her, long, slow, sweet kisses that started at her forehead and worked down to her lips, her throat, her breasts. He found the bare flesh of her belly, and finally his tongue glided between her folds. . . .

During their first night together, they'd made love more times than she could remember, but they'd never got to this point.

So it was a delight to discover how thoroughly Rurik knew a woman's body . . . where to lick, how much pressure to apply, how to build desire in slow swells of pleasure.

She wasn't surprised; he exuded that masculine aura of expertise that promised so much, and he delivered with languid enjoyment.

Then, at the moment her senses began to crest, he pulled back.

She forgot dignity and grabbed for him, but he slipped from the bed and stood, proudly naked, his erection prominent and tantalizing. "We need to get going."

Had she thought he exuded a masculine aura of expertise?

Yeah, he was masculine, all right. He was a big, fat jerk.

"That was mean." She sat up and yanked the covers back, hoping the cold air would subdue her rampant libido.

Unfortunately for her libido, he walked

across the room to get his clothes, and his butt reminded her of Michelangelo's *David*. Only living.

"Yeah. Almost as mean as spending a great night making love to me, then running away without a word like I was some kind of monster." He turned, T-shirt in hand. The tattoo that had fascinated her before snaked down his arm, along his shoulder, and across his chest, a great, glorious slide of color to his waist.

He caught her staring, and in a slow, exotic reverse striptease, he lifted his arms over his head and pulled on the stretchy material.

Her mouth dried at the panorama just inside the window.

"Maybe you'd like to tell me why you chickened out?" he asked.

"I didn't chicken out. I just . . ." She was just afraid. Afraid he was the one man who would stick with her. Afraid he was the one man she could love.

Then, if anything happened to him . . .

But she couldn't say that, could she? That revealed way too much of a soul scarred by loss. "I always knew there was a chance the Varinskis would catch up with me. I didn't want you to get hurt."

"That's noble. So noble." He didn't sound

like he meant it. "It was so good of you to make the decision to save my life from possible injury by slinking away in the early morning like some prima donna photojournalist afraid I'd ask for an autograph."

"That's not what I did!"

"Then tell me why you left."

He didn't believe her. How could he not believe her? "I'm afraid you'll get hurt," she said stubbornly.

He crossed to the bed in one smooth, fast move.

She tried to avoid him, and got caught half on, half off the bed, off-balance and vulnerable.

Holding her pressed against his body, he kissed her, a slow rekindling of barely controlled desire. When all her resistance was subdued and she held him with her arms around his neck, he let her slide back onto the sheets.

Matter-of-factly, he went back to his clothes.

She shoved her hair off her damp forehead. "Why are you doing this?"

"Because I want every breath you take to be empty unless you're close enough to smell me. Every word you speak to be unimportant unless it's to me. Every sound you hear empty unless it's my voice. I want you to remember that whatever pleasure you have from now on, you'll have it from me." He looked into her eyes. "I want you to trust me enough to tell me the truth, all the truth — about Tasya Hunnicutt."

Funny how he put the trouble with the Varinskis right into perspective.

Six feet four of trouble stood right in front of her, putting on his pants.

CHAPTER 14

Tasya and Rurik stood on the curb in front of the Edinburgh train station and watched Hamlin and Serena Kelly drive away.

"That was the longest trip of my life," Rurik said.

"How would you know? You slept through most of it." Tasya hadn't. Tasya had been awake, listening to the Kellys and their constant prattle about their home, their neighbors, their travel, their lives. And just when she thought she would kill if they didn't change the subject, they did — and gleefully pointed out that, yes, indeed, she and Rurik were steaming up the back windows.

Since by then Rurik was snoring, Tasya didn't know why that was so funny, but it kept the Kellys entertained for miles.

If it had stopped raining, Tasya could have rolled the windows down and let the wind whisk their voices away. But no, the mist continued unabated, and she had been stuck.

Stuck between a happily sleeping Rurik, two exuberant Canadians, and the memories of the night before.

Damn Rurik. Because of him, she walked carefully, sat gingerly, and wanted all the time. He'd turned her into a horny teenager again, and she did not appreciate having her every thought consumed by one thing — sex. And more than that — sex with him.

Now Rurik hailed a cab, and she asked, "What are you doing?"

"We're going to see when the ferry leaves for Belgium."

"The ferry for . . . ? But we told Mrs. Reddenhurst and the Kellys we were taking the rail line through the Chunnel."

"We lied." He held the door of the cab while she climbed in, and gave the cabbie directions. Sliding his arm across the seat to rest on her shoulders, Rurik murmured in her ear, "Someone we don't like may question them, and the less they know, the better."

"Oh." She was used to being cautious; a single woman who traveled in the parts of the world she visited had to be. But this trip felt like *The Bourne Identity,* only with someone better looking than Matt Damon.

She glanced out the window.

She had to stop thinking like that. She used to know Matt Damon was the best-looking guy in the world. Surely, if she avoided looking at Rurik, she could convince herself again. "Do you think we were followed?"

"Anything's possible." He put his finger on her lips, and indicated the cabbie.

In fifteen minutes, they had their tickets for the ferry. The boat took eighteen hours to make the crossing to Zeebrugge, Belgium, and included restaurants and casinos. The boarding was in two hours, the departure in the early evening, and Rurik decided that was enough time to visit a secondhand clothing shop.

Tasya found herself trading in her casual khakis for an outfit that looked vaguely Goth and totally outrageous.

Afterward, as they walked down the street, she looked down at the black swirl of cotton gathered around her hips, and at her cleavage, bared in a bright pink shirt with Marilyn Monroe's face embossed on her midriff. "I thought we were trying to look inconspicuous."

"No." Rurik wore a black leather duster that covered him from his neck to below his knees, faded black jeans, and a snap-front shirt. All he needed was a cowboy hat and he could pass for a Texan. "We want people to look somewhere besides your face. We have the added bonus that now, with your hair and that outfit, you look fifteen. If someone has to describe you, that's a good thing."

"They're never going to believe you're a cowboy," she informed him.

"I'll be satisfied if I look a little less massive." He held the door to a coffee shop. "It's my size I can't disguise."

The place was large, smelled rich with coffee and scones, and had televisions high in each corner and computers lining the back wall. Going to the counter, he bought them two cups and the password for the Wi-Fi, and settled her before one of the empty computers.

He took a chair beside her, faced out into the room, and in a soft voice said, "Send those photos to your boss."

Funny, to have her heart thump with excitement as she did something she'd done hundreds of times — upload and send pictures to Kirk Lebreque at National Antiquities. She imagined him receiving the files, studying the photos, putting them in production, and from there spreading them across the country. He would realize she was still alive, and he'd be so glad — he liked her as a person, yes, but he *loved* her as a reporter.

And what a relief not to have the whole responsibility for the record of the finds.

The entire process took less than fifteen minutes, and as she slid the memory card back into her backpack, she nudged Rurik. "We can go now."

But he sat rigid, staring at one of the televisions.

She heard a voice she recognized. She turned and looked.

Mrs. Reddenhurst stood sobbing in front of her smoldering bed-and-breakfast, saying over and over again in a broken voice, "I don't know why they did it. Those men just walked in and set my house on fire. I've lost everything. Everything."

Kirk Lebreque sat watching the photographs pop up, one after another, and desperately tried to memorize details, estimate sizes, materials, age.

When the last one had come through, he carefully placed them in a folder in Photoshop. He sat, his hand hovering over the mouse.

The cold end of the revolver touched his neck. "Do it." The voice was harsh and

Russian-accented.

Swallowing the lump of dismay in his throat, he took the folder over and put it in the trash.

"That's not good enough." The pistol poked Kirk again. "Wipe the computer's memory."

Kirk couldn't help it. He snapped, "Why don't you just shoot the computer?"

"You try to fool me. Do you think I am stupid? That computer backs up to the mainframe. Until you wipe the memory, it will make no difference." He sounded reflective. "Perhaps I will shoot it later for fun."

"But the society has important information on these computers!"

"Wipe it clean."

Kirk rubbed his damp palms on his pants, and pulled up the Utilities file. He found the Erase command, highlighted the hard drive. . . . "This is a crime. There are things on this computer that can never be recovered."

"Exactly."

Kirk couldn't look at the guy anymore. He'd been looking at him for six hours, arguing at first, telling the guy Tasya was dead, then keeping quiet to avoid those big fists.

He didn't know the guy's name. He knew only that he was big and ugly, and something was wrong with his face — his nose looked almost like a rat's, and he seemed able to see in the dark.

He gave Kirk the creeps to start with, and the way he handled the knife, and that semiautomatic pistol . . . Kirk clicked Erase, and watched as the computer started the process of cleaning the hard drive.

He turned his head away. He couldn't watch. Looking up, way up to the guy's face, he said, "You won't get away with this, you know. I can identify you."

He had one second to realize he'd underestimated the situation.

Then the close-range shot blew his brains all over the room. Stanislaw Varinski viewed the mess with satisfaction. "Not anymore, you can't."

CHAPTER 15

Rurik caught a glimpse of him as they boarded the ferry. Just a glimpse. That was enough, and he knew — a Varinski had found them.

He led Tasya to a public area where they could watch the rest of the passengers embark. The broad, flat-bottomed boat held 830 passengers and 120 cars, at least according to the company's literature, and he saw no sign of more assassins.

But on a ferry this size, a Varinski could all too easily stow in a car trunk or work the crew.

Nowhere was safe from the Varinskis, unless Rurik made it safe.

"Shall we go to our seats?" Tasya asked. "Or do you want to go to the casino? Or one of the restaurants?" She was being sarcastic. She was upset about Mrs. Reddenhurst and her bed-and-breakfast, and all of Rurik's assurances that his family would render assistance hadn't wiped the hatred and despair from Tasya's gaze. She took their responsibility in the matter very seriously, and made Rurik remember what his mother always said — the toll of murder and plundering was in more than life and possessions. The Varinskis destroyed every sense of security, and shadowed every sunny day.

"Let's locate our seats first." The seats were airplane-style, facing one direction in a huge room. They reclined, and Rurik had paid for first-class tickets, so he had room to stretch out his legs.

The cabin was crowded with people settling their belongings, but a quick glance showed him no sign of the Varinski. Seating himself next to Tasya, he asked, "Do you have the map of the ferry?"

She handed it to him and closed her eyes.

He unfolded the map and studied the arrangement of the public areas, the crew quarters, and the storage closets, noting everywhere a Varinski might hide. "When we land in Belgium, we'll buy passes for the train and go from there."

She opened her eyes. "Don't be silly. The train'll take too long. We'll fly to Lorraine."

He paused. "The train will be —"

"Slower?" She sat forward. "Right now we

hold the advantage over the Varinskis. They don't know where we're going, and a quick hop on an airplane would throw them off, at least for a little while."

"You learn quickly." *Damn it.*

"We'll catch a quick flight to Strasbourg and be done. At least — I hope we'll be done."

First, they had to get off the ferry alive.

He looked back at the map. The restrooms were always a danger; everyone had to visit them, but no one lingered, and the chances for a solitary attack were good. "The Varinskis will be watching the airports."

"Like they won't be watching the trains?" Her tone hitched up a notch. She physically relaxed back into the seat, and modulated her tone. She was the voice of reason when she said, "I've made this trip before, Rurik. I know what I'm talking about."

"Yeah. I know you do." The lower corridors where the crew, the cars, and the luggage were stowed — they looked good, too.

But Rurik bet on the deck. It was still raining and as night came on, the air grew chilly. No one was out there, and a smart Varinski could lurk until most of the passengers were either asleep or gambling. All he would have to do was find Rurik and Tasya alone, and the hits would be oh so easy.

"So we'll do the plane," she said.

He looked at her. If Rurik didn't catch the Varinski, they'd never get off the ferry. Right now, he was willing to fight for their lives; fighting with Tasya about how they traveled seemed less important. After all, he'd flown in the ultralight. Surely he could stand a flight across France. "Okay."

"Okay." She watched him curiously. "What's up?"

The ferry was under way, pulling out of the harbor and into the North Sea.

"I'm going to stretch my legs." He stood. "You remain in your seat."

"What if I have to pee?"

"I'll take you now if you like, but after that, I'd like you to remain in your seat."

She glanced around. "Are we in danger?"

"I'm cautious."

"I don't have to go." She pulled out her travel blanket and draped it over her shoulders. "I'll stay here."

With the people close and the stewards cruising the aisles, she would be safe. He hoped.

He opened the outside door, and the wind almost ripped it out of his hands. The mist had developed into a storm, and the clouds and the setting sun made the deck a shadowed, empty, rain-swept place. Stairways loomed; the lifeboats held corners where a Varinski could hide — especially a Varinski who kept himself in the animal state. Patches of light from the windows created weird shadows, and as Rurik softly trod the decks, he slipped his knife from the sheath around his waist.

He reached the stern. Paused for a minute and looked across the choppy wake left by the ferry. Listened for movement — and heard something, the faintest flick of a feather.

Only that split second of warning saved Rurik's eyes.

The peregrine came right at his face, claws out.

With his arm, he smacked the bird aside. A blinding pain sliced across his chest.

In an instant, the peregrine changed, becoming a man, as tall as Rurik with arms half again as long and a lethal, intent gaze.

Rurik didn't stop to stare. He charged, lunging with the knife — and the knife made contact, slicing into the flesh over the Varinski's throat.

The guy reared back in surprise.

Good. These bastards always underestimated Konstantine's sons.

Rurik laughed. "Did they send only one of you?"

The guy wiped his hand across the blood dripping down his throat. "Only one Varinski is needed." He caught Rurik's knife hand in his huge grip, and pounded his chest with the other fist. "The best one."

The knife turned toward Rurik, headed toward his chest.

Rurik concentrated, opened his fingers. The knife clattered to the floor. Rurik dropped to his knees, his weight throwing the Varinski off-balance. Coming up underneath the Varinski, he used his shoulder to pull the man's arm out of its socket.

The Varinski roared in pain.

Then he put crushing pressure on Rurik's hand.

Apparently, pain made him mad.

Rurik's bones begin to crack and separate. The pain was horrible; his vision began to fade.

He was going to pass out.

Faintly in the storage bank of his memory, he heard his father yelling at him to think. He heard his brothers mocking him for fainting, for being a girl.

Against the Varinski gorilla, he had only one chance. He focused until he could work his other hand around and open the switchblade hidden in his sleeve — and he placed it between the Varinski's ribs.

The Varinski hung there on the blade, his eyes wide, his grip unyielding. Then, in a gush of blood, he died.

Rurik caught him as he fell. Checking his pulse, he found nothing. Without pausing, he dragged him to the side and hefted him over the rail.

He didn't stop to listen for the splash. The bloody stain would disappear under the lash of the rain, but he couldn't depend on the passengers and crew not to have seen the fight. He needed to get cleaned up and out of sight before someone came along.

He broke the lock on one of the janitors' storage closets, and blotted himself with the paper towels. Removing his duster, he shook it out and examined it. It was wet, but not bloody.

He frowned at his chest. The peregrine had opened an eight-inch slash across his shirt and over his right pec. It burned. His tattoo had jagged edges. But the skin would heal. The shirt wouldn't, and it left all too graphic evidence of his fight.

With a shrug, he put the coat back on. Taking great care, he made a tour of the rest of the boat, pausing and listening, examining the other passengers. He stopped in the gift shop, bought himself a T-shirt that said *Ferry Me Away,* and changed in the men's room. Finally he made his way back to his seat.

He would watch throughout the night, but he believed he and Tasya were safe.

Tasya roused as he sat down, blinking at him. "Oh. It's you."

"Yeah. It's me." And he remembered something that hadn't mattered before. He had agreed to fly with her to Lorraine.

The missile was almost on them.

Rurik drove the plane up and to the side.

They weren't going to make it —

"Did everything go okay?" she asked. "Are there any Varinskis on the ferry?"

He stared blankly, then settled down. "You tell me. Have you felt the presence of any Varinskis?"

He'd caught her half-asleep, all her barricades down. She bit her lower lip, glanced aside.

"What?" Her obvious discomfort intrigued him. Satisfied him.

She made him fly.

He made her reveal herself.

She'd already confessed to her premonitions. Why was she uneasy now?

"I wouldn't feel a Varinski unless he was very close, because when I'm with you, I always feel a low-level sense of . . . something." She put her hand on his arm as if to reassure him. "I think it's just that, in your own way, you're dangerous."

"I see." He had wondered. Now he knew. Her instincts about him were good.

Just not good enough.

Boris Varinski sat in front of his computer, by the phone in his office, searching CNN.com for the news he wanted.

Nothing. Not a word about the mysterious murders of Rurik Wilder and Tasya Hunnicutt.

Why not?

Duscha was one of Boris's sons, a skilled assassin blessed with long arms and an overwhelming muscle mass. He loved the kill, insisting he execute each and every assignment by hand.

They — Boris and his brothers — had thought that Konstantine's weakness for the Gypsy woman must breed inferior sons.

Yet Jasha Wilder had proved impossible to kill, and now, for every minute that went by without a phone call from Duscha, Boris's hopes failed a little more.

The door banged open. One of the younger boys stuck his head in. "Hey, Uncle, want to play poker?"

Boris loved to gamble, and lately, all too often, the family played without asking him to join in. Their disrespect was another sign that his status as their leader had slipped, and this was a good opportunity to reinforce his control over them.

But if he left the office tonight, he might miss the call from Duscha.

Worse, he might see Uncle Ivan.

"I'm waiting for a call. Can't you see I'm waiting for a call?" he snapped.

"Yeah. Sure. Wait for your call." The boy shut the door with a slam.

While Boris stared at the phone.

CHAPTER 16

Rurik sat in the aisle row, staring at the door that stood between him and the pilot, and tried to penetrate the barrier with his mind, to figure out whether the pilot was sober, how many years of flying he had, whether he could change into a bird and soar on the wind currents. . . .

Tasya caught his hand. "You okay?"

He rolled his head toward her. "I'm fine."

"You didn't sleep a bit last night, did you?" She squeezed his fingers. "Why don't you take a nap?"

"I can't sleep until we're off the ground."

"Yeah, right." She wore this crooked smile. "You're about to drop off right now."

"No. Really. I . . . I'm afraid to fly." Okay, the biggest lie he'd ever told, but that girl on the plane from the States had believed it. Why shouldn't Tasya?

Because she knew he'd been a pilot. "Oh, just shut your eyes."

But with his eyes closed, he could listen to the sound of the plane as it joined the queue, analyze the sound of the engine, the noise the wing flaps made as they prepared for takeoff —

In the air over Afghanistan
Five years ago

The XF-155 Blackshadow sliced the pale blue sky, leaving a white vapor trail. Below, at the edge of the Afghan plain, the earth buckled, rising abruptly from the flat brown plain into the soaring mountain heights. For four thousand years, the plain, and the mountains, and the heat and the cold and the drought and the enemy that slipped unseen into the caves and through the passes made Afghanistan a bitch of a country in which to make war.

But that wasn't news. The U.S. Air Force had never bothered to station Captain Rurik "Hawk" Wilder anywhere but in the piss holes of the world.

And he went, gladly, for the chance to fly airplanes like these — jets the Air Force didn't talk about, airplanes that didn't yet officially exist, airplanes that flew under the radar, both literally and figuratively, without raising so much as a ripple.

From the copilot's seat behind him, the newbie asked, "Hey, Hawk, what are we looking for?"

"I don't know." Rurik scanned the ground, looking for some . . . *thing.*

"We've got no clues at all?"

"I only know the brass are behaving like boys with their dick in a twist."

"Worse than usual?"

"Think about it, Jedi. We're flying a plane so secret, not a hint of her existence has leaked to the press. It's my third time in the pilot's seat, your first time as WISO, and you only got to come because I asked for you. And General Garcia calls from base, gives us coordinates, and says to reconnoiter?" Rurik whistled his contempt. "Please. Until they've run a dozen missions on this baby, they won't be convinced she can stay in the air." Hawk continued to scan the terrain below. "I asked the general if there was any satellite intel he could pass on to us. You know what he said?" Hawk didn't wait for the reply; he continued. "He said that satellite intel was what caused the mission to be given to us. Their info wasn't conclusive, but it was good enough to cause us to get the nod for an eyeball rece. I'm here to tell you, Jedi, there's some very, very serious shit coming down."

"Is that the official U.S. Air Force terminology?"

"Yeah — sort of like *FNG*."

Jedi laughed.

FNG loosely translated to "fine new guy," and Matt "Jedi" Clark was an FNG. He had finished his theater training with his instructor pilot. It was Jedi's ninth operational mission as a Weapons Information Systems Officer — WISO — in a hostile area with Hawk as the pilot, and the other WISOs thought he had it made. Rurik Wilder was the best pilot in the Air Force. Everyone knew it; everyone knew Jedi had been the lucky one because he had the best potential to take Rurik's place in the food chain.

Jedi was good. Really good. Brave, strong, and true. That's why they called him Jedi. The kid was Luke Skywalker without the whining.

But Rurik was "the Hawk." At twenty-eight, he had spent a lot of time fending off challengers from his own country's services, as well as more than a few from other nations — some friendly and some definitely aggressors. So far, no one had come close to his abilities. None of these boys knew it, but no one ever could.

He glanced up at the rearview mirror on the canopy bow.

On the other hand, Jedi was prettier. He had brown eyes, red hair, a body toned by weight lifting, and that I'm-a-hot-shit swagger so many pilots had perfected.

Rurik grinned.

Girls loved Jedi.

Women loved Rurik.

Still, Jedi was swift and smart with a knack for flying. He'd go far.

"Give me a view of the mountains," Jedi called.

Rurik dipped the left wing.

Below them, the plain shimmered in the summer heat, and Rurik didn't see a damned thing of interest. What could there be? The terrain was brown and flat, then brown and sharp, rising rapidly toward the sky and shimmering so hard. . . . What the hell was happening down there?

"Earthquake." Jedi's voice rose with excitement. "Earthquake!"

Boulders tumbled down the mountain slope. The air shook as hard as the ground. And right there in the fold of the mountain, Rurik saw the ground rip open.

No, not the ground.

He pulled up the visor of his helmet and looked again.

There was *material* ripping open — *camouflage* material. The *something* they were looking for was down there, a something exposed by a trick of nature.

This was what the brass had sent him out to

see. An enemy installation of some kind . . .

"Son of a bitch," Rurik whispered.

"What is it, Hawk?"

"What do you think it is?" Rurik thought he knew. He also knew he had to be absolutely sure.

"I think it's . . . I think it's some kind of military camp or . . ." Jedi sounded strained. "It needs to stop shaking, and I need to be closer. Can you get us closer?"

"Can't. We don't want them to get a good look at this baby." The plane, he meant, the Air Force's new toy. Besides, Rurik had another option. He only hoped the FNG could hang on to his training under pressure. "I'm in front. I've got a view. You take the controls."

"You want me to take the controls? Of the *Blackshadow*?"

"Now."

"Got it." Jedi sounded steady as a rock as Hawk felt him wiggle the control stick.

Good kid. Because Rurik knew even while he was flying, Jedi must be planning the whole scene — the bar, the pilots, the announcement that the Hawk had let him fly the new plane. . . .

"Concentrate on flying. Keep her straight, keep her steady."

"Okay, Hawk. I've got it."

Still Rurik waited, watching Jedi in the rearview mirror.

The kid really did have it. He was as good as he thought he was.

Rurik took a long breath. For the merest second, he relaxed and closed his eyes.

Deep inside, he felt it. The shift, the rush of exhilaration . . . the sense of *superiority.*

It had been so long since he'd allowed himself to change, and he'd forgotten . . . forgotten about that silent, sibilant whisper in his brain, telling him *he* held the power. He could take a woman. He could help a child. He could crush a man.

He was a god.

Then, like a slap, a deeper, sterner voice superimposed itself in his mind.

Not a god. A demon.

Opening his eyes, he glanced again at Jedi.

The kid had his head in the cockpit watching the gauges.

So Rurik focused on the camp so far below. Closer and closer, picking out details he could never have seen with his normal sight.

Trucks. Men.

Shit.

Taking another long breath, he sharpened his vision again.

A nuclear installation. Enough warheads — *How many? Count them.* Enough to vaporize the Americans *and* the Pakistanis, and, from here, the whole Indian subcontinent. . . . Rage rose in him. Those stupid, petty little tyrants. They could kill *everyone.*

Again, the small sibilant voice whispered in his mind.

He had the power to finish them *right now. . . .* He wanted to finish them *right now. . . .*

He heard a strangled noise from behind him, and that, even more than the memory of his father's deep, stern voice, dragged him back from the brink.

Right. He had a job to do. Absolute power over life and death would have to wait.

"Don't panic, Jedi. We caught them in time." He reached for the radio transmit button — and snapped to attention when he heard the click of the safety on Jedi's pistol.

Glancing up into the mirror, he observed his own eyes — the red flash deep inside the long pupils, the sense of the Other.

He met the kid's gaze.

Jedi's eyes were human, so human, and fierce, angry . . . afraid.

Jedi was first an Air Force pilot, then a WISO, exceptionally well trained to deal with every circumstance the military could imagine.

The military just hadn't ever imagined anything like this.

Jedi pointed his pistol at Rurik. "Put your

hands on the canopy bow where I can see them."

Rurik made his voice soothing, endeavoring to take command of an untenable situation. "Jedi . . . Jedi, fly the plane."

"I am. And do what I told you."

Slowly, Rurik did as instructed; he put his hands on the canopy bow while keeping his gaze steady on Jedi in the mirror.

Jedi's cheeks turned a blotchy cherry.

Trouble was, the kid didn't have enough experience to hold a gun on Rurik, keep complete control of the Blackshadow . . . and handle his fear. A fear that was rapidly turning to anger.

Furiously, the kid asked, "What makes your eyes like that? What are you on?"

Damn it. Rurik had told Jedi to concentrate on flying the plane. Hell of a time for him to not follow orders. "On?"

"No wonder you're such a hot shit. You're on some kind of —" Jedi pressed the mike button.

Puffy — Major Jerry Jacobs — answered the call, and that more than anything told Rurik how seriously they took this flight and his observations. Puffy had security clearances so high that the fact that he had them was classified. "Go ahead, Blackshadow."

"Captain Wilder is on drugs," Jedi blurted.

Son of a bitch. They were in trouble now.

"Newbie, do you know what you're saying?" Major Jacobs sounded wholly offended.

"He's on some kind of designer drug. His eyes flared red. Like he was the —" Jedi stopped. Swallowed. "Red like a fire. Then his pupils changed size. It was a pronounced change."

Jacobs's voice slid into a low, controlled burn. "Do you realize how serious this accusation is?"

"I saw it clearly, sir." Jedi was righteous — and terrified. He knew the severity of his accusations and actions, but more than that — Rurik scared him pissless. "I have the controls."

Because it wasn't drugs. Somewhere in his mind, Jedi knew it. He knew he'd seen a small part of Rurik shapeshift from a man . . . into a hawk.

But Jedi was a modern man. He didn't believe in demons. He didn't believe the devil walked the earth making deals with mortals. He didn't believe, and he didn't want to know.

"Did you take the controls from Captain Wilder?" Jacobs's unyielding voice demanded a reply — the right reply.

No Air Force pilot ever took the controls by force. Never.

"I relinquished the controls to Captain Clark

so I could concentrate on my reconnaissance," Rurik said. No use making a bad situation worse.

"And?" Jacobs wanted something from Rurik — a reassurance, a denial, something.

"When I get on the ground, I have a report to give."

"All right. Clark, bring her in." The mike clicked off.

Jedi continued to fly the plane, but his control was becoming ever more erratic as he tried to keep one eye on Rurik and his sidearm close.

The plane was too new, and too many mountains loomed around them for that kind of flying.

"Stay calm." Bit by bit Rurik lowered his hands. "Just get us back to the base. You can fly her. You can land her. I'm not going to interfere."

"Shut up," Jedi said fiercely. "Just shut up and keep your hands away from the controls."

Rurik knew this wouldn't turn out well for the kid — or for him. They'd land; they'd have him pee in a cup. They'd test his blood, his liver, his skin. They'd by God find his tonsils, which he'd lost in a hospital in Seattle twenty-two years ago.

Every test would be clean.

Then the FNG would be tested, and when

he came up negative, he'd be disciplined. They'd pull him out of training and send him to a psychiatrist. And all the while he'd be swearing he saw what he saw, Rurik would be saying as little as possible, everybody would be taking sides, and the whole thing would be FUBAR.

In the meantime, there was a previously unknown nuclear installation on the ground, with a bunch of maniacs manning it, and if he didn't handle this right, at any moment a bomb could be exploding over —

The threat warning alarm sounded. It was designed to get attention — it was eminently successful. One glance showed the situation. The installation below had spotted them. Sent a missile after them.

"Let me fly her." Rurik started to put his hands on the controls.

"No, sir!"

"Then put the gun away and fly the damned airplane right!" Rurik didn't even realize he was using his command voice.

"No, sir!"

"You've got to fly. That son of a bitch will come right up our ass." Rurik couldn't tear his gaze away from the missile streaking toward them.

"I'm flying!" Jedi was, but not well. Not well enough to save them. He wasn't concentrating. He didn't have the experience. Worst of all, the kid was more afraid of Rurik than he was of dying.

Jedi sent the Blackshadow into a spiral. He twisted, flipped.

The g's pulled at Rurik's face and arms and belly until he thought he'd pass out.

The missile was tracking them, and gaining.

"We haven't got time for this!" Rurik didn't intend to end in a fiery explosion. Stretching behind him, he yanked the pistol right out of the kid's sweaty hands.

The kid screamed.

"I've got the plane," Rurik shouted as he grabbed the controls.

A stark mountain face loomed before them.

The missile was almost on them.

Rurik drove the plane up and to the side.

They weren't going to make it —

And they were clear.

The missile hit the mountain and exploded.

At the same time, the canopy blew.

What the fuck?

Jedi had ejected. Ejected over enemy territory.

Because he thought they were doomed to crash into that mountain and die a fiery death? Or because he was too terrified of Rurik to stay in the plane with him?

Stunned, Rurik watched the parachute

descend. He marked the spot, then streaked toward the base, determined to head back out there as soon as possible to save that kid.

But it was too late.

Too damned late.

Chapter 17

But it had been too late.

Too damned late.

Ever since, Rurik had weighed every option, then moved with lightning precision. He would never be too late again.

Life and death, heaven and hell, depended on him.

Now he stood in the middle of the village of Toul and methodically made plans to find the icon.

"Here's what we're going to do. We'll go to the local historical society and ask them about the one-eyed king. If that doesn't get us any information, we can try the local library, and if the librarians can't help us, we'll use their computers to search the Internet."

"Hm." Tasya looked around at the streets, heating under the morning sun. "Do you speak French?"

"Not well. Why?"

"Because talking to historians and librarians may require some linguistic prowess."

"If we have to, we'll hire an interpreter. And we'll probably have to, because if we can't find any evidence of the one-eyed king and the gift he received, we're going to have to consider the local archaeology society. Usually they're amateurs, but frequently they know the surrounding countryside better than anyone else." Rurik rubbed his hands together. He almost hoped that was the route they'd have to follow. The local archaeology society always contained his kind of people.

"Stay here. I'm going to go to the visitors' center." She strolled toward the largest building on the modern thoroughfare.

For the restrooms, he figured, and called, "Get a map while you're in there."

She waved back at him.

What a hell of a dream he'd had on the plane.

No, not a dream. A reenactment.

Every damned time he got on an airplane, the memories swamped him.

That poor kid. When Rurik recalled finding Matt Clark's body, tortured, shredded, destroyed . . . when he recalled writing the letter of condolence to the kid's parents . . . he writhed in remembered guilt.

He'd vowed not to fly. Commercial, sure — he couldn't avoid that, and no one liked to fly commercial. But the ultralight had been pure pleasure, and in the small plane he'd experienced every air current as the wind had held his wings aloft. . . .

No more. No more flying. Not for any reason.

Rurik owed Jedi to hold to his vow.

As Rurik waited for Tasya, he scanned the locals who hurried to their jobs and the tourists who wandered along the picturesque streets. The Varinskis weren't used to failure, and when their assassin failed to call in, they'd send out reinforcements, and fast. But he saw no signs of danger.

Well, except for Tasya, who came out of the visitors' center. She was dangerous — to him and his peace of mind.

"I've got it." She flapped a brochure under his chin.

"What's that?" he asked.

"The directions to the winery that displays the famous tapestry featuring the one-eyed king."

Dumbfounded, he stared at her.

She shrugged. "I figured the visitors' center was a great place to start, especially since in there, someone has to speak English. Come on, the winery is only a few blocks from here."

Rurik followed, watching Tasya as she charged through the crowds, smiling until the Frenchmen and the tourists fell back and let her pass.

He'd been so intent on protecting her from the Varinskis, he'd forgotten how experienced a traveler she was, and that as a reporter, she could, and would, scout out the information she needed.

The winery was a medieval building that had been remodeled to accommodate the influx of tourists that visited every year. It overlooked the Moselle River, and when they stepped inside, Rurik felt as if he'd been transported back five hundred years. The ceiling was low in the cool, dark sales center. The place smelled like fermenting wine and hummed with the voices of a group preparing to follow a guide down the path to the wine cellars.

"There," Tasya said. "That's the guy we want." She headed toward the stooped old man, who stiffened with disapproval at the sight of her black-and-white spiked hair. But she was not daunted; she fixed him with a blinding smile, and spoke French to him, badly, until he broke down and smiled back.

The next thing Rurik knew, the haughty Frenchman was ushering them into a long, empty gallery at the back of the building. He turned on the lights and gestured to the wall, then disappeared back into the sales center, shutting the door behind him.

Rurik found himself staring at a tapestry that stretched the length of the room and filled the wall from eye level to the tall ceiling.

"Good God." He walked along the velvet cord that kept any tourists out of range. "What is it?"

"It's a tapestry made in the twelfth century celebrating Lorraine's history. The language used is Latin. Not a lot is known about its origins, but the workmanship is believed to be local." Tasya slowly walked along ahead of him, her hands clasped behind her back, and scrutinized each scene the tapestry represented.

"The people at the visitors' bureau said the one-eyed king is here?" Rurik could see scenes of battles and coronations, passages of text, and a blinding complexity of events.

"He's not a king," Tasya corrected. "His name is Arnulf, and he's a warlord, just like Clovus. Clovus probably said he was a king to make his defeat at Arnulf's hands less humiliating."

"More PR."

"For sure." Her expression was intent, and

she halted more than once to examine the figures sewn on the brown linen background. "This is more of an embroidery than a tapestry, but the detail is amazing. The whole story of Alsace-Lorraine is here, including —" She stopped. "There he is. Arnulf the One-Eyed."

Rurik joined her at the rope.

The colors were still rich, the figures clearly drawn. Obviously, Arnulf didn't pay his biographer, for while the scenes were much the same as the ones that portrayed Clovus, the attitude of achievement was missing. Arnulf stood atop piles of bodies, but according to the tapestry, he sacrificed his eye and his nobility for power. The tapestry showed him slashing and burning his way through the countryside until one day, he received a gift from afar.

"Look." Tasya pointed.

"I see it." The gift was the Hershey bar shaped and surrounded by a halo.

"There it is," Tasya whispered.

"Look. Arnulf accepts the tribute gladly, but at once his luck goes sour. He's wounded, put to bed. I'd guess the injury turned gangrenous?" Black spurted from the wound, and his enemies gathered around his bed in attitudes of triumph.

"Serves him right." Tasya smiled. "He

blamed the gift for his misfortune, and sent it away to be hidden in a nunnery in the hopes he would be cured."

Rurik could see a lot represented in that tapestry, but he couldn't see that much detail. "Where do you see that business about being cured?"

"It's in this tourist guide." Tasya showed him the pamphlet.

She was such a smart-ass. "If all the information is in the tourist guide, then what are we doing here?"

"The tourist guide doesn't tell us where the nunnery is." She stood staring at the last scene involving Arnulf the One-Eyed. "I hoped that the information was somewhere on the . . ." Her voice trailed off.

He followed her gaze to the small picture of the dead Arnulf, his eyes x-ed out, a flower clasped in his hands. "There's writing there." Drawing on his feeble Latin, he read, " 'But it was too late for Arnulf. The . . .' I can't read that for sure, but I think it means the holy object —"

"So it is an icon."

"Yes." That he could have told her, but she wouldn't have believed him. "The holy object came to rest in a nunnery in the kingdom of . . . I don't recognize the title." He moved closer, trying to match the ancient name with the modern name. "Wait. The nunnery is in . . . I've almost got it. . . ."

Tasya didn't stir, didn't take her gaze away from the tapestry. Speaking in a voice so low, he almost didn't hear her, she said, "Ruyshvania. The nunnery is in Ruyshvania." She lifted a trembling hand to her forehead. "I have to go back to Ruyshvania."

Chapter 18

Tasya pulled herself together; she didn't think Rurik noticed her small panic attack in front of the tapestry. He didn't say anything, anyway. Instead he briskly arranged their travel schedule.

Rent a car. Drive it to Vienna. Arrive in the late afternoon. Wait four hours for the night train from Vienna to the town of Capraru in Ruyshvania. Shop while they wait.

By the time Tasya settled in the private compartment on the night train, she had a whole new persona. She wore makeup, an expensive pair of jeans, black boots, and a white button-up shirt belted at the waist. The entire studiedly casual ensemble cost more than her camera, and the conductor on the train had bowed and scraped as he saw them to their car.

What did she expect? This was Europe. They worshipped fashion.

Although Rurik had also bought a new

shirt, he still wore that long leather duster.

He said he liked it because it gave him anonymity.

She thought he liked it because it hid the variety of weapons she now knew he carried.

As they pulled out of the station, he said, "I'm going to walk the train. Do you want anything?"

"Walk the train. Is that a euphemism for look for trouble?" He didn't answer, nor did he invite her to come along. She'd already figured out he liked to patrol on his own.

"A glass of wine would be nice," she said. "Maybe even a bottle."

He put his hands on either side of her, leaned down close. "The tension gets to you after a while, doesn't it?"

The tension? It wasn't the tension that had got to her. It was their destination. She couldn't believe . . . well, of course, she could. No one knew better that fate was a bitch who always demanded payment.

Rather than answer him, Tasya placed her hand on his cheek and kissed his mouth. "Be careful."

"Always." He kissed her back, his lips lingering, then straightened. "And you lock the door behind me."

She did. She took the opportunity of

privacy to shower in their tiny private bathroom and, with a sigh, put her clothes back on sans belt.

Usually she liked to travel, and travel light. But it seemed every leg of this trip involved another disguise — and another revelation. She wanted nothing more than to go home to the States, to her spare apartment, and veg out on the couch, television blaring, remote control in hand, and try to remember who she was.

Or was that — who she had taught herself to be?

When she came out, clean and damp, Rurik was back in the room. Their dinner waited on the miniature drop-down table covered with a white tablecloth, the requested bottle of wine uncorked and breathing.

At the sight of her, his brandy-colored eyes warmed as if heated by a flame.

Oh, yes. The man had plans. Plans to torment her some more? Plans to make her the happiest woman in the world?

How did she feel about that?

She didn't know. If he was less intense . . . if this train were headed somewhere else . . .

Yeah. If.

So a purposely casual Tasya brushed at the wrinkles where the belt had sat, and asked, "No trouble?"

"Not a sign. Let me wash up, and we'll eat."

"Right," she said to the closed bathroom door.

When he came out, his hair was wet and his face was damp. "I didn't see a Varinski on the train."

He was buttoning his new shirt over his broad chest, and she wanted to whimper as she watched. The man must work out all the time, to have sculpted those pecs — she straightened, riveted by a knife wound that ran eight inches across the right side of his chest, ripping through his tattoo, shredding his skin.

He continued. "I think we lost them in —"

"What happened to you?" She stood, pushed his hands away, and parted his shirt. The wound looked red, sore, and fresh. "You've been in a fight."

"It's nothing."

"A Varinski."

He paused, then inclined his head.

She put the pieces of the puzzle together. "On the ferry. You killed him."

"Yes."

"Varinskis are supposed to be indestructible."

"I can kill them."

"I know it's a myth," she said impatiently, "but I figured they were good fighters."

"They are. So far, I'm better."

She lightly touched the skin around the cut. "I'm pretty good with first aid. Do you want me to —"

"It'll heal."

"It's deep. You should have had it stitched."

"I promise it's fine. I have a very fast metabolism."

"At least tell me you're up on your tetanus shots."

He caught her hand and pressed it to his heart.

The steady beat warmed her palm.

But Tasya couldn't ignore the proof, right before her eyes, that Rurik was willing to put himself in danger for her. "First the explosion, then you're almost killed. I shouldn't have dragged you into this."

"Sit down." He ushered her into her seat. "Relax." He poured the glass full of shimmering red wine and handed it to her. "You didn't drag me into it. Have you not thought that the Varinskis want the icon destroyed, and that's why they bombed the excavation?"

"That's true." She took a sip, and the

depth and richness of the vintage warmed her. "But that would be mission accomplished. Why are they still chasing us? You should let me go on by myself."

"I'm not leaving you."

Her heart, her stupid heart, made a bound of rapturous pleasure.

"It was my site, and that's my icon," he added, and pulled the covers off the plates. "The steward said this is spaetzle with cheese, whatever that is. It smells great." He picked up his fork and dug in.

She watched him.

She didn't believe him. She didn't believe any human being would risk death for what he called *a Hershey bar.*

He was doing it for her. To keep her safe.

She had to tell him the truth.

She owed him the truth.

CHAPTER 19

Tasya ate. She finished her wine. She waited until he was done.

Then she said, "The Varinskis killed my parents."

Rurik heard the words — and rejected them. It was impossible. The kind of tragedy too hellish to imagine.

But Tasya seemed oblivious to his horror. She recited the events calmly, as if the drug of time insulated her from the pain. "They came in the night. My mother picked me up out of my bed. She handed me to Miss Landau, my governess. She kissed me good-bye. I saw my father getting out his guns. He kissed me, too, as he handed my mother a rifle." Tasya took a long breath. "That was the last time I saw them."

Rurik had so many questions to ask . . . but first he wanted to shake his fist at the sky and howl in fury.

He understood now, understood only too

well. Now he knew why she was so strong, so resilient, and so admirable in all the ways he thought were important.

Now he understood why they could never be together.

"The Varinskis . . . of course. It would be Varinskis." He laughed shortly and without humor. "Those bastards."

What evil fate had thrown them together? The night he'd made love to her was the first night in five years he'd been happy.

"Bastards, for sure. Bastards for generations." Tasya faced Rurik across the table, and with fierce scorn said, "Men who turn into predators. Oh, please! I visited the Ukraine, and I swear, they've got everyone believing this stuff."

"You went to the *Ukraine?* Are you *crazy?*" He shouldn't shout. He would not shout. "If they had discovered you were alive and had escaped them —"

"I know. I know." She waved a dismissive hand. "But I didn't understand the danger then."

"That wouldn't have saved you." He might never have met her.

"I'm pretty sure they don't know I'm alive, or Miss Landau wouldn't have fled with me in the first place."

"That's right." He leaned back against the

seat. "You're right."

"In the Ukraine, it doesn't matter what the Varinskis do — kill, kidnap, torture, rape — no one touches them. They never go to jail. They're never brought to trial. They live in this compound — it's a guy's paradise."

"You went to their compound." He closed his eyes, trying to block out the knowledge of what could have happened.

"I drove by."

"How often?"

"Often enough to get some pictures taken."

"You stopped and took pictures." He could scarcely believe the depths of her foolishness — or the extent of her luck.

"I am a photographer." She acted as if that was the most normal thing in the world. "There are these cars they're working on sitting around with the hoods up, and the ones they've abandoned that are rusting. The grass grows every summer and no one cuts it. The house is unpainted. When they need extra room, they simply tack on some ridiculous-looking addition. And do you know what they have by the gate?"

"A place for the women who were impregnated by a Varinski to leave their infant sons. They ring a bell and run, and the Varinskis take the child in and celebrate the birth of a new demon."

"You know a lot about them."

"Yes. I do." *You have no idea.*

"Then tell me this. How have they managed to perpetuate this atmosphere of terror all these years?"

"They have a firm grip on the local imagination." He couldn't sit there and look her in the eye any longer. He stood and rang for the porter, then piled the dishes onto the tray.

"They're extortionists. They're murderers. They're kidnappers." She was coldly furious. "They're an affront to civilization, and it's time for it to stop."

"I agree, and I intend to do everything in my power to stop them." For more reasons than she knew. "But I can't do anything right now, and I've got questions." He removed the tablecloth and pushed the table up into the wall. "The Varinskis don't kill for free. Who were your parents? Who wanted them dead?"

"What did I know? I was four." She shrugged.

"You're a reporter. You've looked into the records. What did the police say about the attack? Who did they blame?"

"The police report blamed my parents. They said it was a murder/suicide, and that my father torched the house before he killed himself."

"That's a good, standard story. The Varinskis are fond of that one. What about your governess? Where is she now?"

"I don't know. Pardon me for being uninterested in finding Miss Landau." Tasya stood as if she wanted to pace, realized there was no room, then sat back down again. "She took me away. She put me in foster care. And she disappeared. I find being abandoned makes me bitter."

Someone knocked on the door. Rurik checked the peephole, then let the porter in. He took the tray; Rurik tipped him, shut and locked the door, and turned back to Tasya. "You weren't abandoned. She took you to safety and for whatever reason — fear of the Varinskis, probably, but maybe the fear you'd be easier to trace if she was with you — gave you over to foster care. If she had put you down outside your house and left you for the Varinskis to find and kill, then you'd have cause for a grudge."

"Tell a four-year-old who's lost her parents and her home, who's lost the governess she's known her whole life, and who's been put with people who regularly foster at least ten children at a time, that she hasn't been abandoned. I doubt if that child will listen."

"You're not that child anymore." Her capability for carrying a grudge worried him . . . when she had so much more reason to hate him.

"When I need the motivation to do what needs to be done —"

"You mean, when you want to thoughtlessly charge into the fray."

"Whatever." She made a shooing gesture toward him. "Whenever I need to overcome fear or fury, I remember my parents, and the Varinskis, and I plan my revenge. That's why I wrote a book guaranteed to tap into the public's fascination with religion and legend, murder and oppression. That's why I'm willing to travel the world and face the Varinskis to get the icon. If I can bring proof to the National Antiquities, have them verify the authenticity of the icon, and give witness to the Varinski legend, that'll capture the world's attention, focus the spotlight on the Varinskis, and the rulers in Sereminia will be forced to convict them."

"And what will that accomplish?"

"The Varinskis make millions every year performing assassinations. They have a mythological prestige among the criminals of the world. It'll be the beginning of the end for them, and I will be the person who pulled the trigger." Her smile was a symphony of white teeth and vengeful satisfaction.

"You'll be the target." He didn't know why he bothered. This was Tasya Hunnicutt. She wouldn't listen. She would do as she thought right. And when she found out who he was . . . who his parents were, what his family name had been before it had been Wilder . . . that he was a Varinski, that he lived with the devil's pact every day of his life, that he would take the icon from her to free his father . . . she would never forgive him. Never.

And yet he loved her. She was his woman, the one fated to find the icon.

He knew it, and the tragedy of his life was that who and what he was could never be changed.

And who and what she was would never accept him . . . when she knew.

But she didn't know yet.

Something of his thoughts must have shown in his face, for she scooted back. "Why are you looking at me like that?"

Perhaps, if he made the right moves, said the right thing, showed her how he felt, she would remember him, and understand why he'd done what he intended to do.

"Soon the porter will be by to make the bed." He stood. "You're tired. Go ahead.

Get some sleep. We're coming into a stop. I need a few things, and I want to think."

"All right," she said slowly. "Are you okay? You look funny."

"I'm fine."

"Are you sure? Is your wound bothering you?" She pressed her hand to his chest and left it there, worried about him. Trusting him.

The spur of guilt dug into his side.

She didn't trust anybody, and for good reason.

He stood hastily before he betrayed himself with the truth. "Lock the door behind me. I've got the key."

He paused outside the door until he heard her turn the lock before he walked to the end of the car. He waited for the train to stop. He disembarked, and bought everything he needed from the row of vendors lined up selling food and sundries. He very carefully chose what he needed, and when he boarded again, he held a bag in his hand.

At least, when he finished with her tonight, she would never forget him.

Chapter 20

Rurik stood in the viewing car, watching the passengers board the train. When it pulled away from the station, he made a sweep of the cars, examining every person, making sure that once again he and Tasya were safe.

Tonight he needed to know they would be safe.

Tonight he would concentrate on Tasya. Only on Tasya.

When he was satisfied, he went back to their compartment.

Tasya was deeply asleep. She lay facedown on the covers in her clothes, snoring lightly. He smiled to see her so relaxed . . . and locked the door, taking precautions to ensure no one — not an enemy, not a friendly porter — could enter.

She'd left the blind open so that the lights of the passing towns shot through the window and covered the wall in ephemeral bursts of red and blue and white.

He shut it, making sure no beam could penetrate. He shoved a rug forward to block the glow under the door. In here, the darkness was complete. No human eye could see . . . anything.

Taking care not to wake her, he removed her clothes. Using the oils he'd bought, he rubbed her back, her thighs, her calves. He took his time, liberal with his attentions, using the opportunity to stroke every part of her, to learn her body as she would never allow him if she were awake. He rubbed her earlobes, the soles of her feet, the bones of her hands. He stroked her breasts, probed her navel, spread her legs, and explored, arousing her gently, but not seeking response.

Response he would demand later.

She slept still, but she moaned and stretched like a baby in the hands of one she trusted.

"Yes," he murmured in her ear, and he stroked her hair back from her face. "Sleep."

He shed his clothes and climbed on the bed. The scents of sandalwood and orange rose from her body, stirring his senses . . . stirring hers. Or perhaps it was his hands, kneading her muscles, that brought her to wakefulness. He heard her breath hitch as she realized she was in the dark, that she rested on her stomach, and a man was above her.

"Sh," he said. "It's Rurik."

Convulsively, she tried to rise.

He held her down with his weight across her thighs. Sliding his hands up her hips, over her waist, up her arms, he caught her wrists and lifted them above her head. "You knew I wouldn't wait forever."

"Don't!"

"Trust me," he murmured. In a long, slow undulation, he settled atop her. He held her legs together with his knees. He pressed his chest to her back, his penis against her bottom.

He felt the heat of her skin as her passion blossomed.

She struggled against his grip. She said, "No . . ." But she whispered.

He rubbed his body on hers, using the oils to ease the friction, reveling in the sensations of her skin against his. Her body was built to contain him, to please him. He pressed his cock between her legs, seeking the silk there, the warm skin, the glory within her. He rubbed himself between her thighs, enjoying the sensation of skin against skin.

"No." It was more of a breath than a word.

"Do you know what I feel when I'm inside you?" He used his cock like a ram, thrusting against the gates of her body, and the oil he'd used on her allowed him to open her. Just a little. Just enough to almost enter her.

Then he slipped toward the front of her body, and the most sensitive part of him rubbed against the most sensitive part of her.

She caught her breath.

He groaned.

"You can't do this." She turned her head from side to side, tried to lift herself off the bed.

Although he had no intention of hurting her, he enjoyed controlling her. He had a point to make.

"Trust me." Her personal scent was strongest at the back of her neck, and he breathed it in, and kissed the tender skin. "I love the taste of you. Do you know, since that night when we made love, all I have to do is stand close, and I can taste you again?"

"You cannot."

He put both of her wrists in one hand, and slid the other between her rib cage and the bed to cup her breast. "When I rubbed oil on your nipple, you moaned in your sleep."

"I imagine I did." She sounded snappish, more Tasya, less vulnerable.

Yet her nipple beaded in his palm. She might not want to want this: the dark, or him. But her body betrayed both her fear and her desire.

"Damn you. Get *off!*" She tried to turn over.

Gently, he squeezed the tiny bead. Once. Again. Again. A slow, steady rhythm guaranteed to irritate her senses.

Her exertions, and that inexorable rhythm, worked their magic. She panted, and perspiration formed on her skin. The scents of her body grew stronger, blending with the perfumes. Beneath him, her movements made him aware of her strength, her weakness, the promise of her femininity.

And he could see her.

The dark was not dark for him.

He saw the mixture of anger and fear on her face, the dawning of passion, the strength with which she held it back.

Yes. This was the right thing to do. For she didn't stand a chance.

In a single quick motion, he let her go and donned the condom.

She hesitated not at all, but made the dash for freedom.

He caught her, put her back where he

wanted her, and started again. Holding her down, massaging her, arousing her.

She yielded more easily this time, forgetting for many long seconds the dark and her rebellion. Whenever he touched somewhere new, pushed her toward some new pleasure, she would struggle again. But her resistance grew less and less, and finally she accepted his attentions, relaxed into the mattress, waited for the next caress.

Again he pressed her legs together, then slid his cock between her thighs and higher, finding the entrance to her body and seating himself. He held her arms above her head, held her down with his weight, and murmured softly in her ear, "When I am here, where your body begins to yield, the pleasure is only at the tip, and yet so strong and concentrated I want to scream. Then I push a little" — he did — "and you accept me, squeezing me and promising paradise."

"Please. It's dark."

"You're afraid of the dark."

"No, I'm not. I'm not afraid of anything."

He kissed her ear, bit her lobe, tasted her skin. "I get about halfway inside, and you flex. You welcome me."

"That's not welcome."

"Isn't it? Let me convince you." He slipped one well-oiled hand beneath her, down her belly and between her legs, and on one finger, he had attached a tiny vibrator. He flicked the switch, bringing her to instant, unwilling ecstasy — while he thrust all the way inside.

She writhed beneath him. She whimpered in desperation. Her fingernails clawed at the sheets.

Inside, her climax squeezed him, caressed him.

"When . . . when I'm as far inside you as I can go, you're still so tight" — he should have spread her legs, this ecstasy was almost painful — "so tight and hot. . . . Inside, you're so hot . . . and the folds inside you tug at me, begging me to come. To fill you . . ." He was losing the ability to form words. As her spasms dragged him into heaven with her, the primitive beast within him clawed to get out. He thrust faster and faster, desperate for release, determined to claim her, to show her the man he was and make her know she was his.

Their climax built to a crescendo, then gradually faded.

He turned off the vibrator, dropped it on the floor, listened as she sobbed the last of her release.

She was exhausted. He could feel it in the trembling of her muscles, the way she rested, quiescent, beneath him.

Good. That would make the rest of the night easier.

He lifted himself, rolled her over, leaned down between her legs, and kissed her there.

She gasped, tried to scoot away.

He pressed his hand to her belly. "I want you to forget about the dark. I want you to forget where we're going. I want you to forget who you are. I only want you to know what pleasure is — and who is giving you that pleasure." He tasted her, a long, slow savoring of the flavors of aroused woman and satisfied man.

She couldn't believe he wanted to continue as if he'd never come. As if he hadn't held her down and forced orgasm after orgasm from her until her legs trembled. "You can't . . . you can't do me again. Not so soon."

With a bound, he rose above her. Taking her hand, he wrapped it around his arousal.

It should be impossible, but he was as hot and hard as he had been the first time.

That first night, he'd been like this. A man of massive appetites, tightly leashed.

Tonight he'd let those appetites slip the leash. He was an animal, a stranger to civilization — and he made her an animal, too.

Pressing a foil-wrapped packet in her hand, he said, "Put it on me."

"I will not!"

She couldn't see him. She couldn't see anything, only a black so dark it pressed against her eyeballs and threatened to break her will. But she could smell him as he leaned close to her ear, and as he spoke, she felt his breath against her neck. "I would like to impregnate you, Tasya. I want to see you with my son in your belly, and know you suckle him at your breast. If I could, I would make a dozen sons with you, and my pleasure would be increased a hundredfold when I filled you with my come, over and over and over again. So you decide, Tasya Hunnicutt. Condom or no?"

She feared the darkness as much as ever . . . but he made her forget everything except him, and the fury and delight he aroused.

Her hands were shaking as she tore the foil. Taking the small roll, she slid it over the tip of his penis, then eased it down to the base.

He didn't move. He remained so still, he might have been a statue.

When she finished, she still held him in her hands. She thought about the many self-defense moves she knew. She'd used them before, and without hesitation; a woman who wandered the earth alone sometimes found herself in a dangerous situation.

But this was Rurik. He didn't doubt her story about her parents' assassins, and he had come with her every step of the way of her journey.

Unhurriedly she caressed his thigh.

She felt as if he'd seen her yield. She was sure he knew he'd won.

Sliding his arms around her, he lifted her.

She groaned, knowing what would happen now.

"Trust me." He thrust inside. "Trust me now. Trust me forever."

When at last Rurik lifted the shade, morning was well advanced and Tasya barely remembered what it was like not to have him inside her. He'd kissed her lips, filling her with his tongue. He'd taken her with his mouth, with his penis, with his fingers. He'd knelt beside the bed, held her in his lap, and entered her. He'd taken her so many times, and every time he was strong and full, larger than any man she'd ever imagined, tireless, determined, and a man with a mission.

Trust me.

He'd said it over and over.

Trust him? She had made it her policy to never trust anyone, and that policy had stood her in good stead.

So why now was she tempted to discard a lifetime of hard lessons? Why did it seem possible that at last she could dredge down to the bottom of her soul and come up with emotions she thought vanquished?

Love and trust . . . how bright and shiny those emotions looked this morning.

Slowly she sat up, pushing her hair off her forehead. She glanced at Rurik, stretched out beside her, still naked, still large, still watching her as if he would never stop wanting her.

She didn't know what to respond, what to say, how to be the woman he adored.

So she looked out the window.

They'd reached Ruyshvania.

She recognized the mountains, rugged, rock-strewn, shadowy.

She recognized the valleys, filled with rushing rivers and occasionally a farming hamlet.

She recognized the ruins of medieval castles and the Bronze Age standing stones that crowned the peaks.

She recognized this place because, for the first time in twenty-five years, she was home.

Home.

She looked down, and she recognized Rurik, too. Recognized him from the days of travel, from the night spent entwined with him while the train rolled along beneath them. My God, she could never forget him now, although she half wished she could.

If only . . . if only it didn't seem as if Rurik was willing to risk his life for her and her mission.

He was beginning to assume the proportions of a hero.

He watched her now, his eyes alive with some earnest emotion . . . the kind of emotion that made her far too uneasy. Taking her face between his hands, he pressed a kiss on her lips.

"Trust me, Tasya," he said again. "Trust me forever. I will never hurt you. I will never betray you. I swear it on my father's immortal soul. Trust me."

CHAPTER 21

"Talk about terminally quaint." Rurik stood outside the old-fashioned railway station and looked around.

Time had left Capraru behind. Crumbled remnants of its medieval walls snaked through the town. Not far away, a massive clock tower loomed over the square. Bavarian-style scroll decorated the two- and three-story buildings, and cobblestones lined the narrow streets. A few of the cars were new, but he saw well-kept sixties and seventies and eighties models threading through the pedestrians that thronged the streets.

"Ruyshvania lived under the hammer and sickle until the Soviet Union fell. Then their puppet leader, Czajkowski, seized power and kept it until nine years ago. After a cruel reign, he was deposed and executed, and since then, the people have struggled to join the twenty-first century. In the end, the quaintness has paid off — Americans like the clean streets and the old-fashioned hospitality, and tourism is doing well." Tasya sounded like a guidebook, cool and well-informed, and her expression couldn't have been more undemonstrative.

That surprised him. At every stop, Tasya had been enthusiastic about their surroundings, interested no matter how many times she'd visited before.

Perhaps the tension of seeking the icon and failing was getting to her. Or after last night, perhaps she felt awkward as she tried to fathom what it was he wanted.

And he'd told her so many times. . . . *Trust me.*

"Let's see if we can find someone to take us up to the convent." Rurik put his hand on the base of her spine.

Tasya adjusted her backpack, moving her shoulders as if she couldn't find a comfortable position for the straps.

Good. Maybe last night had exhausted her, made her ache in every sinew and muscle. Maybe every time she moved today and her bones protested, she would think of him and his dedication to her pleasure. *Trust me.* "Let me carry that for you." He reached for the backpack.

She jerked aside. "No, I'll carry it."

And maybe his plan had backfired. Last night she'd clung to him, yielded to him, let him take her beyond fear and into passion. Perhaps now her irritating and compulsive independence had caused her to panic . . . but that was all right. She couldn't flee. She had an icon to find.

"I like the way the people look here. I like the way they act." Almost everyone on the street had dark hair and strong features, and they moved purposefully, as if they held their fates in their own hands. "They remind me of my mother."

She gasped softly, as if he'd surprised her. "They remind me of my mother, too."

Her mother? She spoke of her mother? Perhaps she was coming to trust him, after all.

He listened closely to the dialect. It sounded similar to the Russian his parents had taught him, much like Portuguese and Spanish. . . . He couldn't quite understand it, no matter how hard he tried. "Do you know any of the language?"

"No! Why would I?"

"I don't know. I've heard you speak French —"

"Badly!"

"— German, and Japanese to those tourists —"

"I don't know every language there is. Okay? I'm just a photojournalist, not the Tower of Babel."

"Okay! I thought you might know a few words of Ruyshvanian." Man, she was snappish. When his mother and his sister got like this, he and his brother knew better than to tease them — about anything. PMS was no joking matter . . . well, except he and his brothers used to say it stood for "Pack My Suitcase," and they'd use it as an excuse to run for the hills. There they'd camp and fish, and feel sorry for their father stuck at home with two really cranky women.

But Rurik couldn't run from Tasya. She wouldn't be safe, and anyway . . . he didn't want to.

Maybe that was why his papa stayed home instead of joining his sons for some recreation. No matter what her mood, he still wanted to be there for Zorana.

No wonder people claimed that love was three parts glory and one part suffering.

"Shall we try the visitors' center?" he teased.

She relaxed and grinned. Briefly, but she grinned.

He found a policeman who spoke English, and that policeman directed them to the

243

hotel on the square.

As they walked, Tasya glanced over her shoulder.

Rurik glanced, too.

The policeman was watching them. Watching her.

She turned to face front, and she looked . . . uneasy.

"It's all right," Rurik said. "You're a pretty girl. Men gawk at you all the time. Haven't you noticed?"

"You're right, I am a pretty girl." She clutched the straps of her backpack. "This place is just creepy, that's all."

Rurik glanced around. "Twenty thousand people, nice and clean, lots and lots of restaurants. So what's creepy?"

"Nothing."

He raised his eyebrows at her.

"Really. Nothing!"

He held the hotel door for her and followed her inside. Nice place. Small, clean, and there was a woman behind the counter.

She was about his mother's age, and she smiled at him like a woman smiles when she sees a man she likes.

Good. He'd been chasing Tasya so hard, and she'd been running so earnestly, this woman's appreciation was balm on his wounded ego.

"You're swaggering," Tasya murmured.

"And I'm good at it." He glanced at the woman's name tag, leaned across the counter, smiled his most charming smile at the desk clerk, and asked, "Bela, can I hire a guide here?"

"You have come to the right place." Bela picked up a form, placed it on a clipboard, and held her pen at the ready. "Do you want to go any place in particular, or would you like a tour of our lovely countryside?"

"We want to go to the Convent of St. Maria," Rurik said.

Her pen ripped the paper. "The convent? Oh, but there is nothing up there. It was not a rich convent to start with, and Czajkowski stripped it of everything of value. The countryside around it is not attractive. The relics are long gone, as are the nicest of the holy objects. Can I interest you in Horvat?"

"No," Rurik insisted. "The convent."

Bela's smile faded. She put down her pen, leaned on the counter. "I can't get a guide to go up there."

"Why not?" Rurik asked.

She led them to the window. "See that hill?"

It looked more like a mountain to Rurik, looming over the town, craggy and forested, rising toward the sun, catching wisps of clouds as they whirled past.

"People say that hill is bad luck. Not me, of course, but people. They say it's haunted. They say it's no place to be at night, and since the road is in such bad shape, it's almost impossible to get up there and back in one day. The convent's on that mountain. The convent and —" Bela shivered. "That mountain is not a good place."

Tasya apparently couldn't stand to be silent anymore. "We have to get there."

Bela seemed to notice her for the first time.

Eyes narrowed, she considered Tasya, then nodded as if, for the first time, she understood their resolve. "Of course. The stories are superstition, but this is Ruyshvania. Superstition is difficult to overcome here. You understand."

"Yes," Tasya said. "Yes, I understand."

"May I suggest a rental car and a good map?" Bela was the desk clerk, travel agent, and car-rental counter. She got out a different form, put it on the clipboard, and pushed it across to Rurik. "There is still one nun left alive, but I hear she's a little batty."

"One nun?"

"Sister Maria Helvig." Bela shook her

head. "She refuses to come down and live in town. Well, she has lived up there since she was eighteen, and she's watched all the sisters pass away or be — well, they're dead, and she's alone."

"That's enough to make anyone crazy," Rurik agreed.

"She is harmless," Bela assured them. "As is the mountain, I am sure."

As Rurik handed back the filled-out form, Bela smiled hugely and he saw the flash of a gold tooth.

Bela added, "At least — nothing will hurt *you* up there."

Oddly enough, she spoke only to Tasya.

CHAPTER 22

An hour later Rurik and Tasya found themselves driving up a steep, winding grade. When Rurik glanced back, he could see Capraru appearing and disappearing behind the curves.

The clutch was loose, the five-speed transmission ground every time he shifted gears, and the driver's seat was on the wrong side. But Rurik had driven mountain roads all his life and this one held no surprises for him.

So why did Tasya flinch every time they rounded a corner? Had he scared her crossing Germany to Vienna? He'd been driving like a maniac, yeah, but he'd been driving a Mercedes, the road was the Autobahn, and he hadn't slipped a tire.

He could snap at her — that's what his father did when his mother grabbed at the dashboard — or he could distract her. So he said, "It looks as though Ruyshvania has

248

recovered from the dictator well."

"Yes." Her teeth snapped when the car hit a pothole.

"Sorry," he said. "Bela was right. The road is lousy. But the town is thriving — you'd think they could fix it."

"Not if they're afraid to come up here."

They came around a corner, and there was a fork in the road. One way, to the right, was paved. The other way was graded gravel. Both looked rough and ill-used.

He started to take the paved way.

But Tasya said, "Take the fork to the left."

He slowed almost to a crawl. "Bela said —"

"Take the left."

"The other way's paved."

"I'm looking at the map. This way is shorter."

He turned to look at her.

She wanted to be anywhere but here. Because he'd scared her to death last night with his promises of loyalty and demands for trust?

Or did she sense something about this place? A malevolence similar to the coldness she'd sensed at the burial mound?

"Okay, we'll do it your way." He rested his hand on her knee.

She hesitated, then put her hand over his.

"Yes. Please. Let's do it my way."

Maybe she was beginning to soften toward him, after all. Putting the car in gear, he took the left.

To his surprise, she was right. They traveled ten miles of bad road before they rounded a corner . . . and drove through the gate to the Convent of St. Maria.

He parked, and they got out. The convent was old and handsome, and should have had his full attention.

But the view! He'd lived his life in the Cascades in Washington. In his travels as a pilot and an archaeologist, he'd been awed by many a breathtaking spectacle.

But the mountains of Ruyshvania felt . . . ancient. The peaks alternated light and shadow. They whispered of treachery and devotion. And in the distance, another mountain clawed at the skyline, and another, and another, until the pale blue faded into the horizon.

When he could pull his gaze away from the vista, he saw the same clashes of soft and hard on this mountain. Tempestuous outcroppings of stone punched through the billowing, emerald grass. Here and there, cliffs broke the conifer groves into halves. Dense underbrush covered the rugged mountain with green, and beneath it he could see the stiff branches and long thorns that repelled invaders.

He turned to face the convent.

Stone by stone, the walls had been constructed, and stonecutters had created filigrees and gargoyles. High atop the cloister, crosses probed the clear blue skies. The chapel was old, the oldest, tiniest building on the grounds, with small, stained-glass windows and a beautiful door carved with the figures of saints. Just as the mountain was primal, the convent breathed holiness.

This place held contradictions, and hid secrets. He knew that without a doubt.

A tiny woman dressed in black and white stepped out of the cloister.

Sister Maria Helvig.

A pair of Coke-bottle-thick glasses enlarged her faded blue eyes and pale lashes. Her wimple wrapped around her chin, and crepey, finely wrinkled skin draped over the stiff edge. A smile lit her face, and she hurried toward Tasya, hands outstretched.

Tasya shied from her, a movement so quick, only he recognized it as reluctance. Then she smiled and accepted the nun's welcome.

Sister Maria Helvig held Tasya's hands, kissed them with enthusiasm and, in heavily accented English, said, "I've been waiting for you to come!"

He stood, arms crossed, staring at the nun. She came toward him, hands outstretched — and he put his hands behind his back, and he bowed from the waist. "I am honored to meet you, Sister."

Sister Maria Helvig stopped short. She smiled. "Of course. I should have recognized you! He told me about you."

"Who told you?" Rurik asked sharply.

Sister Maria Helvig pointed toward the skies. "*He* did."

Rurik's face softened. He smiled and, like a kindergartner in a Catholic school, looked at his feet. "Did He tell you how this would turn out?"

"He doesn't know. But He hopes that you make the right decisions."

Rurik looked up, and he wasn't smiling. "I hope so, too."

Sister Maria Helvig etched a cross in the air over his head. "I get so lonely here since the other sisters died. I'm so glad you came to visit. . . . Do you have the key?"

Tasya stared at the good sister. "Do we have the key? To what?"

"I'm sorry." The sister looked confused. "They said someone could come for the icon."

Both Rurik and Tasya stiffened and stared.

"The icon? You know where the icon is?"

"No, but it's here. The legend says it is."

"What legend?"

Sister Maria Helvig tucked her hands into her sleeves. "Almost a thousand years ago, a great king from the west received a tribute from a conquered warlord. The gift gave the bearer power — or so the warlord said. But the warlord hated his conqueror, and it was a cruel trick. For the gift was a holy object, a picture of the Virgin and her son, and if a man possessed the icon and possessed no good in his heart, bad luck would follow him."

Rurik's heart began to pound as he listened. This was the place. He knew it.

Sister Maria Helvig continued. "The warlord withered and died, laughing at the trick he'd played on his liege, and soon the king's might failed him. He was helpless against his enemies — and he had no friends. He sent it here for safekeeping. And so we've held the icon ever since."

"What does it look like?" Rurik asked.

"I don't know. I've never seen it." She smiled sweetly.

"Where do you keep it?" Tasya asked.

"I don't know. No one does."

"So you don't know if you have the icon?" Rurik hid his frustration beneath logic.

Sister Maria Helvig laughed, a light, tinkling laugh, and one that didn't fit her plump frame. "Of course we have it. Don't we, Sisters?" She turned to the side and stared fixedly at the door of the church.

Rurik also turned, expecting to see . . . someone. More than one someone. Not no one. Not empty air.

Sister Maria Helvig nodded as if the invisible sisters had agreed with her. "Where else would it be? This is the holiest place in Ruyshvania, perhaps in the whole empire."

"Empire?" Rurik rubbed his forehead.

"I think she means the Holy Roman Empire," Tasya said.

"Of course. Come, let me show you." Sister Maria Helvig might look old, but she walked like a much younger woman, and straight uphill.

Rurik and Tasya hurried to follow her up the narrow path. It cut through a forest grove, and when they stepped out into the sunshine, they found themselves facing a cliff that rose above them and plunged below them, cutting the mountain in two — or perhaps uniting two peaks into one.

As if she hadn't a care in the world, Sister Maria Helvig walked out onto the narrow path that sliced across a cliff.

Tasya stopped at the precipice. She peered

over the edge. The drop was a thousand feet straight down onto sharp-toothed boulders. She stepped back. "Rurik, I don't mind heights. I like to fly. You know that."

He grinned at her stiff back. "I do know that."

"I'd take my ultralight anywhere." She pointed up, then down. "But one step wrong on that cliff, and I won't fly — I'll plunge."

"You're right."

"But what am I supposed to do when an elderly nun just strolls out there? Tell her I'm afraid?"

"She's very sweet. I'm sure she'd understand." Rurik didn't have to wait to know what Tasya would say — and do.

"Don't be an asshole." Tasya took her first step across the cliff.

Rurik followed. "I can't help it. It's in my nature. My mom says so."

The path looked as if it had been cut by God's finger through the rocks, and once upon a time, it had been smooth and straight. Years of freezing and thawing, heavy rains, and piles of snow had changed the path, fraying it like an aging ribbon. The rock crumbled beneath their feet, and here and there gullies cut the ground away completely, and they had to jump to the next level.

Ahead of them, Sister Maria Helvig leaped like a mountain goat from perch to perch, scrambling ahead and calling back, "Hurry! As slow as you are, we'll be stuck there after dark."

"There where?" Rurik asked.

Tasya didn't answer. She just leaped across the next chasm, and froze when a layer of rocks tumbled down the mountain behind her. Pressing her back against the cliff, she looked at Rurik. "Can you make it?"

He leaped, and landed pressed against her. "Don't worry about me. If I have to, I *can* fly." He leaned on her, body to body, and kissed her. "Don't be afraid," he whispered. "After all we've been through, I don't think our fate is to plunge to our deaths."

Tasya clutched her hands in his shirt, her blue eyes warm as she held him. "Perhaps God doesn't like a smart-ass."

"If God doesn't like me, it's for a better reason than that." He took her hand. "Come on. I'll lead you."

He thought it was a mark of how discomfited she was that she let him. Each time they came to a place where the path had sloughed away, he jumped, then held her hand while she jumped, and he laughed at himself for feeling so strong and protective when he knew very well, if left on her own, she would make it across without harm.

They reached the other side to find Sister Maria Helvig standing, staring at the view.

It was spectacular. This part of the mountain faced a different vista, one that stretched for miles in three directions. It overlooked the juncture of two rivers, the joining of two roads, and a series of hills that diminished until they touched the horizon.

"I had no idea this country was so beautiful," Rurik said.

Sister Maria Helvig smiled. "This spot is the first place in Ruyshvania deemed to be holy. But it was the pagans who worshipped here." She gestured up the hill, and there it was — an altar stone of carved granite, eight feet wide and four feet deep, balanced on squat pillars that held the monument up out of the earth and presented it to the skies.

Rurik recognized the stone. It was related to the menhirs and standing stones that dotted Europe and Great Britain, stones placed four thousand years ago and more in miracles of engineering by primitive man.

"The Church came to Ruyshvania very early," Sister Maria Helvig told them, "at least by the third century, and no effort of theirs could dislodge the stone. So they took the other half of the mountain as their own. There has always been a house sacred to our Lord located on the other half of the mountain, while this place silently worships nature, and together we've lived in harmony."

"No wonder the pagans decided this place was holy," Rurik said.

"That's only half the reason." Sister Maria Helvig took his sleeve — only his sleeve, not his arm — and led him to a rocky outcropping marked by the blasted and burned trunk of a great old tree.

In the middle of the mound of rocks, he saw a hole, black and impenetrable.

Tasya hadn't followed them, and he called to her, "Look. A cave!"

She stood gazing toward the top of the mountain, and she shook her head.

"An entrance to the underworld. It's said that's the way to hell." As if she'd been pushed, Sister Maria Helvig staggered sideways. "Oh, all right, Sister Teresa! I'll tell them the other story. There's no need to be so snappish." With a martyrish sigh, she added, "It's also said that it's a secret escape route used by the royal family of Ruyshvania in case of emergency. They say it passes under the mountain and comes out on the other side, in Hungary. But the story about the way to hell is certainly more colorful, isn't it?"

Rurik liked Sister Maria Helvig. He liked her childlike exuberance, her refusal to judge and condemn the pagans who had worshipped here so long ago. "It's very exciting, Sister. Where do the royal family live?"

"The Dimitrus are all dead now. Or so people say. But they lived right up there." Sister Maria Helvig pointed toward the top of the mountain.

His instincts stirred. "What happened to them?"

"They were murdered. Twenty-five years ago, the night was bright with the fire and shrill with the screams."

He scrutinized Sister Maria Helvig, who spoke softly, remembering.

He scrutinized Tasya. Still she stared up the mountain, her usually animated face without expression.

"The sisters say to tell you — this tree was ancient, tall, green, the symbol of the royal family. They burned it, too, and that night, all Ruyshvania mourned." Sister Maria Helvig crossed herself, and her lips moved silently.

Tasya heard her. She turned her head.

259

"We'd better go."

But he had to be sure. "Tasya, look at that cave. When we're done, I'd like to map it. Are you in?"

Tasya glanced at the hole in the ground, then, as if caught, stared without blinking. "That cave does lead to hell, and I won't follow the path no matter what the peril — or the reward." She looked at him, her chin firm and her eyes so blue they looked like chips of the winter sky. "I've been in that cave before. I am a part of the royal family. I escaped through the caves. I'm the last remaining Dimitru on earth, and now you know all my secrets — and you hold my life in your hands."

CHAPTER 23

"The sisters suggest you would like a tour of the abbey." Sister Maria Helvig stood in front of the cloister, as chipper as ever, just as if the three of them hadn't made a trip to old, bad memories and back.

"Of course. If the icon is here, there has to be some way to figure out where." Rurik sounded absolutely confident, a man who had probably never heard screams or smelled burning flesh, and who thought hell was in the afterlife.

Sister Maria Helvig held up one hand, and cocked her head as if listening. Then she said, "Time is getting short."

Tasya glanced at the sun. It had dipped to the west, and she didn't want to be up on this mountain when it got dark.

"The sisters suggest that you, young man, look around the grounds and in the outbuildings." Sister Maria Helvig took Tasya's hand. "This young lady and I will look in the chapel."

Rurik got a funny expression on his face, sort of like he was relieved, and also not at all surprised. "Good plan."

Tasya was glad to see the back of him. Right now, she resented him and his family back in Washington and his clear conscience and his self-assurance so *much,* she could scarcely look at him.

They paused in the doorway of the chapel. It was narrow and tall, with stained-glass windows set high on the walls, and broken pews set among the whole ones. Spiderwebs festooned the ceiling and hung on the chandelier, but the altar was spotless; the altar cloth was embroidered with gold thread, clean, white, and so thin, so old.

Sister Maria Helvig blessed herself with holy water from the font, then dipped her fingers again and etched a cross on Tasya's forehead. "It's better if I do it," she said. "You're too angry at God to do it for yourself."

True — but how did Sister Maria Helvig know?

"I always thought the icon should be in here." She led Tasya down the aisle toward the front. "The boys get to have all the fun, and I think it would be nice if one of us girls had some for a change. So you find it."

"Any idea where to look?"

"I have lots of ideas!" Sister Maria Helvig clasped her hands together. "I thought — what?" She looked at one of the invisible someones beside her.

"What?" Tasya asked.

Sister Maria Helvig sighed heavily. "Sister Catherine insists I can't help you."

Tasya bit her lip. This was not the time or the place to say, "Bullshit," nor was Sister Maria Helvig the person to whom she could say it.

But she wanted to.

While Sister Maria Helvig watched, Tasya walked to the altar and looked at the floor, the walls, the ceiling. She paced up first one side aisle, then another. The chapel was old stones and crumbling wood, and if there had at one time been an arrow and a sign saying ICON HERE! it was long gone.

"Perhaps if you sat down and thought about it," the nun suggested.

Tasya suspected her suggestion was nothing more than an attempt to make her spend time in religious contemplation, but she wasn't getting anywhere on her own. The old training couldn't be denied; Tasya genuflected and slid into the pew close to the altar.

"If you need me, call me." Sister Maria

Helvig drifted toward the back of the chapel, her habit rustling in the quiet.

Tasya sighed and looked around. She'd been here before, a child looking up at the lines of nuns. . . . Her eyes slid almost shut.

She existed in that state between waking and sleeping, when nothing made sense . . . and everything was possible. Her mind floated free of her body. She looked down at herself, poor thing, slumped exhausted in the pew. Her hands rested palms up in her lap. Her chin leaned on her chest. Her eyes were closed.

She could see a tree, its branching reaching up to the sky, its leaves coolly green and promising. She heard a man's voice. . . . *Tasya, little one, as long as you live, that oak will never die.*

But the oak did die. It died a fiery death.

She lived. She lived for vengeance, and for her vengeance to be complete she needed the icon.

It was close. So close.

The light of her consciousness spread out in all directions, searching for the key, and the lock to put it in.

Some force tugged the light toward the altar.

That made sense, but Tasya had looked all over the chapel . . . yet the light sank, and sank, onto the floor and into the cracks between the stones where once-hard mortar had crumbled into dust.

Someone was buried beneath the altar.

Of course. Rurik and Tasya's adventure had started in a tomb in Scotland. It would end in a grave in Ruyshvania.

The light found a treasure chest, a match to the one in Scotland.

And the light hovered there. Waiting.

I don't have a key! Tasya floated in the chapel, arms outstretched. *I can't use what I don't have!*

And all at once, she was wide-awake and on her feet.

She did *too* have the key.

Sure for the first time in this whole journey, she fumbled for her backpack. She dragged it up off the floor by her feet. Placed it on the pew.

Unzipped the main compartment.

The key wasn't there.

It wasn't in the side compartment.

It wasn't in the stupid little compartment for the cell phone, or the one for the business cards, or the Velcro pocket for the pens. It wasn't in the mesh zip for the overnight change of clothes, or the padded computer compartment.

Frustrated, she pushed her hair off her

forehead.

Someone had stolen it.

"No," she whispered.

It had to be here. She lost stuff in here all the time.

She groped the bottom of the backpack. The sides . . . and in the water-bottle pocket, she found the shape she'd been looking for. That of a long, rust-encrusted steel blade.

But it wasn't a steel blade.

All the way through Europe, the artifact had been rattling around in that pocket on the outside of her backpack. It had been smacked against doorframes, dropped on the floor, stored in overhead bins at the bottom of piles of luggage. As she opened the pocket, flakes of rust, large and small, made a grinding noise in the zipper, and when she delved inside, her hand came out red with rust — and she held a key.

The teeth were now clearly visible beneath the crust formed by a thousand years of being hidden in the ground on the Isle of Roi.

"Did you find it?"

She whirled to see Sister Maria Helvig sitting in the pew behind her. The old nun was smiling, as always, and nodding.

"Yes. I had it all along." Tasya showed it to her.

"Of course you did."

"And I know where the icon is."

Sister Maria Helvig's gaze shifted to the stone floor on the altar.

So the good sister had always known the icon's location.

"Will you take the icon?" she asked.

"Of course! That's what I came here to do." Tasya edged out of the pew.

"For your revenge?"

Tasya stopped. "How did you know that?"

"I see my sisters around me. They wait for me to join them."

She sounded so convinced, Tasya turned, half-expecting to see a line of nuns dressed in black and white, seated in the pews.

"But I'm not dotty." Sister Maria Helvig turned to the side and spoke to . . . no one. "Am I?"

Maybe she wasn't crazy or senile. Maybe she saw things that no one else saw, but were there. Maybe she knew things no one else knew. . . . Tasya walked to the sister's pew, grasped the finial tightly. "Will I succeed?"

Sister Maria Helvig pushed her glasses up her nose, and looked solemnly at Tasya. "You don't understand anything at all. You're involved in a great battle. Good and evil hang in the balance, and the actions of every person, no matter how small, will make all the difference."

Tasya waited for more. More enlightenment, more specifics, more anything.

But the nun tucked her hands into her sleeves and bent her head, and Tasya couldn't tell whether she was praying or asleep.

"All right, then." Tasya went up to the altar. Carefully, she placed the key on the railing, and knelt on the granite.

As she'd seen in her vision, the grout was long gone. The stones were loose. Large stones, the length and width of her forearm, squared off by master masons and worn smooth by generations of the faithful. With her fingers, she pried the first one up.

Dirt . . . and bones. Bones picked clean by time.

She'd come to the right spot.

She pried up another stone, and another one. She bent a fingernail back to the quick, and held back a curse.

Not here. Not with Sister Maria Helvig listening.

The bones were old, covered with shreds of a wool burial shroud dyed brown by long contact with the earth. The man, when he'd been alive, had been tall and broad. His femur was long and thick; his hip bones were sturdy. Someone had crossed his hands over his chest. Finger bones were scattered among his ribs, one still wearing a hammered gold ring.

Tasya paused, disappointed and panting. She'd thought he would be holding the treasure chest.

"Keep looking." Sister Maria Helvig's voice floated faintly from the pews. And then, so faintly Tasya almost didn't hear her, she said, "There's no time left."

Tasya looked around. "No time for what?"

The nun didn't reply, but still sat with her head bent.

The stone over the king's head was four inches thick and half the length of Tasya, and probably weighed half a ton. Briefly she considered calling Rurik to help, but she'd seen his reluctance to come into the chapel.

So she wouldn't call him, nor would she pray for help from a god in whom she'd lost faith so many years ago. Instead, she did what she always did, and depended on herself.

Saying, "Brace yourself, Sister, this is going to be loud," she used the rocks on either side of the grave as a firm foundation for her feet. Sliding her hands under the edges of the huge headstone, she labored to lift one end. The other remained firmly braced on the ground. The muscles in her arms and stomach screamed under the strain, yet slowly, slowly the monument rose. She got it almost to the halfway mark. . . . Almost there . . . almost . . . she was going to drop it. She had to drop it. She had to!

She glanced down at the body, hoping to see the treasure chest.

Instead the king's skull grinned up at her, mocking her efforts.

In a surge of fury, she shoved the massive slab over.

With a mighty crash, it smacked the smooth, broad surface of the floor, and broke in two.

She stood panting, staring down at that smirking skull. "Take that," she said.

Above his crowned head, she saw an eight-inch square glint of gold.

The chest.

"It's here," she called. "Sister, the chest is here!"

Careful not to disturb the bones, she knelt and brushed the dirt away. Yes. The work on the top was a match to that of the chest in Scotland. Impossible, but somehow this chest had traveled across an island, across a sea, across a continent, to end here in a kingly grave in an old and honored convent.

She looked around for something to dig

with, but the altar was still bare, and anyway, she might not have forgiven God for allowing her parents to die, but that didn't mean that she would use just anything in the church as a shovel. "Sister, are you sure the icon's inside?"

Sister Maria Helvig didn't answer, but that didn't surprise Tasya. The nun was given to cryptic commentary. Why would she give Tasya the answers she sought now?

With an eagerness that had no time for fear or fastidiousness, Tasya dug around the chest with her fingers.

Once she glanced longingly at the key waiting on the railing . . . but no. She didn't dare use it in the hard-packed dirt. If the rust had weakened the shaft, and she broke the key . . . a thousand years, and Tasya Hunnicutt would blow the whole setup by breaking the key while digging out the chest. The thought made her shudder.

At last the chest shifted in her grip, and gradually she managed to inch it up, out of the hole. She held it in her hands, marveled at the workmanship. She wanted to shake the box, like a child with her birthday present, and try to guess from the sound and the weight whether her wish had been granted.

She wrapped it in her arms, and wondered

271

what was contained inside. For one moment, she closed her eyes and clutched the crusty, hammered gold box in her arms. Was the icon in here? Had she found her proof at last? Was her revenge only the turn of a key away?

She reached for the key. Dropped it. It hit the stone with a solid clang.

Her heart thumped as loudly.

She hardly dared look. When she did, she saw tiny shards of rust scattered across the floor. But the key remained in one piece.

"It's okay, Sister," she called. "Nothing's hurt."

With the tail of her shirt, she rubbed at the key, cleaning the teeth, knowing that between the dirt stuffed in the lock and the corruption on the metal, it would take a team of experts to open the chest — and that was if her vision was right, and the key matched the lock. She didn't have a chance of succeeding — but she had to try.

Placing the chest on the floor, she inserted the key into the lock. Right away, it stuck on something. She freed the key, wiped it again — the stains would never come out, but she sacrificed the shirt gladly — and tried again.

It still stuck.

Picking up the chest, she turned it so the

lock faced the floor. She took a breath — she knew better than to do this — and gently smacked it with the flat of her hand.

A tiny, jagged pebble clattered on the floor.

This time, the key fit. She turned it.

The lock clicked.

Her heart pounded in her chest. She panted as if she'd been running.

She opened the lid.

For the first time in almost a thousand years, human eyes gazed upon the icon of the Virgin Mary.

And the Virgin Mary gazed back.

The cherry color of her cloak was so rich and deep and glossy, it glowed, and the golden halo around her head glittered in the dim light. Her face was pale and still, her dark eyes were large and sorrowful, and a tear gathered on her cheek. For in her lap, this Madonna held the crucified Jesus.

Tears gathered in Tasya's eyes, too, and one splashed onto the icon. Hastily, she wiped it away and tried to tell herself she cried because this moment of her triumph meant so much.

But she couldn't convince even herself.

The Virgin's sad and tender eyes told the tale. This Virgin was a woman who had lost her child. She was a woman who foresaw untold suffering. And in her face, Tasya saw her own mother.

Tasya remembered the flames leaping upward, devouring the drapes, the walls. She remembered the screaming of the servants. She saw anew her mother's torment as she kissed her little girl good-bye and sent her away.

Tasya had screamed and cried, of course, but she hadn't understood.

Now she did, and the depths of her anguish deepened.

Her mother had let her go, not knowing if her daughter would die, but sure her own time had come . . . and that they would never see each other again.

The pain of that moment, when the bond between mother and daughter had been brutally severed, could never be assuaged.

Tasya sobbed once, a brutally loud, harsh sound that echoed through the chapel. Other sobs gathered in her chest, but she fought them back.

She couldn't cry. She never did. She didn't have time.

Sister Maria Helvig had said time was running out, and Tasya knew it was true. The longer she and Rurik stayed in one place, the more likely the Varinskis would find them. If she was to get this icon back to National Antiquities, they needed to leave before night came, while they could still drive down the road and into Capraru, and catch a train out of here.

She stood and slapped at her clothes. "I have it, Sister. It was here all along."

The sun reached through the west windows, and shone on the still figure of Sister Maria Helvig.

"Do you want to see it?" Tasya hurried down the aisle. "It's beautiful, Sister, and so old and sad. The artist was a master, and —" She stopped and stared at the nun. "Sister?"

Sister Maria Helvig slumped forward and sideways.

"Sister!" Tasya slid the icon in the front pocket of her jeans. She knelt beside the old woman and looked into her face.

Her eyes were closed, her expression serene.

Sister Maria Helvig was dead.

CHAPTER 24

Rurik paced in front of the chapel. He shifted his backpack. He unbuttoned his duster and made sure his pistol was at one side, a knife at the other, and the switchblade was hidden up his sleeve. He checked his watch.

It was three in the afternoon.

He'd waited as long as he could wait. He'd scouted out the whole area, looked through the outbuildings, the cemetery, and even the cloister, but he'd found no sign of the icon. Either it wasn't here — or it was in the chapel.

Didn't that just figure? The one place he dared not go.

He'd seen no sign of either Tasya or Sister Maria Helvig, and his sense of urgency was growing. He and Tasya — and Sister Maria Helvig, if he could convince her — needed to locate the icon or leave the convent, or both. They'd been here too long already.

As he stepped into the doorway of the chapel, he smelled the smell of death. He took in the scene in an instant — the old nun slumped in her seat, Tasya kneeling in the aisle beside her, head bowed.

"Tasya." Rurik stayed where he was, not daring to step inside.

She looked up.

He expected to see her crying.

Instead her face was pale, composed, and tearless — and the pain she projected sent him down the aisle toward her.

He'd gone three steps when the silence struck him.

The chapel was waiting for a decision.

He stopped and waited, too.

But nothing happened. The air didn't burn his lungs; the floor didn't burn his feet. He remained a man and not a flame.

He started forward again.

"She's dead." Tasya placed Sister Maria Helvig's hand back in her lap. "We should lay her out and call the undertaker to come and care for her."

"Certainly we should call the undertaker, but she was ready for this. I found the cemetery. Her grave is dug. Her coffin is waiting. And we need to bury her now." Cautiously, he touched the nun's hand.

Nothing. Not even a tingle.

"She didn't have last rites. Her body needs to be washed. She has to have a proper ceremony!"

"They can exhume her and do whatever's right, but we can't leave her body for the wild animals to find."

"What do you mean?"

He lifted the nun in his arms and headed out the door. "The Varinskis are closing on us. We've got to get out of here."

He had to give Tasya credit. She didn't ask how he knew. She didn't argue. She simply joined him as he strode down the aisle, Sister Maria Helvig's limp body in his arms. They exited the chapel and made a right, then a right again, and walked to the cemetery set behind the chapel in the shadows of a great old tree.

Rurik placed Sister Maria Helvig in the plain wood coffin waiting for her. Tasya arranged her hands over her chest, tidied her cowl and her robe, and placed the crucifix over her heart.

The grave was freshly dug, the coffin clean and dry and resting on ropes, and a shovel was waiting; Sister Maria Helvig had known the hour of her death. Rurik suspected she had known who he was, too, and what was coming for them now.

That was the real reason he wanted her

278

buried deep. If they could, the Varinskis would desecrate her body.

"All right." Tasya stepped back and helped him place the lid on the coffin.

Together, they took the ropes. The coffin was heavy, but once again, Tasya impressed Rurik with her strength and her determination to do what had to be done. She braced her feet and helped him slowly lower Sister Maria Helvig into the ground.

He grabbed the shovel.

Tasya stood, head down, hands on hips, panting.

"Say the prayers you want to say." Every instinct was jangling. "As soon as I'm done, we're out of here."

She nodded and lowered her head.

He shoveled and watched her.

Behind her, the sun was sliding toward the west. The rays tinted her black-and-bleached hair with gold and put a halo around her head. Her skin glowed like fine porcelain, and with her eyes closed, her dark lashes dusted her cheeks. An illusion, of course; Tasya was no angel. But she was a good woman who tried to do her best and help those in need.

He didn't deserve her. But he wanted her, and it killed him that the end was coming.

He glanced around.

279

Coming fast.

He finished mounding the dirt on the grave.

Tasya looked up.

One of the stone crosses on the cemetery fence had broken off and fallen to the ground. He pointed to it. "Put that on her grave."

Tasya picked it up. It was heavy and cool in her hand. She pressed it into the dirt that covered Sister Maria Helvig.

"Good. Let's go." He picked up his backpack and took Tasya's arm.

She went gladly. She felt an oppressive sense of danger. His tension had communicated itself to her — or maybe she sensed a nearby Varinski. Were they close? Were they here?

She still had the icon in her pocket.

She had to get it to safety.

"Have you seen signs of them?" Her uneasiness grew.

"No." He looked up at the trees. He paused and listened. "No. But tracking people is what they do, surprise is their forte, and we've lingered here too long." Keeping her arm firmly in his grasp, he took long, ruthless strides, indifferent to her discomfort.

Her heart sped up, not only because of

the pace, but because he looked grim and worried as they skirted the side of the chapel, walked around the corner — and found three men leaned against their car.

One slouched against the hood, tossing a set of keys.

One lounged on the trunk, head turned, watching them.

One stood on the far side, grinning with his arms folded and placed on the roof.

West Side Story as performed by Cossacks.

She would know them anywhere. She'd viewed photos of them. She'd seen them lingering in their yard. She remembered the choking, horrible feeling they generated in her gut.

Varinskis.

Two had black hair. One of those was stocky. Both were raw youths with sullen faces.

The one with the keys was blond, older, forty or fifty, and clearly in charge.

But all were tall, strongly muscled, with broad faces, high cheekbones, and strong chins.

In fact, they all looked like Rurik.

Her breath caught. She looked between them and the man who held her in his grip. The man who'd brought her to ecstasy. The man she trusted.

Rurik . . . Rurik was one of *them.*
Rurik was a Varinski.

CHAPTER 25

Rurik never even paused.

He used Tasya's arm to toss her forward, toward his relatives.

Toward the Varinskis.

Startled, propelled, she stumbled and fell in the dirt, on her hands and knees. Above the buzzing in her ears, and the shock and pain that made her almost faint, she heard Rurik say, "Here she is. The one you missed."

She took a long breath and looked up at the thugs.

The one with the keys stopped tossing them. He straightened. "What the fuck are you talking about?"

"Does the name Dimitru mean anything to you dumbshits?" Rurik asked.

Tasya closed her eyes. She dropped her head. She fought the pain, but she couldn't hide the truth from herself.

Rurik had broken her trust. No, not just

her trust — her heart.

"I worked the Dimitru case." It was Key-Guy.

Rurik had courted her. He'd wooed her with every sweet word and every gallant deed. He had worked, and worked hard, to convince her that he was the one thing she'd no longer believed in — a human being on whom she could depend.

And he'd succeeded.

"That thing on the ground —" Rurik sounded cool and disinterested. "That is the Dimitru child."

She'd told him her deepest secret. In her life, she had never told anyone else about her family.

She'd given Rurik her trust. Hell, she'd given him her heart.

And for this. So he could betray her to his relatives for . . . for what?

"Impossible," Key-Guy said. "We killed all the children. We burned the house."

"The governess took her away," Rurik informed him.

"He's lying." It was one of the other kids, and while Key-Guy's voice was almost clear of an accent, this boy's voice was deep and very Russian.

"A woman and a four-year-old girl escaped from the big, bad Varinskis. I wonder how the world would laugh if they knew."

She hadn't realized Rurik could sneer like that. She almost felt sorry for Key-Guy.

Until Key-Guy walked over and lifted her chin.

She jerked away.

He grabbed her hair and held her in place. He examined her face — and she examined his.

He had to be fifty if he'd been on the Dimitru raid, yet he was vital and alive, with hair so blond it was silver, and eyes the color of split pea soup.

He used her hair ruthlessly, turning her from side to side. He looked into her eyes. Then, most insultingly, he tilted her head sideways and leaned close to her throat. He snuffled her skin, then slid his tongue in a long, slow lick that started at her windpipe and ended behind her ear.

He stood up and stepped back. "He's right," he said in a flat tone. "She's a Dimitru."

With a disgusted gesture, she wiped off his spit.

He laughed and used his tongue in an extravaganza of lolling and licking at the air, like a dog gone mad with rabies.

She didn't care. She was going to die, anyway.

"You'll like me soon enough," he promised, and switched his attention to Rurik. "What do we owe you for delivering this? Money? Jewels?" He flipped the keys again. "Or maybe we'll just let you live."

She dragged herself to her feet. She needed to pay attention. She had to listen to their plans for her, and if Rurik didn't convince them to immediately kill her, she had to figure a way out.

"You're not going to kill me," Rurik said. "I'm the one with the information you want. Remember?"

"What the hell information is that?" It was the boy with the black, black hair and pale skin.

Rurik lifted his eyebrows at Key-Guy.

Key-Guy shook his head.

"What?" the boy asked. "Are you keeping something from us?"

Key-Guy turned on the kid, and Tasya could have sworn he gave a real dog's growl.

Neat trick.

Key-Guy said, "Don't piss me off, Ilya, or I'll keep the pussy to myself."

"The pussy is mine," Rurik said, "and I'll keep her until I tire of her."

"Varinskis share," Ilya said.

"I'm not a Varinski," Rurik answered.

"You act like one. You're hunting treasure.

You brought along a woman to trade for our goodwill and to relieve you. And, added bonus" — Key-Guy looked her over — "you never told her who you are. She's standing there and she still doesn't know what to think. Does she?"

"She knows very well what to think." Tasya wished she didn't. Right now, ignorance would indeed have been bliss.

"Is that what's the matter with her?" The boy with the dark brown hair sounded incredulous. "You *lied* about being one of us?"

The Varinskis laughed, all three of them, thugs and murderers.

"I didn't lie about it. I told you. I am not one of *you*." Rurik sounded calm and in command.

Tasya refused to back away as he walked toward her.

"I'll keep the woman until I'm done with her, and I'll keep the treasure when I find it."

The treasure. The icon, he meant. The icon that was still in her pocket — and he didn't know it had been found.

He took her wrist.

"You make me sick." She twisted in his grasp.

He turned and walked away.

She tried to set her heels.

He dragged her behind him, bigger than her, indifferent to her struggles.

Then suddenly he shoved her aside.

As she stumbled away, she heard three hard smacks, and by the time she turned, Rurik had one of the boys flat on his face on the ground with his arm jacked up straight behind his back and his wrist twisted sideways.

She hadn't realized. . . . Well, she'd known Rurik was capable of winning a fight, of course. Fool that she was, she'd depended on him for safety. But she hadn't realized exactly how deadly he was.

She'd worked with him, fought with him, traveled with him, slept with him — and she did not know Rurik Wilder at all.

Cautiously she ran her hand over the front pocket of her jeans.

The icon was still there.

Thank God. Thank God, and Sister Maria Helvig, that Tasya hadn't thought to tell him she'd found the icon.

Now she had to figure out how to hide the icon — or at least put it somewhere a little less obvious.

Rurik placed his booted foot in the middle of the kid's back. "What's your name?"

"Sergei."

Tasya glanced around. Everybody was intently watching Rurik.

"Didn't anybody ever teach you about a sucker maneuver?" Rurik asked.

"Yeah."

Rurik twisted a little more. "What did you say to me?"

"Yes, sir. The Varinskis teach the sucker maneuver."

Tasya slid her backpack off.

"And what is the sucker maneuver?" Rurik barked like a drill sergeant.

Sergei responded like a raw recruit. "That's when someone turns his back to lure you into attacking, but when you do, he's prepared and puts you down."

As quietly as she could, Tasya inched the backpack's main zipper open.

"What do the Varinskis say should be done to suckers?" Clearly, Rurik knew the answers.

Sergei paused for a long, long time. "That's up to the discretion of the winner."

Tasya slid the icon out of her pocket and thrust it into the depths of the backpack, and twirled it like a caterpillar in a cocoon of clothing.

"My father said suckers should be put out of their misery." Rurik was toying with the kid. "So the question is — should I kill you now or give you a second chance?"

She zipped the bag closed. It wasn't good, but right now, it was the best she could do.

"Second chance," Sergei said.

"What?" Rurik twisted Sergei's arm so hard Tasya heard something break.

She flinched. She wanted to vomit.

"Second chance, sir." Sergei's voice squeaked. "Please, sir."

Rurik let him go and stepped away. "Either my father is lying, or the training has fallen short since his day."

The blond guy had not budged. He'd watched the whole thing with no apparent interest. "He's in training."

"At what? Eighteen?"

"I'm twenty." Sergei sat up and resentfully held his wrist.

Had she been wrong? Hadn't Rurik broken a bone? Or were these guys so used to pain they were indifferent?

"A bird, right?" Rurik guessed.

"An owl," Sergei said proudly. "They brought me along to hunt you at night."

Key-Guy muttered a harsh Russian word.

"So your daytime vision's not too good. Thanks for the tip." Rurik shook his head in disgust. "You're going to have to do better than that, or you're going to get killed first thing."

"Poyesh' govna pechyonovo," Sergei said rudely.

Key-Guy and Ilya strolled forward, each from a different direction.

"Yes, he's a young fool and says too much," Key-Guy said, "but, smart Wilder boy, you *showed* too much."

They were both going to attack Rurik, Tasya realized. Two trained assassins were going to kill him — and try as she might to steel herself against him, she cared. Because she thought he would protect her at least a little . . . but also because she cared. Damn it, she didn't want to, but she did.

Rurik stood loosely, waiting, while the guys circled him.

She watched, breathless, waiting for the first punch.

Instead, Ilya disappeared, leaving his clothes on the ground, and in a flash of feathers, a huge, black-and-white bird took his place. With a flap of its eight-foot wing span, the eagle took to the air.

Tasya didn't know what to do with her hands. What to do with her feet. Whether to scream or pray.

Then Rurik exploded into a burst of feathers and rose into the air on a hawk's wings.

"No," she whispered. "No!"

She had witnessed the impossible.

Someone grabbed her from behind. "Yes," Sergei whispered back at her. "It's true. You're living your worst nightmare."

Later, she didn't know what she did. She knew her moves: elbow him in the gut, nail him in the instep, twist that hurt wrist. He was a Varinski, but she must have done something, because he was on the ground behind her.

Maybe he wasn't completely impervious to pain.

She stared at the pile of clothes and weapons, Rurik's clothes and weapons, left on the ground. She stared at the skies while the two mighty birds of prey circled and slashed.

Their talons were like razor blades.

The hawk was smaller, faster, dashing in, slashing, dashing out.

But the eagle made each swipe count, cutting deep into the hawk. He slashed the wing, the chest. . . . The hawk spiraled downward.

She thought she screamed.

The eagle swooped down for the kill — and right before they hit the earth, the hawk became a man, taking the eagle and rolling, smashing him into the ground with Rurik's man weight on top of him.

The eagle flapped its wings and went still.

Rurik had won, but at a price.

He gasped and writhed, trying to get his breath. He was naked. He was defenseless.

As the blond man watched, his eyes turned to flame. He stripped off his clothes — my God, he was bigger and more muscular than she'd realized — and Tasya saw his transformation start.

A wolf. He was a wolf. His snout grew long; his teeth lengthened; the pale hair on his head covered his face and neck and down his back.

He'd used the eagle to wear Rurik down. Now he intended to finish Rurik off.

So Tasya lifted her backpack and smashed him across the face.

It must have been her heavy-soled boots hanging by a strap that took him out. Or maybe it was her canteen half-filled with water. For a vital few seconds, he hit the dirt and didn't move.

When he did, Rurik stood above him. His tattoo writhed up one arm and down his chest, and the sky blue and the vivid red seemed almost to glow with menace. "It'll be evening soon. Where's the campground? I hope to hell you had the good sense to stay well away from the holy ground."

The guy in the dirt groaned and turned his head away.

"That way." Sergei pointed, and his voice held a respect she hadn't heard before. "Down the path, then cut a right up into the boulders."

Rurik gathered his clothes, his knives, and his pistol, and handed them to Tasya. "Hold those."

She looked at them, then looked up at him, wanting to see his reaction when she tossed them in the dirt.

Until he said, "Unless you want me to remain naked."

She didn't want to look at him, really look at him, but his words were a challenge, and now he was all she could see. The setting sun shone on the muscles of his chest, still heaving from exertion, and on the knife wound that she now realized was not from a knife, but a claw or a tooth. Blood oozed from the cuts the eagle had inflicted. He was ripped; the six-pack of his belly and his massive thighs spoke only too clearly of a life lived with a regime of weights and long-distance running, of constantly preparing for the fight that might come. And now had.

While she scrutinized him, his genitals stirred. Of course.

He was a Varinski.

"I hate you so much," she breathed. She'd never meant anything so much.

"But you'll carry my clothes."

Yes. He'd won every battle with every underhanded tactic known to man.

And she'd fallen for it all.

Rurik grabbed his backpack in one hand and her arm with the other, and started for the camp.

The blond guy, no longer a wolf, staggered to his feet. "The bitch needs to be taught a lesson."

Rurik faced him. "What's your name?"

"I'm Kassian."

"Well, Kassian, I'd say she learned one. She can't kill a Varinski, but she can knock him unconscious with a swift blow to the head." Rurik turned and walked her down the hill.

She'd learned another one, too.

That monsters walked the earth, and through her own foolishness, she'd become their prey.

CHAPTER 26

"Let go of my arm." Tasya marched stiffly beside Rurik as he strode down the hill toward the camp.

"I have things to tell you and no time to do it."

She tried to yank herself free.

His grip tightened. "Stay close. Their job is to kill you. If you get away from me, they'll finish the job."

"What a wonderful choice you're offering."

"Do *not* chop off your nose to spite your face."

"I am a fool. Just not that kind." She looked at him, trying to see the man she had known so well.

A Varinski. My God. The man she'd worked with, the man she'd slept with, the man she'd trusted . . . was a Varinski.

She'd seen him change into a hawk. She'd *seen* it. Still she couldn't comprehend, and she couldn't keep silent. "But rest assured, you've proved to me I am a fool. In every way. You screwed me in every way possible."

He jerked her to a stop. "Okay. First — when I met you, I didn't know you had a beef with the Varinskis. So don't convince yourself I screwed you because it was funny. I screwed you because I wanted you. I still want you, and I'm going to do my damnedest to make sure you come out of this alive."

"Yeah, sure." He made her dizzy when he bent his gaze on her and spoke so forcefully. She could almost believe him. "That's why you told them who I am." Her hand tightened on her backpack.

She needed to concentrate. She had the icon. He didn't know it. She intended to keep it that way.

"I used you as a bargaining chip so they would accept me." He started forward again, dragging her along behind him. "In case you didn't notice, there's some tension between the Russian Varinskis and the American Wilders, and I'm worthless to you dead."

"You never *told* me you were a Varinski."

"I'm not. I'm a Wilder. I'm my father's son. My mother's son." He pulled her to a stop in a grassy hollow beside the pile of Varinski duffel bags — and rifles and semiautomatic pistols. He scanned the area, then dropped his backpack beside a pile of boulders. Taking his T-shirt from her, he pulled it over his head. "And when you told me your story, we were already on the run."

"You didn't have to stay with me." She watched him pull on his underwear, strap on his knives, pull on his pants. "All that crap about, 'Trust me, Tasya. I won't betray you, Tasya. I swear on my father's soul.' Your father's soul must be so stained from your swearing, he'll go straight to hell."

Rurik looked at her. Just looked at her, and for one moment, she saw straight into the depths of grief.

She recognized those depths. She'd lived in those depths.

Her spine stiffened.

She would *not* feel empathy for him. For a Varinski.

She dropped the rest of his clothes and his shoes in the grass, and dusted her fingers. "*Why* am I holding those for you?"

He leaned against the boulder and put on his socks and shoes, then picked through the pile of Varinski weapons and chose a semiautomatic pistol. He loaded a clip into the handle. "Let's get out of here."

"Sounds like a good idea to me." She leaned down to pick up a pistol.

He caught her hand. "Do you shoot?"

"I've had training."

"Well, then." He sounded grimly amused. "While I would love to know you could defend yourself against the Varinskis, I'm afraid I'll have to err on the side of remaining alive myself."

He was wary. Good. "According to you Varinskis, I can't kill you."

"That's true. But if you shot me, you could certainly slow me down."

"Good to know." She fixed her gaze on his.

"Slow me down and piss me off." He looked right back at her. "How about this? I'll explain first, then give you the pistol."

"Sounds like a deal." She didn't want to be the one to break eye contact, but the way he looked at her, so knowing, so determined, made her turn her gaze away.

He thought since he'd seduced her once — well, more than once — he'd be able to sweet-talk her into believing his lies again.

Why wouldn't he? She'd been a sucker all the way.

"Come on." He tried to take her backpack.

She balked, her fingers tightening on the handle, her heart pounding with sudden alarm.

He was a supernatural *thing.* Did he sense

the icon inside?

"What are you doing?"

"We're leaving stuff here so they know we're coming back." He tugged again. "Where we're going, you don't need your backpack."

No. He didn't know about the icon.

Face it, Tasya, if he knew about the icon, he'd take it and run — no, fly — and leave you for the Varinskis.

The bitterness of that truth made her lift her chin and stare him right in the eyes. "Then I'm keeping it. It's . . . got my camera in it."

He looked back, just as angry, just as hostile.

As if he had the right!

"Fine." He tossed his leather duster down beside his stuff and took her arm again.

She shook him off. "I can walk."

"Fine." He let her go and headed up the hill.

She shrugged into her backpack and, fueled by her anger, hurried to catch up. "Where are we going?"

"To the other side of the mountain where we can talk in peace."

Across the narrow rock path that cut across the cliff, he meant. It wasn't a walk she cherished making twice in one day. Or ever again. "How do you figure? At least one of those guys are birds. If they want to fly over and poop on us, they will. They're Varinskis. They can do whatever they want." She shuddered. "And so can you."

"No, I can't."

"I *saw* you."

"You saw me turn into a hawk for the first time in five years. I broke my vow because —" He took a breath and gathered his thoughts. "The two young Varinskis are hurt. They're going to need to recover — which they will, and quickly, because that's part of the deal with the devil. You humiliated Kassian, and that's going to take a longer recovery, because he's going to have to reestablish his authority over the kids. We've got a couple of hours before they come looking for us."

"Because they know that now they've found us, we can't get away." It seemed as if the icon made the backpack weigh more.

"That's exactly what I intend."

"Or maybe they didn't find us. Maybe you brought me here to deliver me to them." It hurt to even say the words.

"If that was the truth, why would I go through the trouble of lying to you now?" He had the guts to snap at her.

Her frustration boiled over. "I don't know.

I don't freaking understand why you did any of this — excavating that site, following me around Europe."

"I did it for my family. I did it for my father."

"Isn't that touching? I did it for my family, too! Only I want to take the icon to the National Antiquities Society, and you want to take it to . . . ?" She raised her eyebrows at him.

"To my parents in Washington State." He added bitterly, "But what's the point of fighting about that? We didn't find the icon."

She stumbled.

He caught her arm.

She'd almost betrayed herself. She'd almost let slip that she had found the icon, that she had it in her possession, and if she could, she'd take it away. "So all this — the excavation, the race through Europe after a Hershey bar — was about your family and your father?"

"The legend is true. The devil did divide the icons. He flung them to the four corners of the earth." Rurik flung out his arm as if he were the devil — and right now, to Tasya, that seemed a fair description. "My family has to reunite them to break the pact with the devil."

"How touching."

They reached the ledge that clung so precariously to the cliff.

He offered her his hand to help her along.

"Do you want to hear this or not?"

She did. She wanted some explanation. "Sure. It beats hanging around with the Varinskis." She walked forward without fear. How could she fear a fall when she'd slept with her greatest enemy?

Rurik followed close behind, out onto the stone path.

She couldn't stop — didn't want to stop — the sarcasm that bubbled from her like an endless spring. "Oh, wait. I forgot. You are a Varinski."

He caught her arm and halted her, right there on the narrow path. He didn't do anything. He just waited.

She wouldn't look down. She wouldn't look down. She would not. . . . She looked down. All the way down to the jagged rocks below.

Tearing her gaze away, she looked back at Rurik.

Clearly, the son of a bitch could stand here all day. Yeah, because if he fell, he *could* fly.

She surrendered. "Please tell me your story. It beats —" No. No more scorn. "Just talk."

He let her go and followed her as she edged along with more caution this time. "My father is one of Konstantine's descendants, his generation's leader of the Varinskis — and the first Varinski to fall in love."

"With your mother?"

"With my mother. When they ran away to be married, his family and her tribe went after them. To say the least, neither group approved. In the fight, Konstantine killed his brother. The Varinskis would never forgive him, so Konstantine and Zorana escaped to the United States, changed their name to Wilder, and made their home in the mountains of Washington. They had three sons." His voice grew reverent. "And then a miracle happened. My mother gave birth to the first girl in a thousand years."

Clearly, Rurik adored his sister, and unfortunately, his affection plucked at Tasya's sentiments. "I feel as if I've wandered into *Monsterpiece Theater,*" she said, but as they reached the end of the path, and safe ground, she could feel her anger cooling.

Which was exactly what Rurik intended, for he walked beside her, his long stride confident and relaxed. "My parents hoped that the pact had been broken, but when Jasha passed through puberty, he changed into a wolf. Adrik changed into a panther. Firebird . . . well, my sister, Firebird, doesn't change into an animal, but she's strong and smart, and dear to us all."

"And you're a hawk." Tasya didn't want to go near the entrance to the cave. So she headed for the top of the hill.

Rurik joined her. "When we boys were teenagers, it was so cool. We couldn't let anyone know about us, of course, but we'd sneak off and run or fly, and we thought we were the hottest guys in town. I'm the only son who can control the transformation. My father says I'm the only male ever to be able to do that. I can turn an arm into a wing, or a foot into a claw, or change my eyes to see with the acuity and distance of a hunting hawk."

"You're swaggering." He was. Swaggering at the memory of a youth spent with a freedom and a power Tasya could never have imagined.

"Yeah. I was really hot shit. My father claimed each transformation brought us closer to the yawning pit of hell, but I was sure I could make the shape-shifting work for me." As he spoke, his gait changed infinitesimally. "Bad things happened. When Adrik was seventeen, he got in trouble and just . . . disappeared. We traced him to Asia, but . . . nothing. Still I thought I could handle the hawk thing without any repercussions. Flying was just so glorious!"

She watched him and knew — these memories were bittersweet. "So you became a pilot."

"Then everyone knew I was the best pilot in the Air Force, the guy who got to fly the experimental airplanes and train the best recruits."

She heard the longing in his voice. Told herself she didn't care. And found herself asking anyway. "What happened?"

"I used my hawk vision when I was flying recon and scared my WISO so much he ejected into enemy territory. Before we could get back to him, the enemy had caught him and tortured him to death." He spoke with a low intensity that made her look at him, really look at him.

Guilt hung on him like mourning clothes. Regret choked him like a noose.

She felt . . . she felt almost sorry for him.

"My father was right. The devil's gift *can't* be used for good, and it cost a good man his life for me to learn that lesson. So I made a vow to never turn again."

She did *not* want to feel sorry for him, and she *refused* to feel an obligation because he'd broken his vow to save her life. "Did anything good come out of the flight?"

"I confirmed an enemy nuclear site, and we took it out."

He was being so stupid she couldn't stand it. "So you saved how many lives? Did you not think the devil manipulated the circumstances to stop you from using your gift for good?" she snapped. "Come on, Rurik, don't be an idiot. If you're going to battle the demons of hell, you'll need every weapon in your arsenal. Just be careful and don't change when you're around an idiot, that's all."

"Matt Clark was not an idiot."

"Any man who'll eject out of a perfectly good airplane into enemy territory for any reason is an idiot."

He laughed, a brief, violent burst. "That's what my sister said when it happened."

"Why didn't you listen to her?"

"She was seventeen, and I was . . . I was pretty screwed up." He rubbed his forehead. "Maybe she had a point."

"Maybe she did." Tasya stopped beside the stone altar and looked out across the country. Her country. Right now, she needed to see the mountains, the valleys. To see as far as she could.

There was still a thread missing from his story. "You've got the ability to change into a hawk. To fly whenever and wherever you please. Your brothers can change into animals, too. So why do you want to break the pact?"

"If I don't — if we don't — my father is condemned to burn in hell for all eternity."

He, too, stared out at the distance.

"Can you see farther right now?" she asked.

"No. When I change, my eyes are different. Visibly different." He turned to her, and his eyes looked like Rurik's. Like those of the man she loved.

How could she? How could she love a Varinski? How could she stand on the soil of her forefathers, betray her father and her mother, forget their deaths, and abandon her revenge?

No. *No.* She would *not.* She had come too far to change her course.

The knowledge of the icon burned in her mind. If she could somehow live through this meeting with the Varinskis, she could thwart Rurik. But . . . if his story was true . . .

Her mind veered away before she allowed the thought to form. "Who told you that reuniting the icons would break the pact with the devil?"

"My mother had a vision."

"Your mother had a vision," she repeated, deadpan. "And we believe this because . . . ?"

"Because I was there. Because something was speaking through her, and I saw it. Heard it."

"Does she do this often?" She used that really logical voice, the kind the guy on The History Channel used when he was explaining something simple for the hundredth time.

Rurik responded with a flash of red in his eyes. She'd dissed his mother, and she'd pissed him off.

Good.

"I've never seen her have a vision before, and more to the point, the first two parts of her prophecy immediately came to fruition. My father dropped like a felled oak. And my brother's woman found the first icon."

That shook her, but she hid it beneath mockery. "That must have frustrated you, to have a mere woman find one of the icons."

He considered her coolly. "My mother said, 'Only their loves can bring the holy pieces home.'"

"What the hell does that mean?"

"I think it means that perhaps I can find

the icon, but it's up to you to take it to my family."

Panic hit first, starting her heart beating too fast. "I am not your love!"

He smiled, a slow curve of the lips.

Disappointment hit next, low and in the gut. "But if you think I am, it certainly explains a lot about why you've been hanging around with me instead of going after the icon by yourself." Thank God she'd found it. Thank God she had it. And if his story had made her waver, that little tidbit fired her resolution to diamond hardness.

"You are determined to make a difficulty where none exists. If the prophecy is true, if some greater power is working through my mother for good, do you believe that power would be fooled if I faked love for you?" He stared at her, demanding logic where all she wanted was to slip back into the old, familiar anger.

The anger was easier. So much easier. "I don't know. I don't know why I should believe you. All I know is what I've seen and heard and felt." She pointed. "My father used to pick me up and carry me to the tree down the hill, the symbol of the Dimitru family. He would climb with me to the top branches. He'd point out to the countryside — almost the same view as we see from here — and he'd say, 'This tree has grown on our mountain since the dawn of time. It symbolizes the Dimitru royal blood, and as long the tree grows and flourishes, so shall the Dimitrus.' "

Rurik tried to put his arm around her.

She pushed him away. "Do you know what happened? The dictator Czajkowski hired the Varinskis to kill my family, kill us all, and he gave special instructions that the tree be burned so everyone in Ruyshvania knew their royal family would never return."

Rurik physically took her in his embrace, restrained her when she struggled. "Tasya, honey, why don't you cry?"

"Don't you think I wish I could?" She hated this. She didn't want to feel this ripping, tearing anguish in her guts, and if she had to, she really didn't want him to see it. "I still hear the screams. I still see the flames. I dream of my parents burning in agony, of the tortures they put my father through, of the people who died for us, and I bleed for the Ruyshvanians who lost a child or a parent. They curse our name, I know it, and I want to do something to bring them peace. I want to destroy the Varinskis for them."

She wanted to be as strong as she pretended to be, not this weak child who didn't dare look on the remnants of her life for fear she'd break apart.

Worse, his touch steadied her, although why it should, she didn't know.

And that was another betrayal of her parents, a betrayal so much more painful. In a rage of pain and fury, she said, "So your family can call yourself Wilders if you want, but scratch a little deeper, and you're Varinskis. You always knew what I was seeking, and you kept the truth from me. I will never forgive you for lying to me. For using me. I will never forgive you."

CHAPTER 27

Rurik looked at Tasya for a long time.

The bones of his face seemed carved of granite. His eyes were brown, yet heated by red flames. The curve of his mouth was cruel. And his body was as still and as strong as a predator's as it waited to deal death.

Tasya realized something — she had never really feared him.

She feared him now.

In a voice as cold as the Arctic, he asked, "What is your petty damned revenge when compared to breaking a pact with the devil?"

She could scarcely catch her breath for outrage . . . and terror. "Petty?"

"*If* you manage to find the icon, and if you manage to bring it to National Antiquities, and *if* they manage to document it thoroughly enough to prove your theory about the Varinskis is the truth, *then* you'll go on the morning shows and get your publicity.

You'll get your book published and maybe, *if* you can keep the world's attention for more than fifteen minutes and *if* the Varinskis don't threaten or bribe the jury, Yerik and Fdoror Varinski will go to prison." Rurik slowly closed his hands on her arms, leaned down to eye level, and stared at her so directly, she dared not blink. "Where they'll live like kings and get out in six months for good conduct."

"But the bad publicity —"

"Will do what? Give them a little black eye in the assassination business, and bring them to the attention of the world? Who will undoubtedly be fascinated by their evil." He gestured toward the east, toward the Ukraine and the Varinski home. "*Sixty Minutes* will send some old-guy reporter to interview Boris. The publishing company you've pinned your hopes on will rush to give them a contract and a ghostwriter to sensationalize their tale. Before you know it, there'll be a movie and a television miniseries about them. But it won't matter to you."

She stiffened. "Why not?"

"You won't live long enough to see any of it."

"I'm not afraid to die."

"Then you're a fool, because the Varinskis

are like adolescent boys in the most successful gang in history. They have no conscience. They love to torment the helpless. And they'll beat you, kill you slowly, and rape you while they do it."

"Like they did my mother?" She fought back, but she knew she was losing ground.

"Like they did your mother," he agreed. "But let's talk about the flaws in your plan. National Antiquities hasn't got the security to keep the icon safe."

"They have good security!"

"The proof will be gone before the first expert looks at it. So the rest of the plan is already a bust. Oh, except the part about you dying. They *will* kill you."

She lifted her chin. "They're going to anyway. I'm the Dimitru that got away, and the Varinskis don't leave survivors."

"That's true." Rurik straightened. "But if you can get to my family in Washington, they can protect you."

"How would I get there without leading the Varinskis to them?"

"I'll tell you how to get there, and I'll provide the distraction."

"The hell you will!"

"We've run out of options. One of us has to come out alive to find the icon."

"You're the only one who has a chance of

surviving."

"I'm also the only one who can fight the Varinskis. Listen to me. If you could find that icon and take it to my family, we have a chance of defeating the devil." He took her shoulders and shook her lightly. "Think about it. If we can put an end to the pact, the Varinskis would be nothing more than a bunch of pathetic humans who don't know how to function in the real world. No one would be afraid of them. They'd be vulnerable to prosecution. They would have lost everything. Look at the big picture, Tasya! There's your revenge!"

He'd backed her into a corner, and worse — he done it by making her face the facts.

Her plan never had a chance of succeeding.

At least one of them was going to die.

And that was the ultimate failure.

Frustration held her in its heated grip. "I don't want to be here. I don't want to be in a corner. I want —"

"What do you want?"

You.

Rurik and a return of her naive belief that if she just got her hands on the proof, she could defeat the Varinskis and find peace with her parents' deaths.

Rurik and some semblance of the comfort

he'd given her on the train.

Rurik and that vague sense that this was a man she could love.

But now she'd seen him change into a predator. . . . She'd seen proof of the devil and his work.

Every dream crushed . . . and Rurik had crushed them.

With a growl, she dropped the backpack and the burden of the icon, and heaved them under the altar.

She shoved him in the chest. She shoved him with all her might.

He barely swayed.

He was immovable: strong, tall . . . right.

It felt good to shove him, so she did it again. And again.

And he, who had been standing there a pillar of reason and calm, picked her up, crushed her against him, and kissed her.

Not a kiss like the ones on the train. Not the gentle, slow, reassuring seduction of mouth against mouth, but a kiss of heat, fury, and frustration.

He crushed her lips, opened them with his tongue, and took without asking.

She wanted that. For a few precious moments, she wanted the fire between them to burn away the painful truths and give her forgetfulness.

So she answered him with the same fierce passion, holding his head in her hands, sucking at his tongue, making him groan.

He adjusted his hands, cupping her bottom and lifting her legs, matching them so that his erection rubbed against the seam of her pants.

She broke the kiss, arched her back, as orgasm, swift and unanticipated, burned through her.

He held her, thrust at her, prolonging the pleasure, but as soon as the passion crested, he turned, pressed her against the altar, and pulled her shirt over her head. He flicked her bra open with one hand and her belt with the other.

"You son of a bitch." Did he think he could strip her, just like that, and do her?

Not without getting naked himself.

She pulled his belt loose and unzipped his jeans with enough violence to make him mutter, "Careful!"

He shoved her pants down to her ankles.

She toed off her shoes, abandoned everything — Levi's and panties — then pushed his pants down. In one graceful move, she followed the pants to kneel before him.

"Careful!" It was more a grunt than a word.

She didn't need to be careful. She knew

exactly what she was doing.

She took his erection in her mouth in a long, deliberate motion that moistened the silky skin. The tip felt like heated velvet, and she savored the first drop of semen, welling up and filling her with his taste.

Their nights together had been about him taking her, pleasuring her, indulging her. Now, here, at last and at least, she was in control.

She sucked on him, taking as much into her mouth as she could, then slowly releasing him.

His hips jerked as if he couldn't stand still. His dick twitched in her mouth. He swore, a long string of cursing that utilized desperate words and unknown languages.

God, revenge was sweet.

He must have seen her smile, or who knows? Maybe he felt it, because he stripped off his T-shirt, toed off his jeans, leaned down, and picked her up by her armpits.

He lifted her, put her on the altar, spread her legs, and followed her up.

The stone was rough and warm beneath her back. He was scorching and ready above her, his dick squeezed so tightly against her, it was slick with come.

So she said, "No."

He stopped. His arms trembled as he held

himself in position. His eyes were hot coals, and whips of red flame flickered in their depths. "No?"

Would he stop if she told him?

Fat chance.

She grasped his arms. "You get on the bottom."

His chest heaved, and his teeth clenched. He looked down the hill toward the Varinskis, then back at her. "Woman, you push me too far."

But he did as she commanded. He rolled with her.

"Perfect." She sat up straight on him, groin to groin. Here, on top of the altar, she could see for miles — down into the valley, up the far mountain range, and through the horizon into eternity. Up here, they were on top of the world, and she was on top of him.

The breeze was just cool enough to make her nipples tighten . . . or maybe his gaze aroused her. . . .

The contours of his mighty chest and arms shone in the sun, and the light dusting of dark hair emphasized the definition of each muscle. That tattoo, that wild, primitive tattoo, strutted across his skin in a bright, archaic design. His lids drooped as he watched her, half-concealing his eyes, but she saw the truth. Deep within his pupils, the red flames flickered more strongly.

He was a predator. He was wild. He was savage.

And for this moment, she had wrested power from him.

She stretched her arms over her head, laughing in a wicked burst of triumph.

He reached for her.

She caught his wrists in her hands.

For a moment he resisted. Then he allowed her to bend his arms over his head.

She stretched out on him, the hair on his chest lightly brushing her breasts. She smiled into his face. "I'm not afraid of you."

"You should be."

She laughed again, and slid her tongue into his mouth.

He dueled with her, his tongue against hers, wet and warm.

He let her hold him captive, yes.

But he moved between her thighs, heightening her sensations, tempting her . . . but she was strong. She didn't take him inside. Instead, she rode his hard-on in gentle waves, pleasuring herself without giving him a damned thing — except, perhaps, the satisfaction of knowing that with nothing but the memory and the promise of his dick inside her, touching that place deep within, he could make her want him.

She wanted to provoke him to madness.

And maybe she did. But two could play that game, and while she provoked, he drugged her with sensation. He plumped her breasts in his hands, moving her nipples in the rough hair on his chest. His mouth slid away from hers, along the ridge of her jaw to her ear, then down her throat in a long, slow, damp caress.

Her heartbeat strengthened. She was alive as she had never been in her life — perhaps because death hovered so close

Shuddering with need, she pulled away from the addictive intensity of his mouth.

She sat up again, but she wasn't laughing this time. Blind with lust, she groped between their bodies, took his dick in her fist, and held it, squeezed it, knowing that she could finish him with the stroke of her hand, trying to convince herself she could live without him inside her.

But she couldn't. This might be, probably would be, the last time they had sex. Even if they both lived, could she sleep with the enemy?

No. *No.* This was it. The last time.

"Do it." He watched her, his face hard-edged with need, and she would have sworn he knew every thought in her mind. "You've tormented me enough. Do it now."

She placed him at the entrance to her body and pressed down, taking him inside. She was wet with desire, but her tissues yielded slowly, wrapping around him, and he groaned as if he were in agony.

Yes. If this sex, this dilemma, this pleasure, broke her will and stole her breath away, then it was only right that it should be a two-edged sword.

That night on the train, it had seemed as if he'd been inside her every way possible, that they'd explored every sense, every feeling.

But no, this time was new, different. She was on top, in command. She set the pace, developed the rhythm. As she rose and fell, the stone scraped at her knees. The sun shone on her head, on her shoulders. The scent of pine, fresh air, and Rurik filled her lungs. She saw Rurik, glorious, muscled, damp with sweat, beneath her.

He strained, his rugged face transformed by sunlight and dark obsession. Fierce passion colored his eyes. He held her thighs in his hands, flexing his fingers, lifting her, caressing her, over and over, as if he couldn't get enough of touching her. She could almost see the restraints he placed on himself — he was one second, one motion, one breath, away from seizing command of the day and of her.

He possessed the power, and as he held himself back, his power grew.

She experienced him, large, strong, and vital, inside her. His hips drove up at her; she met his thrusts with her own motion. Together they traveled a passage as ancient as the stone beneath them, and as new as the dawn.

Her breath rasped in her throat.

Her climax built and built within her, a mighty, feverish tidal wave waiting to crash over her. She lost track of time, of place. There was only Rurik and Tasya, a single being, joined by enchantment.

Then it struck — a single, long spasm of joy, wracking her body. As the oldest glory in the world sang in her ears, she sank her nails into Rurik's shoulders. As he thrust and came, she welcomed and embraced, and she lived this moment as she had never lived before — and would never live again.

Lust gripped them.

She cried out her pleasure to the skies.

He groaned deeply, wracked with pleasure.

And lightning ripped up from the earth, through the altar stone, through him, and into her. The sensation was a fire and a shock such as Tasya had never experienced. She screamed in pain and rapture. The jolt took their mutual orgasm and drove it beyond the bounds of the world, binding them together and sending them into one glorious, final, blissful spasm.

"What . . . ?" She braced herself against his chest, and looked down at him, exhausted, sated, so handsome he brought her to tears. "What was that?"

He smiled a savage smile. "Fusion."

They dressed in silence, but Tasya could see Rurik glancing over at her.

She pretended she didn't notice. Better not to think about what happened on the pagan stone altar in her own country with the sun shining on them like a blessing.

She was tying her shoes when Rurik thrust something under her nose.

The semiautomatic pistol.

She looked at it for a long moment.

"Take it. You'll need to get away." In quick, precise detail, he told her how to find his parents.

She wrapped her hand around the grip. "I don't want —"

"What you want and what I want is not important. One of us has to defeat the devil, and at least, my darling, we've shared a long good-bye."

She looked up at him.

He smiled at her with all the intensity that had first focused her attention and made her realize that this could be a man she could trust. "Believe me, Tasya, it's every man's dream, to share great sex with the woman he loves right before he dies in a fight."

"With the woman he . . . you . . ." He'd said it before, but she hadn't believed him. Now how could she not?

"Of course I love you." Kneeling before her, he finished tying her shoe.

"You do *not.*"

"Tasya, I'm thirty-three years old. I may never have loved before, but I recognize it when I feel it."

She didn't know what to say, or how to say it. He'd made her trust him, shattered her dreams of revenge with a savage dose of the truth, then offered to die for her. And he was a Varinski. Her *enemy,* for shit's sake.

But somehow the word had no meaning.

"It's okay." He helped her up, helped her tug the pistol in her belt at the back. "I know you don't love me. But if I had time, I could change your mind, and that makes me happy, too."

"Maybe," she mumbled. "Sure." She

reached under the altar and grabbed her backpack.

He helped her shrug into the straps.

The bag seemed heavy, as if with each of Rurik's declarations of love, the weight of the icon grew.

The icon was simply a holy object. It didn't have a preference for where it went or whom it served. Tasya needed to get a grip, and get it fast, or she'd be babbling the truth to Rurik . . . and maybe that was what she should do, anyway.

"Come on." She sprang down the hill, away from the idea.

He followed, then took the lead — and veered toward the entrance to the cave.

He stopped beside the sinister, black gash in the earth.

"What?" But she knew.

"I want you to take the path through the cave."

"No."

"You've done it before. You can find your way out."

"No!"

"Two of the Varinskis are birds. They can't make it down there. But if I take Kassian out, you can get away."

"Look. I'm not going down there again." She took a breath. "And I'm not leaving you to die. I'll take my chances with you."

Rurik considered her. He didn't know what drove her more — her fear of the dark and the cave, or her misplaced courage. But he couldn't stuff her down the hole, and if she didn't have that courage, she wouldn't be the Tasya he loved.

So he nodded. "All right. Come on. Let's go."

He set off at a run, listening as Tasya panted behind him. He'd studied the terrain, figured out an escape route.

That was what his father had trained him to do.

He cut around the edge of the mountain, then up toward the peak.

He could fight the boys and win.

Kassian was another thing altogether. Kassian was experienced, deadly, and he'd already proved he was willing to fling the youngsters into the fray to soften Rurik's defenses.

He was in every way the perfect Varinski.

They skirted a grove of trees, ran into a clearing studded with boulders, headed for another grove of trees.

And he heard the sounds he'd been waiting for.

The flap of wings. The soft thud of a wolf's paws.

Kassian must have quickly reestablished his domination.

"They're coming." Anticipation and dread filled Tasya's voice.

Rurik slowed to a walk. There was no need to hurry now.

Putting Tasya in front of him, he said, "Remember, use your head. Stay out of their way. When I see an opportunity, I'll attack and you run like hell. Don't stop, and stay alive, whatever you do."

"Listen, I have to tell you something." She turned to face him.

He glanced up. "No time!" He shoved her out of the way.

In a flash of gray feathers, Sergei sliced through the air, his talons extended. He swooped up, landed on a tall boulder, and changed. And looked down and laughed, a big, stupid, perfect composite of muscles and malice.

A grinning Ilya came out of the grove of trees in front of them.

Kassian came from behind, changing from wolf form to human. His fangs shortened, his snout narrowed, but still a froth clung around his lips.

Kassian wasn't amused. He was furious.

Yeah. It was going to be a long, hard fight.

Ilya and Kassian paced toward them.

Sergei leaped as hard as he could, grabbing for Tasya.

She twisted, smashed her elbow into his ribs, and left him holding her backpack.

Leaping back at Sergei, she landed on his back, grabbing for the bag. "Give it to me!"

Rurik could have killed her himself.

She should have run. Instead she sounded like a thwarted schoolgirl and acted like a dunce.

Of course, Sergei responded with all the maturity of which he was capable. He dumped her in the dirt. Took her backpack by both of the bottom corners. Whirled it in a circle.

"No! Stop that!" Tasya lunged again.

The contents spread across the ground. Her lens case smacked against the side of a boulder. The wrapping on her granola bars sparkled silver in the sunlight. Her clothes scattered in the dirt, and her spare T-shirt unfurled. Something square, something that glittered like old gold, flew through the air and with the distinctive ring of fired ceramic, landed among the rocks.

The icon.

Tasya had found the icon.

CHAPTER 28

Tasya skidded to a halt.

One glance at her guilty face told Rurik all he needed to know. She hadn't forgotten to tell him about finding the icon. She'd chosen to keep it for herself, so she could get her publicity, publish her book, gain her revenge — and bring the Varinskis' vengeance down on her foolish head.

He was furious. He was betrayed. He was hurt.

And he loved her. He'd told her his deepest secrets, thrown himself on her mercy, begged for her understanding.

Loved her.

He loved her.

And she had lied to him.

There was only one thing to do.

"Damn you!" he shouted. Grabbing her shoulders, he shoved her against the boulder. "You little bitch, you betrayed me!" As he pulled back his fist, he whispered, "Go down hard."

He saw comprehension flicker in her eyes. He pulled his punch.

She let his fist hit her cheek. She jumped and landed on her side in the dirt. When he grabbed her and dragged her back to her feet, she cried out as if she'd been murdered.

"That's the way," he heard Kassian say.

Yeah, you prick, you'd know how to beat a woman, wouldn't you?

"Get the icon," he shouted at his damned-to-hell cousins.

He shook Tasya.

She flopped around like a rag doll, her neck snapping back and forth.

Yes, that was his Tasya. Such an actress. She'd fooled him. He'd had no idea she'd found the icon.

Something of his real rage must have shown in his face, for she really flinched, and he saw something — regret? — in her eyes.

A little late for that.

He turned back in time to see Sergei grin that stupid, greedy grin of his, lean down, and pick up the icon. Sergei's eyes grew wide, panicked, surprised. With a scream, he flipped the icon into the air.

It landed in the grass.

Sergei screamed again.

"What the hell's the matter with him?" Rurik demanded. As if he didn't know. No Varinski male could hold the icon. The Madonna would not allow herself to be possessed by a demon.

"Shut him up," Rurik said. "What a wimp."

"Shut up, you dumbshit." Kassian shoved Sergei.

Sergei screamed until Ilya hit him hard in the middle of the chest. Then he sank to his knees and whimpered.

"That's better." Grabbing Tasya's hair, Rurik jerked Tasya's head back, and kissed her hard.

Kissed her good-bye.

At first she fought him. Then she grabbed his neck and kissed him back.

When he pulled back, he said, "Don't rush in to save me. Don't rush in to save anybody. Save yourself."

Perhaps in her mind, she was still fighting the inevitable, but her kiss told him the truth. She knew what she had to do. "Like I'm going to let anyone get killed for me."

"There's a choice here. We can both die fighting them, or you can take the icon and run."

"I don't run."

"Then you die, and the devil takes possession of the icon once more, and the Varinskis win."

She shook her head. Shook it and shook it.

"Yes, Tasya."

Slowly she nodded.

Putting himself between her and the Varinskis, he said, "Make it look good."

"I will."

"Trust me."

"I do."

He stared at her.

Her blue eyes were fierce and hot. "I trust you."

"That's not love, but that's good enough." This time when he slapped at her, she flinched and cried, sobbing, "Stop it, please stop it!" Both of them made the sound of flesh slapping against flesh.

Behind them, Sergei still moaned and complained.

As if he'd had enough, Rurik turned on the others. "For shit's sake, pick up the goddamn icon!" This time he didn't watch, but returned to beating Tasya.

When he heard another Varinski scream, he smiled.

Tasya smiled back, her face red from exertion.

Pivoting to face his cousins, he saw the icon on the ground again, and Ilya holding his hand out, his wrist in his other hand, looking at the damage, screaming, and looking again.

Kassian was the smart one in the group. He understood what had happened. "We can't hold that fucking thing." He pointed at Tasya. "Make her get it for us."

"You finally had a good idea." Rurik started to push her toward the icon.

She stopped him with a hand on his wrist. In a low tone, she said, "I need blood on my face, and I need bruises."

He froze. For all the Air Force bar fights and all the tussles with his brothers, he'd never hit a woman in his life. Hitting Tasya would be like hitting his mother, or Firebird, or Meadow Szarvas, or his old-maid teacher, Miss Joyce.

"C'mon," Tasya said. "I lived in some good foster homes, but lived in a couple of lousy ones, too. I've been hit before."

His hand came up, then fell to his side.

Her blue eyes were as fierce and as bright as a hot coal. "If you don't do it, I'll have to slam myself against a rock, and I'll really hurt myself."

"Right. I'll do it." He had to steel himself. Close his eyes almost all the way. Pretend she was one of his brothers. And smack her hard enough to split her lip and leave a bruise on her cheek.

"Crap, that hurt!" Her fist came up to hit him back, then fell to her side.

Even now her first instinct was to defend herself.

"None of that." Grabbing her by the arm, he propelled her toward the icon, and in a loud, rough tone shouted, "Pick it up. Put it in your backpack. You carry it!"

She fell forward. She crawled to the icon. With a look of misery, she picked it up. When she did, the gilt of the Madonna's halo flashed in the sun.

Rurik hoped that was an omen, a sign of hope that his sacrifice would not be in vain.

She slipped the icon into her backpack, then crept along, gathering her clothes, her granola bars, her lens case, staying low, moving like an old woman scavenging her few precious belongings.

She got within range of Kassian.

He stepped up and kicked her in the ribs.

She rolled down the hill, her backpack clutched to her stomach, and slammed into a boulder.

Kassian was a big man, broad-shouldered, mean, and fast.

Rurik didn't care. He'd been wanting this.

He closed the distance between them, grabbed Kassian by the throat, looked full into the Varinski's red-rimmed eyes. "I didn't tell you to kick her."

"You're not in charge." Kassian's hot breath smelled of garlic and brimstone.

"I am now!" Rurik punched him between the legs.

Kassian doubled over, then came up with a head butt to Rurik's belly.

Rurik fell onto his back, brought his leg up, and, before Kassian could straighten, kicked him under the chin.

Kassian stumbled backward.

Sergei and Ilya jumped Rurik at once.

Tasya dragged breath into her lungs, trying to clear the dark fog that swam before her eyes.

With one hand on the boulder that had stopped her and the other one clutching the backpack, she climbed to her feet and stood, weaving.

She had to focus. She had to get out of here.

They were killing Rurik.

First Sergei and Ilya pounded on him, and took a pounding in their turn. Rurik had told her he could fight; she saw the proof of it now as he kicked and slashed, leaping into the air, moving so quickly she couldn't follow his motions.

It was *Crouching Tiger, Hidden Dragon,* but without subtitles.

A glint of metal caught her gaze. She looked — and there it was. The Varinskis' arsenal. A rifle with scope. Another semiautomatic pistol. A shotgun. And all the ammunition.

Nothing, she discovered, cured a possible broken rib as fast as seeing the Varinskis' firearms lying there unprotected.

She tossed the pistol and the shotgun in the stream. She checked the rifle to see if it was loaded. It was, and she tucked it under her arm. She scattered the ammunition into the dirt.

She looked up at the fight in time to see Kassian charge back into the fray, and the dynamics changed.

Rurik was overwhelmed, still punishing the men with his fists and his feet, but taking more and more blows to his face, his chest, his legs.

Then it happened.

In an action so quick she couldn't follow it, he changed. Rurik disappeared, and in his place a hawk burst forth from the group and flew straight up.

Rurik.

She raised her fist in triumph. Good for him!

She saw the flash as his eyes focused on her.

He'd given her a head start. He wanted her to use it.

Flinging her backpack over one shoulder, she ran up the hill toward the convent, and escape.

That kick Kassian had given her didn't make it easy; she had trouble catching her breath. The cumbersome rifle weighed her down, too. But she wouldn't give it up — that, she might need.

Yet she kept glancing over her shoulder, desperate to see Rurik's battle.

A huge black-and-white eagle raced after the hawk.

Ilya.

She ran on, and glanced again.

The birds engaged in an aerial battle, swooping and screaming. Ilya's wings beat at Rurik, but Rurik was smaller and faster, dashing in, tearing at the eagle with beak and talons.

The combat was beautiful, and deadly.

"Come on, Rurik," she whispered. "Come on. You can win this."

For the first time since she'd walked out of that chapel and into the arms of the

Varinskis, hope lifted her heart. Maybe the two of them could survive this attack. Maybe he could forgive her for keeping the icon for herself. Maybe . . . maybe she could live with a Varinski, as long as his name was Rurik. Maybe none of that mattered. Maybe all that mattered was surviving —

She glanced. Halted. Turned.

She was high on the mountain now, looking down on the tumble of rocks and groves of trees that made up the countryside. The birds of prey still wheeled and fought, but the eagle was wearying, failing.

She couldn't see Sergei; he was hidden from her sight.

But she could see Kassian. He stood on a boulder, holding a bow and arrow — and he was aiming at Rurik.

CHAPTER 29

The arrow flew, not in slow motion like in the movies, but so fast Tasya didn't have time to scream a protest. It stabbed the hawk in midair, ripping it from its flight path, and for one horrifying second, she saw the red flare in its eyes. Then the flare was extinguished.

The bird plunged toward the earth and vanished in a grove of trees.

She screamed, putting all her energy, all her anguish, all her emotion, into a protest against the life that had led her inexorably to this . . . this *destiny*.

Kassian Varinski heard her. He turned to face her. He smiled, his teeth glistening. And he pursed his lips in a kiss that promised humiliation, rape, death.

The old, familiar rage against destiny took hold of her. She took one step toward him.

But no. If she threw herself headlong at saving Rurik, everything — the icon, Rurik's family, humanity itself — would be lost.

And she couldn't save him. She'd seen his life vanish in a blink of an eye.

She knew now. She'd been a fool, chasing the wrong dream. The bitter dream. Revenge for her own family, even if it was possible, would be an incomplete victory.

But she could save the Wilders. They were Rurik's family, the people who had brought him into the world, the ones who formed him, shaped him into the man who had given his life for her and for the icon.

His sacrifice would not be in vain.

She would follow Rurik's directions. No matter how hard the road, she would take the icon to Washington.

But while she could not kill a Varinski, she knew she could hurt him. Hurt him badly.

Without compunction or pity, she lifted the rifle to her shoulder.

Kassian took one look at her steady hand, and ran downhill toward the place where Rurik had landed.

She shot and missed.

He vanished from sight.

"You coward! You son-of-a-bitch coward!" She wanted to kill him. She so badly wanted to kill him —

The eagle gave a screech of triumph, tucked in its wings, and dived down. . . .

Her heated fury vanished under the surge of cold hatred. This time, she aimed coolly, and shot.

The bullet smacked the eagle right in the breast.

The bird exploded in a flurry of black-and-white feathers, and the dive became a free fall.

Take that, asshole.

As much as she would like to savor the triumph, she had only a little time to escape.

Rurik was right. She had only one possible route.

She ran back the way they had come, and watched for the remains of the tree, black and crumbling, that marked the entrance to the cave.

And there it was.

She lowered the backpack and rifle through the little crack in the earth. She easily squeezed through, then lowered herself down until her feet dangled.

Her mission was crystal clear in her mind. Escape through the tunnel. Deliver the icon to safety.

All she had to do was let go.

Let go and disappear into the endless darkness where nothing lived, not even a breath of air. . . .

But in the end, what did her old fears matter?

The worst thing that could have happened had happened.

Rurik was dead.

She had to go on.

So she did.

She landed on the soft dirt floor, breathing the cool, damp air. A sunbeam from above touched her head. The tunnel wound away from her, down into a dark so black it hurt her eyes. At the end, she knew, was safety, another country . . . a different life.

She'd already been reborn once from this tunnel. Now she had to go through the painful process once more.

But this time, she wasn't a child. This was her choice.

Taking up her backpack, she dug through and found her flashlight.

The plastic case was cracked.

Of course. On this journey, she could have no light.

She placed her fingers on the small ridge in the rock and started forward.

If only she weren't alone . . .

She strangled that thought before it could take over her mind.

She would not think of Rurik, of the flame of his life blinking out.

She would concentrate on getting away. She'd really hurt one Varinski, but the other two were alive. Would they hunt her right away? She thought not. They had a brother to care for, and Rurik's body to . . . to . . .

It didn't matter what they did to Rurik's body. What mattered was escaping.

So she hurried into the endless night.

The light from the hole into the cave gradually dwindled, as she'd known it would, and each step became a step into the unknown.

No, not the unknown. Into the past.

She'd been young, so young, and angry at being dragged away from her mother. She'd kicked at her governess, trying to get away, to go back and help put out the fire, and make that woman stop screaming. But Miss Landau had dragged her along. It was proper Miss Landau's imperviousness to Tasya's fuss that had finally captured Tasya's attention; Miss Landau always insisted on correct behavior no matter what the circumstances, and Tasya was not behaving properly.

Once Tasya stopped throwing her tantrum and started paying attention, she noticed the dark. She noticed other things, too — the smell of dirt, the slow, erratic drip of water, the feel of the stone beneath her fingers. She noticed that the unflappable Miss Landau shook with a fine tremor.

But it was the dark that had overwhelmed everything. Tasya and her governess were walking — Tasya was putting one foot in front of the other — so she knew they were moving. But it had seemed fake. Like any child — like any person — the young Tasya had measured her progress by what she could see and feel and smell, and down here, nothing changed.

Nothing changed for miles . . . for millennia.

Now Tasya was taller. Her steps were longer. Life had transformed her from the imperious child into someone who believed she could fix everything with her camera, her story, and, if necessary, her fists.

As she moved through the tunnel, keeping a steady speed, she wondered who she would be when she escaped this time.

She walked for hours, stopping only to press the light on her watch and look at the time.

Two hours.

Four hours.

Eight hours.

Sometimes she felt a breath of air as another cave opened onto the main tunnel. Most of the time, it was just cool and pure, but once it seemed malignant, and for just a flash the veil of time lifted, and in her mind, she saw a man, laden with gold. He collapsed under its weight, and died there in the alcove nearby.

She didn't run, but she wanted to, away from the skull's empty eye sockets that watched her in amusement.

Was she going mad?

Her feet hurt. Her eyes ached. She wanted to cry from loneliness, from the thoughts that circled in her brain like the hawk itself — that she'd once lost everyone who loved her, and now she'd lost again. She faced an eternity bleak with loneliness, and maybe, just maybe . . . an eternity of darkness, for there was no way out of this cave.

That made her stop.

Yes. There were more passages than this one, and if she went astray, she could wander, lost, until she died.

Taking off her backpack, she looped her arm through one strap. Putting her back against the wall, she slid down and sat. She'd been walking so long, so fast, so hard, without food or water, that she was starting to hallucinate. She had no reason, none, to imagine a death in these caves, or to despair of escaping when everything was going perfectly well. She had the rock ledge, narrow and comforting, to guide her, and the knowledge she'd come through here before.

No matter how long it took, she would escape the caves and the shadows, and once she was back in the real world, no one knew better than Tasya Hunnicutt how to move from country to country without being noticed.

Well, perhaps Rurik knew better.

A tear slid down her cool cheek.

She wiped it away.

No time for that.

Digging out her canteen, she took a long drink, then found her granola bars and ate one of the poor, crumbled things.

This cave was simply a cave, and part of the real world. She wasn't Luke Skywalker, sent to a place out of time where hallucinations tested her strength and her beliefs. Twenty-five years ago, she'd come through this cave and suffered no harm, had no revelations, learned nothing except that her old life was over and a new life had begun.

Now it was better than before. Twenty-five years ago, Miss Landau had hurried her all the way, and when four-year-old Tasya couldn't walk anymore, Miss Landau had carried her. Then when they at last approached the opening on the other end, Miss Landau had been twitchy. Even the child Tasya had realized Miss Landau feared what she would find.

Today, Tasya also feared.

Yet after more than eight hours of walking, she knew pursuit was unlikely, and if the Varinskis hadn't discovered the outlet to the cave the first time, they certainly wouldn't this time.

So now she needed only to keep her head, stay fed, stay hydrated, and keep moving.

She shook the remains of the granola bar out of the package and into her mouth, took another good drink of water, stood, and dusted off the seat of her pants.

How much longer?

She didn't know. One day? Two? The child Tasya had had no concept of time; it had seemed as if the ordeal would never end. But it had, and it would again.

She groped until she found the ledge, still at waist level, and started forward. She heard a trickle of water, then a ripple, and realized she was walking beside a stream. The air grew fresher, as if somewhere close there was an entrance to the outdoors. Her heart lifted — and for the first time, she stumbled on a rock in the path.

She fell forward, her hands outstretched to break her fall. She scraped her palms and banged her shins on the tumble of rocks, and when she cried out, the sound echoed up and out.

She froze, and listened. Somewhere near, water was trickling. Far above her head, she heard a faint squeaking: bats.

It felt damp in here.

Somehow, she'd reached a huge cavern, and maybe a lake or a stream.

She didn't remember this place, didn't remember it at all.

Cautiously she dragged herself back and onto her feet. She groped for the wall that had guided her here. She found the ledge and carefully inched forward, sliding around the rocks that blocked the path — and without warning, the wall disappeared.

She took a quick, panicked breath.

That echoed through the cavern, getting louder as it expanded to fill the dead space.

She backed up, found the wall again, and the ledge, and started forward once more.

The wall crumbled away beneath her touch.

Sometime in the recent past, a cave-in had made the wall crumble, and, with it, the ledge that would lead her to safety.

She couldn't believe it. This wasn't possible. She'd walked miles underground — if she figured three miles an hour for an average, and a minimum of eight hours, she'd walked twenty-four miles under the damned mountain seeking her freedom — to end here? Standing with her hand outstretched into nothing? It wasn't possible!

She couldn't go back. The Varinskis might not be chasing her into a cave, but she would bet they wouldn't allow her to just sashay back across Ruyshvania to freedom.

She couldn't go forward because . . . because she didn't know where to go. She threw her arms forward, waving them around, trying to find the guidance she needed — and the gravel beneath her foot slipped away.

She fell. For an instant, she kept her footing, skidding down as if she were on skis.

Then the ground disappeared completely, and she fell into darkness.

Boris sat at his desk, staring at the phone, waiting for it to ring. Waiting for his boys to call and tell him they'd destroyed Rurik Wilder, that they had the woman — and the icon.

Boris had obeyed the Other.

He'd found out all about the woman Rurik Wilder had with him, that Tasya Hunnicutt.

Now Boris knew he was in real trouble.

Because in New York City, a book made

its way through the publication process. A book about the Varinskis.

A hundred years ago, even fifty, the Varinskis had had an iron grip on the New York publishing industry. They'd held the companies by their tiny little balls, and for safety, they'd bought the editors' souls.

Then in the last thirty years, women had stepped out of bounds, become powerful editors and even publishers, and those women wore trousers and had piercings in their eyebrows. Some of them were even young and pretty.

Boris had not thought it would matter. What difference would a book make? No one would believe the truth about the Varinskis.

But this author had researched everything about them. She had written a book chronicling their history, their legend, their long stranglehold on the assassin business, the way they tracked and killed for hire, and how governments hired them to perpetrate "crimes." She'd had a story to tell, and the male editor said she had the voice to make it a best seller. The woman publisher smiled with her white teeth and called the author "the next Dan Brown."

As the world turned its attention to the Varinski trial, word of mouth among the booksellers and the press grew to almost mythic proportions. The gathering publicity around the Varinski Twins was ruining Boris's carefully developed Varinski image of invincible, untouchable murderers.

And the author was Tasya Hunnicutt.

Tasya Hunnicutt, Rurik's companion, the female who worked for the National Antiquities Society. She wasn't some old woman with fat, black chin hairs. She was the same woman who had disappeared with Rurik Wilder after the explosion at the Scottish tomb.

She had promised her publisher that before they published the book, she would provide sensational proof of the Varinskis' history, and what had occurred — the discovery of the gold, the explosion at the tomb, her mysterious disappearance — had created a furor far beyond anything she could have imagined. Right now, the American morning shows were bidding on who would first have her as a guest when she reappeared.

When the Other found out about Hunnicutt, how she'd done research on the Varinskis, even going so far as to travel to the Ukraine and take photos of their home . . . when the Other discovered Boris hadn't been vigilant and watchful about their privacy . . . when the Other realized Boris had failed to stop the book before it was even submitted . . . Boris would suffer.

And if the Other asked what had been done to retrieve the woman and the icon, and Boris told him Konstantine's whelp and a mere woman had defeated the might of the Varinskis . . . Boris would die.

He would die, he would go to hell, and he would burn in eternal agony.

He knew it. He could already feel the flames.

CHAPTER 30

Tasya's head hurt. Her cheek was icy cold. She didn't know where she was, and when she opened her eyes, her disorientation increased.

Was she four years old?

Had her whole life been an illusion?

Had she died and found the afterlife one huge dark cavern?

She sat up with a jerk.

The path through the dark.

The wall that disappeared. The cavern. The fall. She remembered now, but remembering did her no good. It was pitch-dark. She didn't know where she'd come from. She didn't know where she should go. She was stuck here, in the mountain under her country, and she would die here.

She would disappear here, and the icon that would help destroy the deal with the devil, avenge her parents, help Rurik's spirit rest in peace — it would disappear, too, never to be found.

The devil had won.

She had failed.

For the first time since she was four years old, Tasya lowered her head onto her knees and cried.

She cried for her parents. She cried for her lost childhood. She cried for all the sights of pain and inhumanity she'd documented with her camera. She cried for the death of Rurik's hopes.

Most of all, she cried for Rurik.

He'd been vanquished fighting for her.

He could have stolen the icon and run. He would have made it to safety and taken it to his family, and they would have guarded it while they waited for the next piece of destiny's puzzle to fall into place.

But no. Rurik had believed she was a integral part of the plan, and he'd refused to abandon her.

Yet that didn't change the fact that she loved him. For the first time since she was four years old, she had dared to love.

Yet she'd been an idiot. What good had guarding her heart, her words, and her affection done her? Rurik was dead, and he would never know that she'd do anything for him — take the icon to his parents, sacrifice her chance for revenge — because she loved him.

Lifting her head toward the unseen sky, she said, "God, for years, I haven't prayed to you. I didn't believe in you. How could I? I saw no evidence of your existence. But now I've seen proof that the devil exists. So you must exist, too, and now I beg you. . . . Rurik Wilder is dead. He's been part of a pact with the devil, but he didn't sign the pact, and he is . . . was a good man. If you're everything that is good, then please, I beg you, take him to be with you. Let him come . . . home." She couldn't talk anymore. Grief and anguish tore at her heart. She curled into a little ball. Sobs wracked her, hurt her head, and tore at her lungs. They echoed through the chamber, through the cracks in the rocks . . . and up into heaven.

She didn't know how long she cried. For an hour or more. But when she finally lifted her head, she felt better . . . lighter, more confident.

When all the days of her life had burned away, and she wandered into the lands of the dead, she would see Rurik again. And in the dark and the damp of the cavern, she made a vow — the first thing she would say to him was *I love you.*

For now — no matter how hopeless it seemed — she had to try to find her way out of this maze of caves. She had to return the icon to Rurik's family, or die trying.

But — how odd! — it seemed as if there was a light in the distance. Not a real light, not sunshine or a flashlight, but this glow . . .

She rubbed her eyes, trying to clear them, but the glow was still there. Two glows, actually.

She glanced around, wondering if the sun had somehow slanted in here. But no, it had to be nighttime. So the moon? Or maybe a phosphorescent fish in the lake or some glow-in-the-dark stalactite?

She laughed a little.

Maybe she'd just gone crazy, because it looked like two people standing across the lake . . . and there was a lake. It filled the cavern, with no way around it.

But the people — it was a man and a woman — gestured for her to climb back up the way she'd come.

Tasya hiccuped. She stood up, her gaze fixed to those people. Who were they?

Were they people? Or were they figments of her imagination?

Was Tasya dreaming? Still unconscious?

Why were a man and a woman underground with her?

She grabbed her backpack and picked her way through the rockfall back toward the wall where she'd started. She could see the whole way; that faint white light bathed everything.

It was weird to view what had been hidden before. The rockfall had been huge; a whole section of wall and ceiling had collapsed, demolishing what had been a smooth path through the mountains, damming the stream, and building the lake.

When she got to the top, she could see back the way she'd come, along the path, and forward where a thin strip of stone path still clung close to the wall.

A *really* thin strip of stone. So narrow that if she inched her way around, following the summons of those luminous strangers, there was a pretty good chance she'd slide and fall, and this time she wouldn't live.

But the people waited for her, and somehow, she knew she had to go to them. Sure — if she didn't, she'd be lost forever. But if she did . . . who were they? Where would they lead her?

They looked familiar.

How could they look familiar?

With her gaze fixed on them, she put her back against the wall and walked sideways along the ledge. She kept her gaze on the strangers, kept her gaze on the strangers, kept her gaze . . . she glanced down.

And froze.

Her toes were hanging over the edge — and the cliff dropped straight down into the lake. It was miles down, and the boulders stuck up like teeth. If she fell . . .

A thin whisper of sound brought her head around.

"Come on, sweetheart. Come on."

That was her mother's voice.

That was her *mother's* voice.

Eyes wide and fixed to the glow, Tasya followed the thin strip of rock around the edge of the lake. It remained sturdy beneath her feet.

Her mother. Her *parents.* She'd prayed, and her parents had come to get her. Or to help her escape the caves. She didn't know. She didn't care. For the first time in twenty-five years, she could see her mother's face, the bright blue eyes, so like her own. She could see her father's face, the determined jaw, the same one she saw in the mirror every morning.

This was the best moment of her life.

This was the moment she realized how much she'd lost. And how much she had.

"Mama," she whispered as she inched forward. "I miss you."

Her mother smiled. *I know.*

Tasya couldn't hear her. Not really. The

360

words were like a breath in her mind.

"Papa . . ."

I know.

The ledge widened. She moved with more confidence. "Is he there with you?"

They didn't answer.

She moved faster, trying to see them more clearly. "Please. Rurik. I loved him. Can I see him?"

Her parents moved away as she came closer. The warmth of their love surrounded her, leading her onward. They smiled, rejoicing in her.

The ledge grew wider, became a path, and Tasya hurried more and more, until she was running after them.

But they weren't talking.

"Oh, please. Oh, please —" The glow was growing brighter, stronger. "If I could just see him one more time . . ." She rounded a corner — and the morning sun struck her full in the eyes.

She flung her hands up over her eyes, and herself backward. "Mama?"

But they were gone, vanished in the light of day. They had led her . . . to freedom. To life.

Now she was again alone.

The sense of loss struck her like a blow.

But she couldn't falter. She couldn't collapse.

She'd been sent into that cave to learn a lesson, and she had learned. She would go forward and do what had to be done.

If her parents were so close, then she had faith that she would see Rurik again someday.

Someday, they'd be together again.

CHAPTER 31

Konstantine pushed the walker, leaning heavily on the bars, as he completed one of three circuits around his home in Washington State. His clothes hung on him, as if he were an old man rather than sixty-six and a Varinski in the prime of his life. He had a stupid tube in his nose, and he was weak. So weak.

Yet every day he walked a little farther, pushed himself to go a little faster.

Every day, Zorana fussed and fumed. She walked with him, and dragged his oxygen on wheels and his mobile IV, but she didn't like it and in her own way, she made her opinion quite clear.

His little wife had barely changed in thirty-five years. She was still tiny, five feet one, with the dark hair and dark eyes that had first fascinated him. Her skin was smooth and tanned, with a little sag at the jaw, but what man looked at a woman's jaw?

Her lips . . . ah, her lips were still as intoxicating, the lips that had changed his world.

He'd seen her glare like this dozens of times when the kids misbehaved. Her jaw was thrust forward, her arms crossed over her chest — she was stalking rather than walking.

She was not happy with him.

Usually, he would indulge her.

But not in this. He would not live out the last of his days as an invalid chained to a wheelchair. He would regain at least a portion of his strength.

He had to. Whether Zorana liked it or not, the battle would come to him.

So now he walked and distracted her with his nonsense. "The house — I like it. Not too big, like those Californians who move in and build the huge mansions on the top of the mountain and tell themselves they are kings. Pigs in fine clothing are still pigs. We have three bedrooms — that is enough for us. And two bathrooms." He paused, lifted two fingers, and used the chance to catch his breath. "In the Old Country, two bathrooms is unheard of. Everyone would think we are rich."

Zorana said nothing.

"Of course, we could remodel and add a

bathroom just for us. It would be a fine thing for when we have grandchildren. The trip to the bathroom is long in the winter, and you are getting older. But you don't want to talk about this bathroom scheme."

Actually, she'd been nattering about a master bathroom for years. And it was a sign of how furious she was that she managed to remain silent when he acknowledged her wish for the first time.

He worried about Zorana — his wife had had to be brave every day since Adrik had run away so many years ago. Now Rurik had disappeared. Jasha said Rurik had used his credit card, the one with the fake name, but the last time was many days ago, and their worry, unspoken but oh so real, gnawed at them day and night.

"It's a good year for the grapes, especially the pinots." The rows of vines, thick with green leaves and ripening grapes, ran through their valley as far as he could see, and they lightened the heaviness of his heart. "If we keep this up, we will kick those Oregon growers' butts."

Zorana didn't look at him. She didn't answer.

But they'd been married for many years. He knew his wife, and this was a battle he would win. "The garden's doing well this year, too, and I don't want you to handle the fruit stand on your own. It is too much work for a woman your age."

She huffed.

He pretended not to hear. "We will hire one of the kids that works at the Szarvases'. What is that girl's name?" He pretended he couldn't remember. "The one who will do anything for money for paints?"

"Michele."

Ha. Zorana had had to say a word. If he kept it up, she'd have to release all that pent-up fury that he knew simmered right below the surface. "That's right. When she works, people would stop to buy."

Zorana froze in place. "*What* do you mean by that?"

He kept walking. "I mean they will stop to look at her pretty face."

Zorana's frustration and fury boiled over, and she hurried to rejoin him. "Are you making now decisions about the fruit stand? The fruit stand I started without any help from you? The fruit stand you thought was a stupid idea? And you think I'm too old to run it?"

He let her natter on for a while, enjoying the flush in her cheeks, the cheeks that too often lately had been pale and drawn with worry. When she finally began to run down, he said, "I think you are too beautiful, and I fear some young buck will come by and take you from me."

She snorted. "We should have your eyes checked next time we go to that Seattle doctor."

"No need. I saw him watching you. He fancies you himself." Konstantine lightly struck his chest with his fist. "But I will not allow him to have you. You are mine, forever."

Her eyes filled with quick tears. She had remembered her own vision, the one that saw him chained in hell for all eternity . . . without her.

"Forever," he insisted. "Now give me a kiss."

She kissed him, a kiss full of her love for him and her rebellion against this cruel fate, and he held her with one arm and cursed this disease that wasted his heart and made him unable to comfort her as they both wished.

Ever mindful of his condition, she released him before either of them was ready, and placed his second hand on the security of his walker.

"Let us go around the house one more time," he said. She began to protest, then he lifted his hand. Listened intently. "I hear a car coming up the road."

She didn't question his statement; his wolf hearing had not failed him. "Do you recognize it?" she asked.

He shook his head, and when he moved as quickly as he could toward the front, she didn't try to slow him.

They came around the corner as the Camry pulled up in front of the porch. The woman inside sat and stared up at the house, then jumped and stared at them as they moved toward her.

"It's . . . that girl, the one he was with when he vanished. I recognize her from the television," Zorana whispered. "That's Tasya — with black-and-white hair."

"So I see." He saw, too, the parade of expressions across Tasya's face: the fiery resolution that had got her here dissolving, becoming tear-filled eyes and a desperate disinclination to do the duty she'd come to fulfill.

"Do you suppose he's wounded? Or coming home later?" Zorana's voice was fraught with hope.

With obvious reluctance, Tasya opened the door and slid out of the car.

No. Tasya showed in her face and her motions that there was no room for hope.

His son, the babe he'd rocked, the boy

he'd taught to be wary, to hunt, to control his wildness, the man who had grown into a pilot and then an archaeologist . . . was dead.

The girl walked toward them, trying to smile with a mouth that trembled.

He stopped, and took Zorana's arm when she would have hurried forward.

As Tasya dug in her pocket, she stopped in front of them, her large blue eyes pleading for their understanding, for their compassion.

Right now, he had none for anyone but himself and his wife.

Tasya pulled out a small square, wrapped in tissue paper, and unwrapped it. She extended it toward them.

The second icon.

He wanted to spit on it. The price had been too high.

Zorana's fingers shook as she took the icon and stared at the face of the Virgin, at the crucified Jesus, at the glitter of gold and the sheen of more than a thousand years. She looked up at Tasya. "Rurik?" she choked.

Tasya shook her head.

As if the icon were too heavy, Zorana sank down toward the ground.

Konstantine reached for her, almost

369

tipped over, barely caught himself.

Tasya sprang to Zorana's side and wrapped her close.

And the two women cried on each other's shoulders.

As he watched them, tears gathered in Konstantine's eyes and trickled down his cheeks.

All right. This Tasya had loved his son. Now she helped his wife.

So Konstantine would take her into his family, and they would love her.

Tasya sat at Rurik's old desk in Rurik's small bedroom in his parents' house.

She'd downloaded her photographs onto his old computer, and now she examined them one by one, reviewing her record of the site, the excavation, the findings. . . . She wanted so badly to send her pictures to National Antiquities, to her editor at her publishing company, to the newsmagazines who had already moved on to a new story. Revenge on the Varinskis had been her goal for so long, she couldn't quite leave it behind. With the proof she had here, she could deal that family of murderers such a blow they might never recover.

Yet for all that Rurik's family had changed their name to Wilder, they were Varinskis, and so was he. Konstantine and Zorana could not have been kinder to her, taking her into their home, treating her with the respect due the one who had found the icon — and with the love due to Rurik's woman.

Rurik's sister, Firebird, had openly grieved for her brother. Then, ever practical, she loaned Tasya clothes from her closet until the Internet order arrived, and as if she was glad of someone close to her age in the house, she talked about her baby.

The sonogram showed a boy. She hadn't decided on a name. She hoped he wasn't too big; all of her brothers had been over ten pounds.

Yet Firebird never referred to the father. Whoever he was, he was completely out of the picture. Tasya would have thought he was just a fleeting mistake, but when Firebird didn't realize she was observed, she stared out the window and stroked her belly, and the expression on her face . . . rage, hurt, loneliness . . . yes, for different reasons, Tasya and Firebird had a lot in common.

So could Tasya publicize the photographs without ruining the chance to break the pact forever? Rurik had desperately wanted to give his father his chance for redemption.

Did Tasya care?

Before she'd met him, she hadn't cared at all.

Then she'd come to this house, and found Konstantine was the one Varinski she watched warily. It didn't matter that he was dreadfully ill, spending most of his time in a wheelchair, breathing with the help of oxygen at night.

He *felt* like those other Varinskis, the bastards who had tried so hard to kill Rurik, and finally succeeded. She knew why she shivered when Konstantine was near; he'd murdered, he'd raped, he'd pillaged, and for all that he'd repented, those sins dragged at his soul.

Zorana's prophecy claimed that unless he and his sons broke the pact with the devil, Konstantine would burn in hell.

When the Varinskis had killed her parents, Konstantine had been long gone from that family, yet she couldn't forget he'd performed deeds equally horrible.

Nor could she forget he'd fathered Rurik, and raised him to be a man she admired and loved.

She didn't know whether to love Konstantine or hate him — or weep for him.

Reaching out, she ran her finger along the edge of the icon. She'd given the Madonna the place of honor. Every time she looked away from the computer monitor, she could see the Virgin's wise, sad eyes and know that in the battle between good and evil, other losses had been suffered, other sacrifices had been made.

Yet seeing the ghosts of her own parents had shown Tasya a very important fact — their pain no longer existed, but their love for her would never fail. Their tenderness extended past death, and brought them back to save her life.

Although those assassins, those murderers, those Ukrainian Varinskis, would hate the idea that they'd in any way given comfort to the child who had evaded them, it was an inescapable truth that in forcing her underground, they'd both cured her fear of the dark and given her peace from the anguish that had fired her resolve.

Now all she had to do was carefully weed through the hundreds of pictures of the Scottish site on the Isle of Roi. She needed photographic proof of what she and Rurik found there. She would hold them until the pact had been broken and she could once again return to normal life . . . as if life could ever be normal again, without Rurik.

As she worked, she took notes writing what she recalled about each photo, until she reached the point when she'd handed

Ashley her camera so she could labor with Rurik to open the tomb.

The first picture Ashley had taken showed Tasya and Rurik from the back, and stiff and reserved, determinedly not touching. For a dozen shots, it was the same — the hole into the tomb got bigger, but Tasya and Rurik concentrated on their tasks.

Suddenly, the view changed.

Tasya had her hand over Rurik's, and the two of them were looking at each other. Looking . . . and between them Tasya saw need and outrage, anger and fear, sexual tension so high the photo blurred on the monitor.

Tasya dashed the tears from her eyes.

The emotions between them sprang forth from the photograph, a record of that moment in time before the booby trap, the treasure chest, the wall carvings, the explosion — and the truth — changed their lives.

Had they been so obvious? Were their passions there for everyone to see?

Since that moment in the cave when Tasya realized she would die, and perhaps spend an eternity without Rurik, she hadn't cried.

Crying was not a habit she wished to cultivate.

Yet again she had to wipe the tears from her eyes, and a single sob escaped her. She covered her mouth, but another followed, and another, and hot, rebellious tears scalded her cheeks.

How dared he be dead? *How dared he?* What ruthlessness made him hand her the icon and force her to bring it here so the pact could be broken . . . and so she could live? Her whole life had been one long stretch of loneliness, and for a brief few days, she had been alive. Not always happy, not always sure, but alive.

Now more bleak years of loneliness stretched before her until she faded into the night, and at last found her parents, and her love, once more.

Downstairs, she heard Konstantine roar.

She gave a laugh, and gave a sob.

She'd been here ten days, and discovered Konstantine roared more than he talked. It gave her comfort to hear him. He was alive — sick, but still alive. Fighting, and still alive. The old man was an inspiration . . . but then, he still had Zorana.

The thought brought another burst of tears.

My God, when had she turned into such a girl?

Easy answer.

When she'd fallen in love.

Out of the corner of her eye, she caught a

movement, and in a reflex action she turned, fists up, ready to kill.

A ghost stood there.

Rurik, with his jacket flung over his shoulder.

She stared.

Had her parents sent him?

He tossed his jacket on the bed.

Bewildered, she watched it land.

It landed with a whoosh. It wrinkled the comforter. It looked real.

He looked real.

Standing, she knocked her chair backward. It hit the floor with a smack loud enough to wake her and frighten the ghost.

She didn't wake.

The ghost didn't move. Instead he smiled, a sort of crooked, self-mocking smile that stopped her heart. "No man is worth so many tears."

"Rurik?" she whispered. "Rurik!"

He was sunburned and thin, with a yellowing bruise from a black eye and a weary sadness around his mouth.

She reached out a hand to his shoulder, thinking it would pass right through his form — and touched warm flesh.

He caught her hand, lifted it to his mouth, kissed it, and his breath touched her skin. . . .

She launched herself at him.

He caught her, lifted her into his arms.

Vaguely, from the doorway, she heard a sob. His parents were there. His sister watched.

Tasya didn't care.

She wrapped her arms around his neck, her legs around his hips.

She kissed him, taking his breath into her lungs, giving her breath into his. And she remembered her vow in the tunnel. "I love you." She took his head in her hands. She looked into his eyes. "I love you. I love you. I love you."

He was another miracle in a life blessed with miracles.

He was alive.

Rurik was alive.

CHAPTER 32

Firebird stood at the open window of the bedroom she shared with Tasya and gazed out into the night. "Look at that moon."

"Wonderful." Tasya sat in her pajamas, stared at the computer screen, concentrating as hard as she could. She had to, to block out the tumult in her body. Her blood sang with need; her legs trembled with desire.

And she lounged here playing solitaire.

"The stars are gorgeous, too. It is so clear and so bright, I can see *clear* to the horse barn." Firebird made that sound like a big deal. "When I was ten, I desperately wanted a horse and Papa said no. He said a horse cost too much to buy and too much to maintain, and we were poor, struggling immigrants with no money for such frivolity. I was crushed."

"Yeah. Bummer." Rurik was in the next bedroom. *In the next bedroom,* and Tasya

378

couldn't go to him. Because the house rules didn't allow unmarried people to sleep together. They'd held hands through dinner. They'd smiled into each other's eyes. Then they'd kissed good night — repeatedly — and gone their separate ways.

Tasya couldn't believe it. She was twenty-nine years old, held to chastity by nineteenth-century morals as applied by a former Varinski.

"But Papa's word is law, so I didn't complain. And on my eleventh birthday, Papa bought himself a horse." Firebird wore a small, reminiscent smile. "He said he had discovered a use for it around the place."

Caught against her will by the story, Tasya asked, "What use was that?"

"Giving me something to ride and care for."

"Nice."

"He has his moments. Anyway, my sweet old mare is still in the barn, so Papa keeps hay in the loft." Long pause. "You know, my brothers used to use that barn as their own private make-out space."

Tasya looked up. Firebird had her attention now.

"Yep. Because, you know, for a guy who used to have no morals whatsoever, Papa's really strict about this no-sex-under-his-roof thing."

"I noticed."

"Papa is a really traditional guy. And traditionally, lovers have to sneak around to get laid."

Slowly, Tasya pushed her chair back. "Firebird, what are you trying to say?"

"Nothing. Why do you think I'm trying to say something?" Firebird leaned out. "Look at that. That's a big bird. A hawk!"

Tasya raced to the window in time to see the huge hawk sailing across the moon toward the barn. "Rurik," she whispered.

"Papa has the hearing of a wolf." Firebird wandered over to her iPod and flipped on her speakers. "Better climb out the window."

Zorana listened to the music playing over her head. Groping under the covers, she patted Konstantine's chest. "Tasya just went out the window."

Konstantine grunted and caught her hand, and held it. "I heard nothing. Now, be quiet, woman. I'm trying to get some rest."

Tasya ran across the lawn, along the path through the trees, to the barn.

She pressed her hand on the door. With a

creak, it swung open. The barn smelled of clean straw, of leather, of a much-loved horse. Moonlight streamed through the open windows, and Rurik stood beside the stall. The mare had her head laid adoringly on his shoulder while he petted her nose.

There wasn't a female in the world who could resist him.

He smiled at Tasya.

Once again it struck her — he was alive. "I must have done something really good in a former life to deserve you." Her voice was husky with unshed tears, and she swallowed to contain them.

Such a girl.

"You did something really good in *this* life." He patted the horse one last time, gently disengaged, and strode toward Tasya, his gait long and easy. "I'm the one who never dared dream I would see you again."

She wanted to fling herself at him as she had done this afternoon, but after that first, instinctive reaction, she remembered . . . the fight with the Varinskis, the way the light in his eyes blinked out. She'd thought he'd been killed. At the least, he'd been horribly injured, and she thought that not even his prodigious healing abilities could take an arrow through the chest without repercussions.

"Are you really alive, or is this another dream?" She reached out to him, her hand pale in the moonlight.

He came to a halt before her, and she pressed her palm over his heart. It beat strongly, reassuring her.

"How did you live through it?" she whispered.

He captured her fingers. "Come on. I'll tell you." He led her to the ladder.

She started up. "Your sister said you guys used this barn for a make-out den."

"Sure. The other guys. But not me. I'm a virgin."

She paused and looked down at him. "Liar."

"A virgin." He looked up, making her dreadfully aware that the light cotton pajamas pulled tight as she climbed, wonderfully aware that he watched and wanted.

She crawled up onto the hay-strewn floor, faced the trap, and watched him follow her up. "I'll have to see what I can do about that."

"I wish you would."

The moonlight shone through the window in a square that lit each straw and made bold shadows of the rafters, the bales, the pitchfork. It was warm up here, the heat of the August sun lingering under the eaves.

She hadn't come prepared for seduction. Her hair was still tipped with white and curled wildly. Her arms were bare; a burst of stars decorated the material over her chest and down her thigh. The drawstring on her pants was knotted, and the waistband rested low on her hips.

"You are the most beautiful thing I've ever seen." Going to the blanket spread over a nest in the straw, he stretched out and tucked his arms behind his head. He was a living, breathing invitation to sin.

All the times they had been together, they'd been seducing, lying, attacking, lusting.

Tonight was different. Tonight she would learn him.

She knelt beside him, the clean straw cracking beneath her knees. Unbuttoning his shirt, she spread it wide, and traced the contours of his chest. She found the shattered skin where the arrow had entered, right below his left shoulder. But there was another wound on his shoulder, larger, uglier, where the skin didn't cover the muscle and the edges of the wound glowed red.

"Rurik." She looked into his face.

He watched her face. "It's over now."

Which meant he'd suffered far more than

any mere man could bear.

She unbuckled his belt, removed his pants, discovered a slice of flesh gone from his right thigh, a chunk of bone from the thrust of his hip. She kissed each injury, her lips lingering, and breathed in the scent of him, reveling in his life, anguished about his pain.

He slid his hand around her neck and brought her close, and kissed her. "It's all right. You're alive. I'm alive. That's all that counts."

"No, it's not all that counts. Those bastards almost killed you. I thought they had. And I hope they burn in hell."

"I think you can rest assured of that." He kissed her again.

"Did you kill them all?"

"I did."

She looked into his eyes. Smoothed his hair off his forehead. "Rurik," she whispered. "Tell me."

He sighed, and leaned his head back. "Only if I can hold you. I need to hold you while I . . . while I remember. . . ."

Stretching out beside him, she wrapped her arms around his waist and laid her head against his chest. "Are you warm enough? Am I hurting you?"

He crushed her to him. "This is the best I've been in three weeks."

She listened to him breathe, and even now she couldn't believe he was here. "You're a miracle."

"Not me. There are other miracles in this world — and so many horrors. I've lived through a few of both."

"I saw you. You were fighting Ilya in the air."

"I shredded him with my talons. I was kicking his ass —"

"I saw you. You had him on the ropes, and then —"

"Kassian shot me with an arrow." Rurik touched the spot where the arrow had pierced him. "The Varinskis are poor losers."

Tasya swallowed over the anxiety in her throat. "I saw that, too. I thought you'd been killed."

"Pretty close. Really close." Tenderly, he smoothed his hand down her bare arm as if he needed to touch something warm and alive. "I knew I was done for it. The injury was too massive for the hawk's smaller body mass —"

"Wait a minute." Tasya half sat up. "Are you saying the arrow would kill you as a hawk, but not as a human?"

"Not exactly." He struggled to explain the fine points. "I didn't know if I could survive as a human, either — the arrow went right through my lung — but I had a better chance in my human form. Unfortunately, I was up high, and I can't fly as a human. I was too injured, and with the arrow in me, too off balance to fly, anyway, and I was headed for the ground way too fast. I caught a glimpse of you." Taking her hand in his, he kissed her fingers. "I saw you turn and leave."

"I hated to run. I hated it so much." She huddled next to him.

"Do you think I don't know that? I also knew that if anyone could make it here with the icon, it would be you." He tilted her head up and looked into her eyes. "Only you, Tasya. Only you."

"Because of the prophecy?"

"No. Because no matter what the odds, you won't quit."

At his avowed faith in her, she half smiled.

"I wanted to give you time to get away. I figured I didn't have a lot of choice — die of the wound, or take a chance, soar until the last minute, then change into human form, and hope I didn't break my neck." Rurik's hand crushed the material of her top. "I didn't break my neck."

She knew what that meant. "What did you break?"

386

"I cracked a few ribs, did something really bad to my shoulder joint." Rurik shrugged in a way that looked more like a test of the joint than an expression of insouciance. "But with what happened afterward, that didn't matter."

She ran her hand over him, reassuring herself, offering comfort to him.

But she had begun to realize he had no time for sympathy. Rurik and his family were involved in a fight to the death — and beyond.

And Rurik . . . Rurik wanted only to win. He wanted justice. He continued. "While Kassian and Sergei ran over, I yanked that arrow out of me and stuck it right through Sergei's throat."

"Good," Tasya said.

"Bloodthirsty girl." Rurik pressed a kiss on her forehead. "But that arrow trick really pissed off Kassian, and he picked up his walking stick — my father says those guys use everything as a weapon, and he's right — and slammed the pointed end through my shoulder. He pinned me right to the ground."

Tasya recoiled, dug her fists into her eyes, trying to shut out the vision.

"I looked up, and Ilya was diving, talons out, right for my eyes — when he exploded in this burst of black-and-white feathers."

Tasya took her hands away from her face. "I used their rifle and shot him."

"That's my girl!" Rurik chuckled, and she heard the sound deep in his chest. "I thought that must be what happened."

"I knew I couldn't kill him, but I didn't care. I hoped I could hurt him badly. The lousy little weasel."

"Eagle, honey." He stroked under her top, finding the soft skin along her waist. "Not a weasel, an eagle."

"I know a weasel when I see one," Tasya said.

"All right," he conceded. "A weasel."

"Keep going."

His hand slipped below the waistband of her pants.

She caught his wrist. "I didn't mean that. Keep going with the story."

He groaned. "We can talk later."

She looked down his body, and saw why he'd lost interest in telling his story. And as his hand skimmed lightly along the skin of her buttocks, she recognized a distinct diminishing of her curiosity.

Yet he'd left too many questions unanswered, and this slow rise of passion could be held off for a little while longer.

She wanted to know, and she had things

to say. "Did he fall on you?"

Rurik sighed, but softly, content . . . for now . . . to touch her. "Barely missed me, which was a good thing, because by then I was half-dead. I could have suffocated under him and not been able to push him away. That ass Kassian turned the color of borscht. He leaned over me, grabbed me by the throat, and said, 'I'm going to finish you. Then I'm going to hunt down the woman and make her suffer.' " Rurik smiled, but it wasn't a pleasant smile. That smile made Tasya very glad she was not Kassian. "You know that trick I told you about, the one where I can will myself to change only one part of my body?"

"Yes?" She wasn't sure she wanted to hear this.

"I changed my hands to talons and sliced his throat wide open." Rurik gestured widely with his free arm. "Then I took out his eyes. Then — Tasya?"

Tasya realized her head was buzzing and her vision blurred. It wasn't that she was squeamish. It was that mental picture of Rurik pinned to the ground, yet fighting for his life — and hers. "You killed him," she said.

"Yes. I killed him." He sat up, leaned over her, his body a protection, his face shadowed in mystery. "All the time I was fighting, all I wanted was for you to get away. Don't cry for me. Don't feel guilty for running. You did the right thing. You brought the icon here, and I'll never forget . . . that you trusted me."

"I did trust you. I do trust you. I'm sorry about the icon." She smoothed her palms down his cheeks. "I should have told you I had it."

"While I was recovering, I had a lot of time to think." He leaned his forehead to hers. "You found it in the chapel, didn't you?"

"When you first walked in, I was holding Sister Maria Helvig's hand. She was still warm. . . ." Tasya's shock had battled with her grief, and above that, she was glad for the nun. Glad she'd gone on to be with her sisters.

"What could you say?" He sounded briskly practical, putting the memories in the past. " 'The nun is dead, but hey! I found the icon.' "

"True. But I just didn't *think* to tell you about the icon. Then we buried her, then the Varinskis appeared, and then —"

"Then you didn't like me anymore." He leaned close and breathed in the scent of her hair.

"No, but I still loved you, and that made me madder."

"You loved me." His warm, deep voice lingered over the words. "Tell me again."

"I love you."

He kissed her, his breath mingling with hers, his tongue exploring, his warmth pressed against her. Each motion was heat and life and heart, and when he slid his hand under her shirt, up her belly, to cup her breast, she wanted to die from the sweetness — and live the rest of her life in his arms. She placed her hands on his shoulders. "Are you going to tell me the rest of the story?"

He unknotted the drawstring at her waist. "Tomorrow. I'll tell you tomorrow."

CHAPTER 33

With great ceremony, Zorana placed the immense pork roast basted with a mustard rosemary sauce on the table in the Wilder kitchen, then stepped back and smiled while her children and her husband applauded and praised.

Tasya joined in; one asset her years as a foster child had given her was the ability to observe a family's traditions, learn them quickly, and blend in without a hitch.

Sometimes it was a matter of being one of the crowd.

Sometimes it was a matter of staying under the radar.

At the Wilders', it was something she did because here, at last, she was home.

This family had taken her to their bosom without reservation; just as Rurik promised, Konstantine and Zorana opened their home to her, not just because she'd brought them the icon, but because she had loved their son. During those dark days when they'd thought he was dead, his parents had talked about him, asked her about his last days, shown her his baby book, cried with her.

Now that he had returned, they didn't claim him as their own. Instead, they paid tribute to her with the place of honor at their kitchen table.

Rurik sat on the bench beside her, dressed in a loose black T-shirt and jeans, and an old pair of running shoes, making sure she had all she wanted on her plate before he dug into his welcome-home dinner.

Firebird had taken the evening off from her job down at Szarvas's art school. She sat beside Rurik, her skin radiant with that special glow only pregnant women possessed.

Jasha and his fiancée, Ann, had flown up from Napa for the reunion. Now they sat across the table from Rurik, opening more bottles of Wilder Wines and keeping the glasses full.

"All right, Mama, the food is on the table. *Now* can Rurik tell us what happened?" Jasha looked as impatient and annoyed as only the oldest son could look when deprived of the information he viewed as his by privilege.

Zorana glared at her son. "Rurik should

have meat. He's still weak."

"Weak from what? What ordeals did he undergo?" Jasha gestured at his brother. "I haven't heard the story yet."

"So weak," Rurik dramatically whispered.

His mother patted his shoulder and gave him the end cut of pork.

"You are such a piece of work." Jasha sounded aggravated, but his fork went to work on his full plate, and never slowed.

"Waiting makes Jasha irritable," Ann confided to Tasya. "If it were up to him, all the icons would be found, the pact would be broken, and we could go back to the business of growing grapes and creating wines."

"And you and I would have time for a honeymoon," Jasha said.

"I haven't agreed to marry you, yet," Ann shot back.

Jasha slid his arm around her shoulders. "But you will."

She turned her head away, a woman sure of her man. "Maybe."

"I would die without you."

She turned back to him, touched the fading scars on his throat. "You almost died for me. That is enough."

The screened kitchen door let in the warm, scented air of a summer evening.

Zorana served the pork with roasted red potatoes and carrots tossed in olive oil, and a massive Greek salad. Everything in the Wilder household seemed so normal . . . yet Tasya never forgot that she dined at the table of her enemy.

Somehow, that seemed to be the right thing to do.

Konstantine sat in his wheelchair at the head of the table, his IV bottle dangling from a hook, and poured enough vodka to fill the Black Sea.

Jasha looked enough like Rurik that Tasya would know they were brothers, yet they were very different. Where Rurik had brown hair and golden brown eyes, Jasha's hair was black, and his eyes were an odd color, like ancient gold coins.

Ann was very tall and very slender, with a shy demeanor that kept everyone at a distance — until she smiled. Then the whole world fell in love with her. Certainly Jasha adored her; he waited on her as if she were the queen and he her most devoted courtier.

Tasya leaned to Rurik, seated at her right hand. "I like the way Jasha treats Ann."

Rurik put a piece of potato in his mouth, chewed, and swallowed. "He is *so* pussy-whipped."

She looked at him out of the corners of

her eyes.

"Not that there's anything wrong with being whipped," he added hastily.

Tasya took an olive from the appetizer plate. She bit into it until her teeth struck the pit, used her tongue to strip the flesh away, then slid the bare pit out of her mouth.

Rurik's color rose, his eyes grew hot, and he leaned close. "Later, I'll make you pay for that."

"But you're weak from your injuries . . . and from our reunion last night," she murmured. "You should rest."

"I'm fine," he snapped.

She smiled. "Then I'll count on it."

"Ma, Rurik says he's fine." Jasha grinned at his loudmouthed brother. "So he can tell us what happened."

Zorana started to shake her finger at her oldest, but Konstantine said, "He's almost done eating, and I, too, would like to know how Rurik survived the Varinski attack."

Rurik put down his fork and knife.

The table grew quiet.

Rurik began, "Tasya told you that she saw me fighting Ilya in the air. . . ."

Just as it had last night, the story had the power to horrify Tasya. Rurik had come so close to death, and as he told of slashing at

Ilya, of the arrow piercing his breast, of turning human to reach the ground alive, she alternately flinched and applauded. She still could scarcely comprehend who and what he was, and how he'd escaped death.

When he got to the part where Tasya shot Ilya, Konstantine poured himself a vodka and passed the bottle. "Everyone! A toast! To Tasya, our new daughter."

Everyone raised their glasses and drank vodka.

Except Firebird, who toasted with water.

"To our three daughters." Zorana dipped her glass first to Firebird, then to Ann, then to Tasya. "They hold our hearts."

Everyone drank again.

"To Rurik!" Jasha said.

"To Rurik!" everyone echoed.

"May he finish his story uninterrupted!" Jasha glared meaningfully.

Everyone laughed, drank, and settled back to listen once more.

"Was Ilya dead on impact?" Konstantine asked.

"No, he staggered to his feet, grabbed Kassian's pistol. I kicked his feet out from underneath him" — Rurik gave a crack of laughter — "and the son of a bitch shot himself."

The table was absolutely silent. Then —

"I guess . . . since he was a demon . . . it was fatal?" Jasha asked.

"Killed him deader than hell," Rurik confirmed.

"A Varinski shot himself? Killed himself?" Konstantine sat and stared into space, his eyes narrowed, his fingers rubbing together over and over again. "Unheard of. Impossible. I wonder what is going on."

"The pact is failing," Zorana said matter-of-factly. "If we're lucky, they'll all kill themselves before they find us."

"You keep hoping, Ma." Only a month before, Jasha and Ann had had their own run-ins with the Varinski clan, and although Jasha had healed, he still bore the scars.

"So they were all dead. You were staked to the ground. And . . . ?" Firebird rolled her hands, trying to get Rurik to finish the story.

"I was done for it. I was exhausted. I'd been shot. I'd lost a lot of blood. I was dehydrated and in pain, and I could *not* get that stake out of the ground so I could get away, get help."

"Don't." Tasya's voice broke.

"It got dark and cold, and I was delirious, in and out of consciousness. It was about dawn when I came out of it, and knew I was dying."

Zorana clutched her fist in her blouse over

her heart.

Ann wiped her eyes with her napkin, and Jasha put his arm around her.

Firebird rubbed her hand on the mound of her belly.

"I was in such pain, I was glad to have it finished. . . ." Rurik looked right at Tasya. "Then two people appeared to me."

"Someone came to help you?" Tasya's bright blue eyes filled with tears, and she looked at Rurik with that expression that both broke his heart — and made it all worthwhile. "God bless them."

He liked this new Tasya, made soft and tender by love. She touched him at every opportunity; she brooded over him while she thought he slept; she waited on him.

He knew it wouldn't last. Well, the love would, but her hanging over him wouldn't. A woman like Tasya needed meaningful employment, and they'd have to find something for her to do, and fast, but . . . a man could get used to that kind of treatment.

"The sun came up behind them, so I never did see their faces." Rurik wanted to get through this part, and at the same time . . . he wanted someone to explain what had happened. "They seemed to glow."

Tasya's chin stopped trembling. She sat up straight, and she stared at him.

"The lady gave me something to drink, water, I guess. Really good, clear water. I've never tasted water as good as that." Even the memory gave Rurik cheer. "And the guy . . . he was sort of talking to me. At least, I could hear him in my head. He said I was never going to be able to yank that walking stick out of the ground, but if I could get my feet under me and use my other hand on the stick, I could pull myself up."

"Why didn't he pull the stick out of you?" Jasha still didn't understand; no one had ever said Jasha was subtle.

Firebird stared at him in disgust. "Because he was a ghost, you moron."

"Oh, come on." Jasha made his disbelief quite clear. "You were hallucinating."

Tasya twisted her napkin between her fists.

"All I know is — it hurt like a bitch when I managed to pull myself free." At the memory, Rurik rubbed his shoulder. The tendons straining, the muscles tearing, the knowledge that he had to deliberately break his own shoulder blade. "Those people led me to this stream coming out of the side of the mountain. I just flopped down in that icy water and let it wash my wounds, and got a good drink. I passed out again, and when I woke up . . . the sun was rising."

"Told you, you were hallucinating," Jasha said.

Tasya looked between Jasha and Rurik. She opened her mouth, and shut it.

"You're lucky you didn't drown in the stream," Ann said.

"According to the people in Capraru, that stream dried up when the Dimitru family was killed."

Even Jasha said, "Whoa."

Firebird shivered. "That's a better ghost story than I ever heard while I was camping."

"Maybe I was hallucinating about the people and the stream, but the fact is, my wounds closed, I was conscious and able to stand, and there were no tracks or scents of that couple." Rurik watched his family absorb that, then added, "I looked. The stick was still stuck in the ground, too."

Tasya swallowed, and in a tiny voice, she said, "I know who they are."

As one, everyone turned to her.

"They were my parents."

As if she'd already guessed, Zorana nodded.

"They saved me" — Tasya lightly touched Rurik's arm — "and they saved you."

Rurik took both her hands and kissed

them, and held them. "Then we can safely say they gave us their blessing."

Chapter 34

"As do we. We — Zorana and I — give you our blessing." Konstantine pounded on the table with the flat of his hand. "Another toast! To Tasya's parents, the Dimitrus!"

"Antai and Jennica," Tasya supplied.

"Antai and Jennica Dimitru!" Konstantine looked into the glass of clear vodka. "*Pahzhalstah*, my friends. Thank you."

Everyone drank again, Konstantine taking the liquor into himself reverently, as if honoring the Dimitrus for saving his son.

Zorana whispered in Konstantine's ear, then stood and started clearing the table.

Tasya and Ann tried to get up and help, but Zorana put a firm hand on both of their shoulders. "The kitchen is small. Let me do it."

"So, Rurik." Konstantine put his glass on the table with a resounding thump. "You had had a spear in your shoulder. You had been shot by an arrow. Your fingers . . . they were broken?"

Tasya frowned in confusion. "His fingers were fine."

Rurik shook his head. He knew where his father was heading.

"Because I have been living here in a house for a week with three weeping women, and all it took was one little phone call." Konstantine's volume swelled. "One phone call, Rurik! You could have reversed the charges!"

Zorana rattled the dishes in agreement.

Jasha relaxed and grinned.

Rurik grinned back and said, "I don't know, Papa. You're pretty strict about not spending your money on long-distance calls."

Tasya slammed Rurik with her fist. "He's right. Why didn't you call?"

With one glance at her furious face, Rurik got serious in a hurry. "Look. I managed to get to the convent. That took me all day, walking and crawling. There was food and water there, and that's where I stayed for eight or nine days. Or ten. I wasn't dying anymore, but I wanted to. I felt like hell, and I couldn't make it down to Capraru on my own."

Jasha raised his eyebrows. "Staying at a convent didn't turn you to cinders?"

"I stayed out of the chapel. I didn't touch any of the holy objects. But it wasn't fun, I can tell you." Rurik shuddered at the memory of the cool cloister, the hard, narrow cot, the nightmares brought on by fever and pain. "Not just because I'm a part of a pact with the Evil One, either. Any guy would be freaked about sleeping in a nun's bed. Lucky for me I was so damned sick I could barely raise my head."

"Sorry, man." Jasha shook his head.

"Finally, a woman from Capraru showed up. Apparently Mrs. Gulyás ventured up once a month to check on Sister Maria Helvig."

"I'll bet you looked bad." Firebird caught the hot, wet washcloth her mother tossed her, and wiped the table.

"Bruises all over, holes in my clothes that went all the way through my body, dried blood . . . and the way Mrs. Gulyás screamed, I was afraid I'd scared her to death." At the memory, Rurik wiped his face with a napkin. "Then she realized the nun was dead."

"Oh, dear." Tasya covered her mouth.

"I didn't speak the language —"

"Oh, dear," Tasya said again.

"I wouldn't have thought a woman of her girth could move that fast" — he rounded his arms to show her size — "but she ran back for her car, and I couldn't catch her. I knew she'd be back, which she was —"

"With the cops?" Ann guessed.

"They dragged me down to the local jail. They went back to the nunnery, exhumed Sister Maria Helvig, discovered I *hadn't* murdered her, found the Varinskis, were quite pleased that I'd killed *them* — Ruyshvanians are not fans of the Varinskis." Rurik smiled at the recollection of the fine, festive meal he'd been served. "When someone finally remembered they'd seen me with you, Tasya, they wanted to know where you were. I told them you escaped through the tunnel. . . . They didn't believe me about that, either, but they went up and checked it out, discovered your tracks going in and coming out. They held a huge celebration. Then they let me go."

Tasya took a long drink of her vodka.

If he hadn't felt such tenderness for her, he would have laughed. She was so brave when it came to physical challenges, and such a coward about feelings — the feelings of others, and especially hers. But she would learn. In a family as demonstrative as his, she would have to.

"Tasya, don't you want to know why they were so happy that you'd escaped unharmed?" he asked.

"No."

"Tasya," he said reproachfully.

She surrendered. "Why?"

"Because they recognized you as the Dimitru princess."

"They couldn't. They didn't." Tasya spoke too quickly, putting words together in an excess of denial. "They didn't say anything. *Who* recognized me?"

"Mrs. Gulyás visited while they were releasing me. She showed me a miniature she owned of a medieval painting. A Dimitru queen. Tasya, she looked exactly like you. Dark hair and beautiful blue eyes. Strong genes in your family."

"No. They can't have recognized me. Why didn't anybody say anything?" Tasya pushed her hair off her sweaty forehead. Clearly, she didn't know whether to be pleased or aghast.

"They recognized you, and your wish for anonymity, and they respected that. Then . . . when the Varinskis came through, they recognized them. They told terrible stories about the night your parents were killed."

Tasya cast a glance around the table.

He could see her thoughts in her eyes. Last night she had slept with a born predator. Today she had dined with her enemies. Incredulity fought with acceptance.

Taking her hand, he cradled it in his. "The Ruyshvanians are kind people. They suffered under Czajkowski. They're cautious, but not cruel. They have long memories, and they are very happy that you survived. Very happy." Leaning forward, he cupped her neck in his hands and kissed her. "So am I."

Her lashes fluttered down, then up, and a half smile lifted her lips.

"And that is why we belong together." How could he resist? He kissed her again. "I love you."

"I love you, too," she whispered.

In that disgusted-brother tone, Jasha said, "Get a room."

"Sh. It's sweet," Zorana said.

Rurik kept one hand on Tasya's shoulder as he said, "Anyway, Papa, by the time they put me on the plane, I figured another twenty-four hours wouldn't make a lot of difference, so I surprised you in person instead."

"All right." Konstantine nodded. "I accept that. And now — we are a family. Both of my sons have won women worthy of them —"

Zorana interrupted. "And if they work

very hard at improving themselves, in perhaps forty years they might be worthy of their women."

Konstantine looked at his wife, then across the table at Tasya. "She says this because we have been together only thirty-five years."

"So you're getting close, Pop," Rurik said cheerfully.

"We'll reassess at forty years." Zorana smiled, but her lips trembled — according to the doctors' prognoses, Konstantine didn't have another five years, and then . . . Rurik couldn't bear to think what would happen if Konstantine died with the weight of all his sins on his soul.

"Sit down, Mama," Firebird said. "I'll load the dishwasher."

"Yes. But first!" Zorana pulled a plate piled high with sconelike desserts out of the refrigerator, and put it on the table. Beside it, she placed a bowl of sour cream. "*Varenyky* with cherries!"

A few minutes ago, Rurik had thought he couldn't eat another thing. Now as he gazed at his favorite dessert in the world, he said, "My most wonderful mother, I adore you."

"As you should." Zorana served Konstantine, then seated herself and let Konstantine break off a piece and feed her.

"Both of my sons have a woman worthy of them," Konstantine repeated, "so I know these women who have chosen my sons will marry and reproduce many children. Many children."

Rurik stopped in the middle of explaining *varenyky* to Tasya. "Now, wait, Papa —"

Tasya's eyes flashed. "Mr. Wilder, I don't intend to discuss —"

"Papa, you are making so much trouble —" Jasha said.

Firebird slammed the dishwasher shut. The sound resounded in the small kitchen, shocking them to silence. Into the momentary lull, she shot a question. "So, Rurik, what are you guys going to do now?"

"I don't know," Rurik admitted. "I want to get back to my site in Scotland and direct the cleanup. Tasya wants to be free to wander to the wild places of the world in search of a story."

"I never said that!" Tasya said.

"You didn't have to." He understood her so well now. Understood her weaknesses, her strengths, her need to prove herself and to help those who were helpless to help themselves.

"The trouble is, both of our vocations put us in the path of the Varinskis. The Varinskis, who now know who Tasya is and that she escaped one of their assassination campaign — they won't stop until she's dead. Plus they know where Jasha and Ann live now, so no one is safe. It's a damned mess." Rurik looked at Jasha. "Do you think we can cause the Varinskis enough trouble to keep them occupied so we can work?"

"You don't have to." Firebird spoke with just enough of an accent to sound like a fortune-teller.

Rurik jumped and stared at his little sister. *Shit, not her, too.*

"What do you know, pip-squeak?" Jasha asked.

"Boris is dead, murdered by his own family," Firebird said in a mysterious tone. "The leadership of the Varinskis is up for grabs."

"Did you have a vision?" Jasha's voice was hushed.

"No. I read it on the Internet!" Firebird laughed so hard she bent over and held her belly. "Jeez, you guys are suckers!"

Ann laughed, too, then Tasya, and finally Zorana.

The men were unified in their disapproval.

"That's not funny," Rurik said.

"I thought it was." Tasya grinned like the Cheshire cat.

"All right, daughter." Konstantine stared disapprovingly at Firebird. "You have had your little joke. Now tell us the details."

"They found Boris's body in a garbage pit outside of Kiev, apparently mauled by" — Firebird made air quotes with her fingers — " 'a variety of wild animals.' The speculation in the international press is that the Varinskis assassinated him because of his failure to halt the trial of the Varinski Twins and keep the whole episode out of the press. One of the Varinskis made a statement which said that while they grieved for Boris, he was their weakest leader in their history and will be replaced by someone who has the strength to bring the Varinski family back to the pinnacle of power."

Ann sat forward. "Who said that? Who's their new leader?"

"He wouldn't say."

"Then they're fighting among themselves for command." Konstantine stroked his chin. "I wonder who it could be."

"There are quite a few candidates, although none of the obvious ones have the organizational skills as well as the ruthlessness needed to maintain control over those boys." Ann shook her head as everyone in the family turned to stare at her. "I'm not psychic, either, but I've done a lot of research in the past weeks."

"If there's a file on a computer somewhere

about the Varinskis, Ann has found it," Jasha announced with pride.

"The younger Varinskis are online a *lot*. They play video games. They look at porn. Some of them even have MySpace pages." Ann smiled with the smug pleasure of someone who had discovered the weak link.

Konstantine rubbed his neck. "Such sloppiness."

"I wonder what kind of information the right kind of interest could elicit from them." Tasya's eyes narrowed, and Rurik could almost see her mind working.

So Rurik gave his first command to his woman. "You are not going to flirt with a bunch of horny young Varinskis so we can find out what's happening in the organization."

"Never crossed my mind." But Tasya wasn't really paying attention to him.

Grabbing her by the shirtfront, Rurik brought her to her feet.

That got her attention.

"Promise me you won't put yourself in their path. They know who you are now. They know you're unfinished business, and they have everything to prove. Don't contact them." He shook her a little. "You owe it to your parents, who came back from the grave to save your life, and mine."

"I promise, Rurik." Tasya laid her hand on his face. "Don't worry so much."

Don't worry?

He slowly sank back into his seat.

A woman like this, who charged in first and thought afterward, didn't want him to worry.

She'd given him everything. She'd told him the truth about herself and the truth about him. She'd made him embrace the wild part of himself. She'd brought the icon to his parents and proved he meant more to her than her own ambitions and her own revenge.

He had to protect her now — from the Varinskis, and from herself.

"Really. Rurik. I won't contact these guys online. Calm down." Tasya took his hand and put a fork in it. "Eat some *varenyky.*"

"Yoo-hoo!" A sweet, high lady's voice hailed them from the open door.

As one, the family jumped and turned.

Miss Mabel Joyce stood there, her face pressed to the screen. She was tall and big-boned, with only the slightest dowager's hump. Her hair was iron gray and had been for as long as Rurik could remember. Once upon a time her eyes might have been hazel, but now they were faded to a wispy gray. Her jowls drooped over her jawline, her

414

cheeks drooped toward her lips, and her whole face was a monument to the softening nature of old age. But her skin was clear of spots; Rurik had never seen her outside without a hat to protect her from the sun.

She held one in her hand now, a wide-brimmed straw hat that would have looked at home on a Cozumel beach.

"Come in!" Konstantine waved a generous hand.

Zorana bustled to the door to flip the lock.

"Who's that?" Tasya whispered as she stared at the old woman.

"She's the retired schoolteacher here in Blythe. In high school, all of us kids had her." Rurik saw Tasya's wary expression. "She's an amazing old lady. Taught way past the age of retirement, and she's only recently needed a cane."

"How come you guys didn't hear her arrive?" she asked.

"She's pretty all-round amazing." Rurik remembered more than once when Miss Joyce sneaked up behind the boys when they gambled or fought.

Tasya moved uneasily in her seat. "Do you think she heard us? Heard what we were talking about?"

"Naw. She couldn't have been there that long." He stood and offered his seat.

Miss Joyce waved him back. "I can't stay but a minute. The Milburns from in town volunteered to bring me. They wanted a flat of raspberries from the fruit stand. They're making jam, bless their hearts, and they'll share with me. I had something for you, so I hitched a ride."

Zorana brought her a glass of iced tea — Miss Joyce didn't drink alcohol — and the teacher drained the glass.

"Thank you. Whew!" She waved her hat before her face. "It is really warm this summer." Digging into her purse, she pulled out a long envelope.

Rurik could see the foreign stamps, the stained paper, the scratchy writing that had etched their address on the front.

"This was delivered to me by mistake — that substitute mailman from down Burlington way is an idiot!" Miss Joyce frowned. "The post office should screen their people better. But when I saw where the letter was from, I thought it might be something to do with, well . . ."

"Adrik," Zorana breathed.

Jasha slowly rose to his feet.

Rurik followed.

Of course. Adrik.

Rurik was furious with his little brother for leaving their parents without a word,

416

but at the same time . . . he was blood of his blood, bone of his bone. Rurik's heart began a slow, hard beat.

Zorana snatched the envelope out of Miss Joyce's hands. She opened it easily — it was so tattered the letter barely hung in there. Dropping the envelope on the floor, she spread open the thin sheet of paper.

Miss Joyce leaned down, picked up the envelope, and smoothed it between her hands.

"Read it to us, Zorana. Let us all hear the news." Konstantine's voice rang with optimism — and fear.

"The American consul for Nepal is sorry to send us such bad news, but Adrik's . . . Adrik's badly decomposed body has been found and identified. He's been cremated." Her voice wobbled, then strengthened. "His remains are being returned to us."

"Oh, no," Ann whispered.

Firebird gave a muffled sob.

"My poor darlings, it's exactly what we all feared. I'm so sorry!" Miss Joyce patted Zorana's back.

Tasya hugged Rurik, and Rurik leaned heavily against her.

"It is as we suspected." Konstantine, who only a few minutes ago had been flushed and happy, was now drawn, gray, and looking fragile. "Our son and brother is dead."

Beneath the family's grief, there was another horrible realization — there was no hope.

Without Adrik, without the woman he loved and the icon he was fated to find, the pact could never be broken.

Konstantine was damned to hell.

They were all condemned . . . forever.

ABOUT THE AUTHOR

Christina Dodd is a *New York Times* bestselling author whose novels have been translated into twelve languages, featured by Doubleday Book Club®, recorded on books on tape for the blind, given Romance Writers of America's prestigious Golden Heart and RITA Awards, called the year's best by *Library Journal,* and, at the pinnacle of her illustrious career, used as a clue in the *Los Angeles Times* crossword puzzle. Christina Dodd lives in Washington with her husband and two dogs. Sign up for her newsletter at www.christinadodd.com.